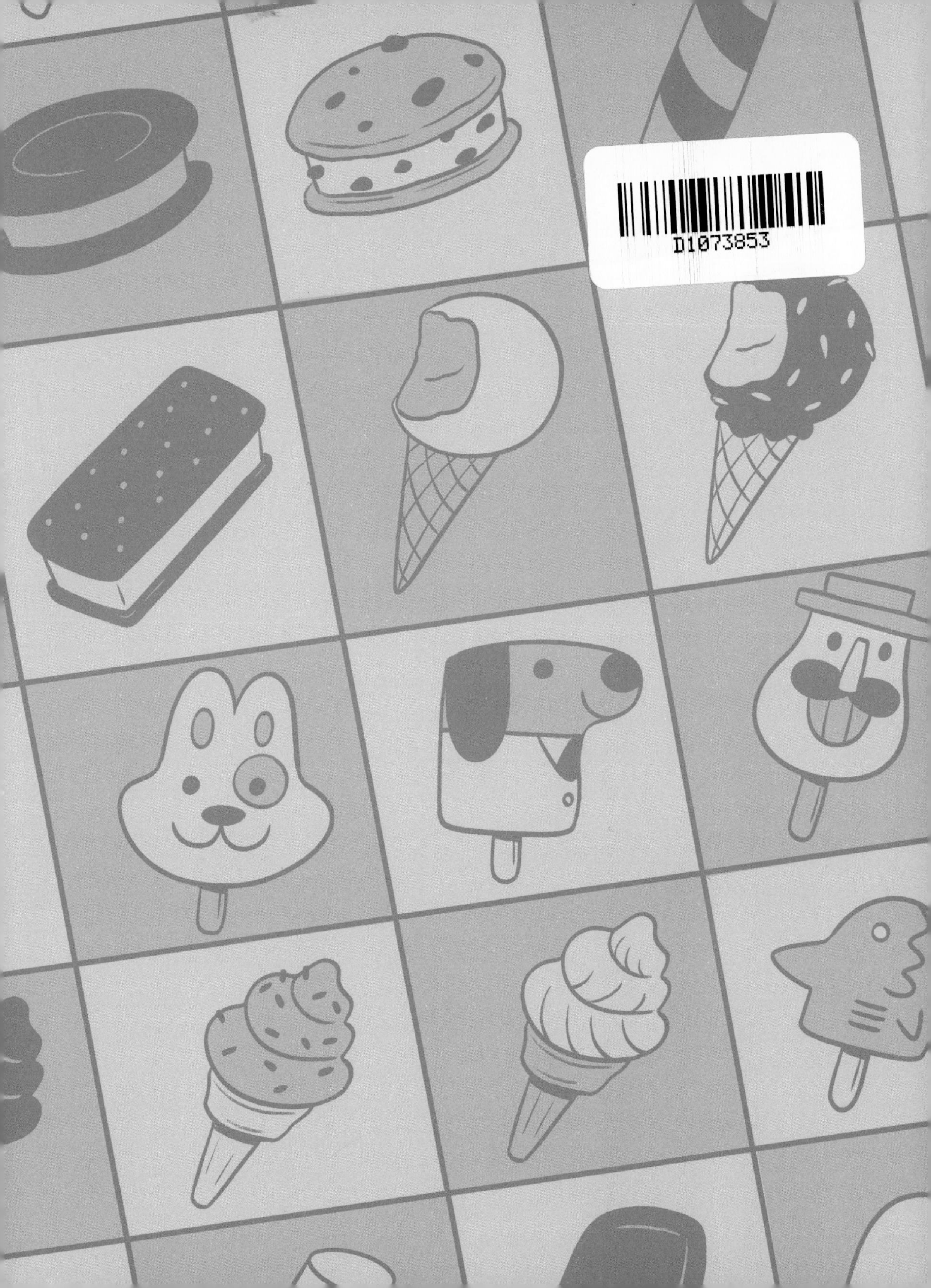

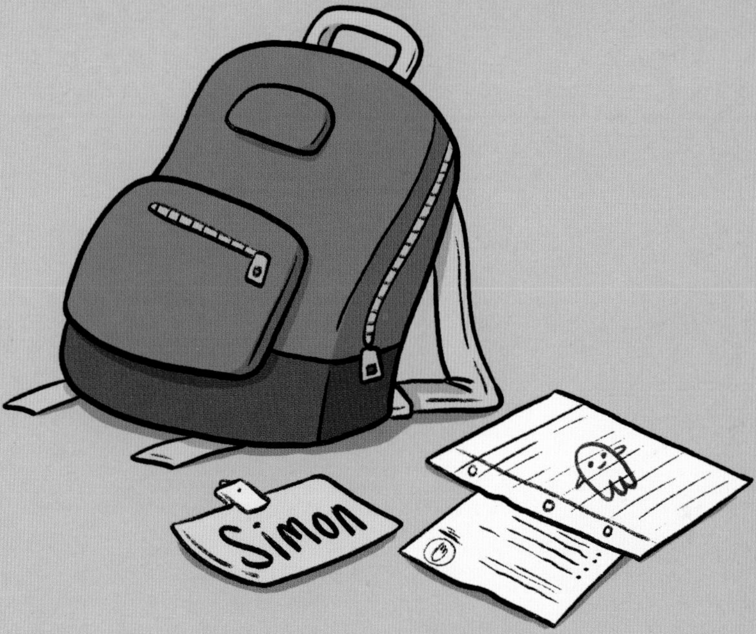
Simon

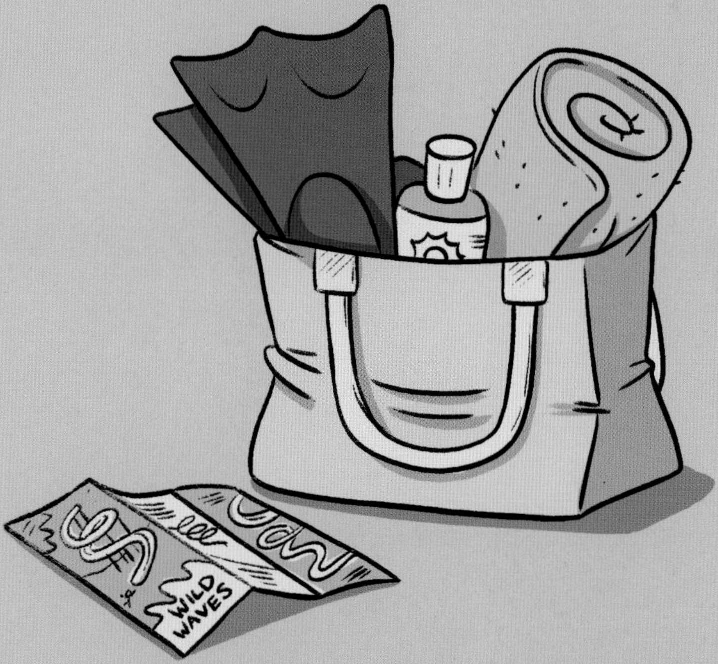
WILD
WAVES

For all the "normal" families out there

Tundra Books, an imprint of Penguin Random House Canada Young Readers,
a division of Penguin Random House of Canada Limited

Library and Archives Canada Cataloguing in Publication

Title: Super family! / Cale Atkinson.
Names: Atkinson, Cale, author, illustrator.
Series: Atkinson, Cale. Simon and Chester.
Description: Series statement: Simon and Chester
Identifiers: Canadiana (print) 20210351616 | Canadiana (ebook) 20210351632 |
ISBN 9780735272439 (hardcover) | ISBN 9780735272446 (EPUB)
Subjects: LCGFT: Ghost comics. | LCGFT: Graphic novels.
Classification: LCC PN6733.A85 S874 2022 | DDC j741.5/971—dc23

Published simultaneously in the United States of America
by Tundra Books of Northern New York, an imprint of Tundra Book Group,
a division of Penguin Random House of Canada Limited

Library of Congress Control Number: 2020950281

Edited by Samantha Swenson
Designed by Andrew Roberts
The artwork in this book was created with missing puzzle pieces, pizza,
astronaut ice cream and Photoshop.

The text was set in Silver Age BB.

Printed in China

www.penguinrandomhouse.ca

1 2 3 4 5   26 25 24 23 22

Penguin
Random House
TUNDRA BOOKS

Simon AND Chester

Super Family!

by Cale Atkinson

tundra

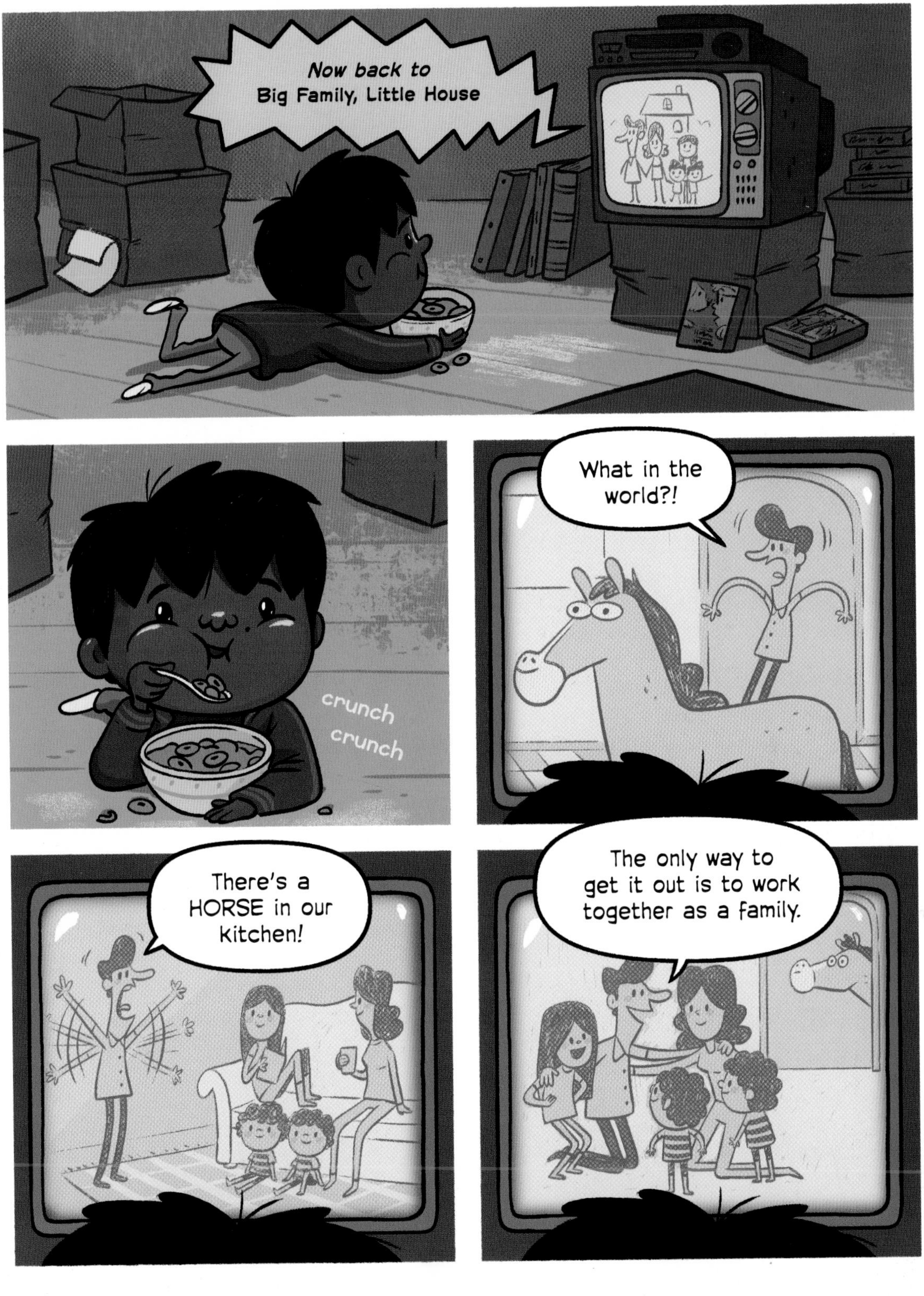
Now back to Big Family, Little House
crunch crunch
What in the world?!
There's a HORSE in our kitchen!
The only way to get it out is to work together as a family.

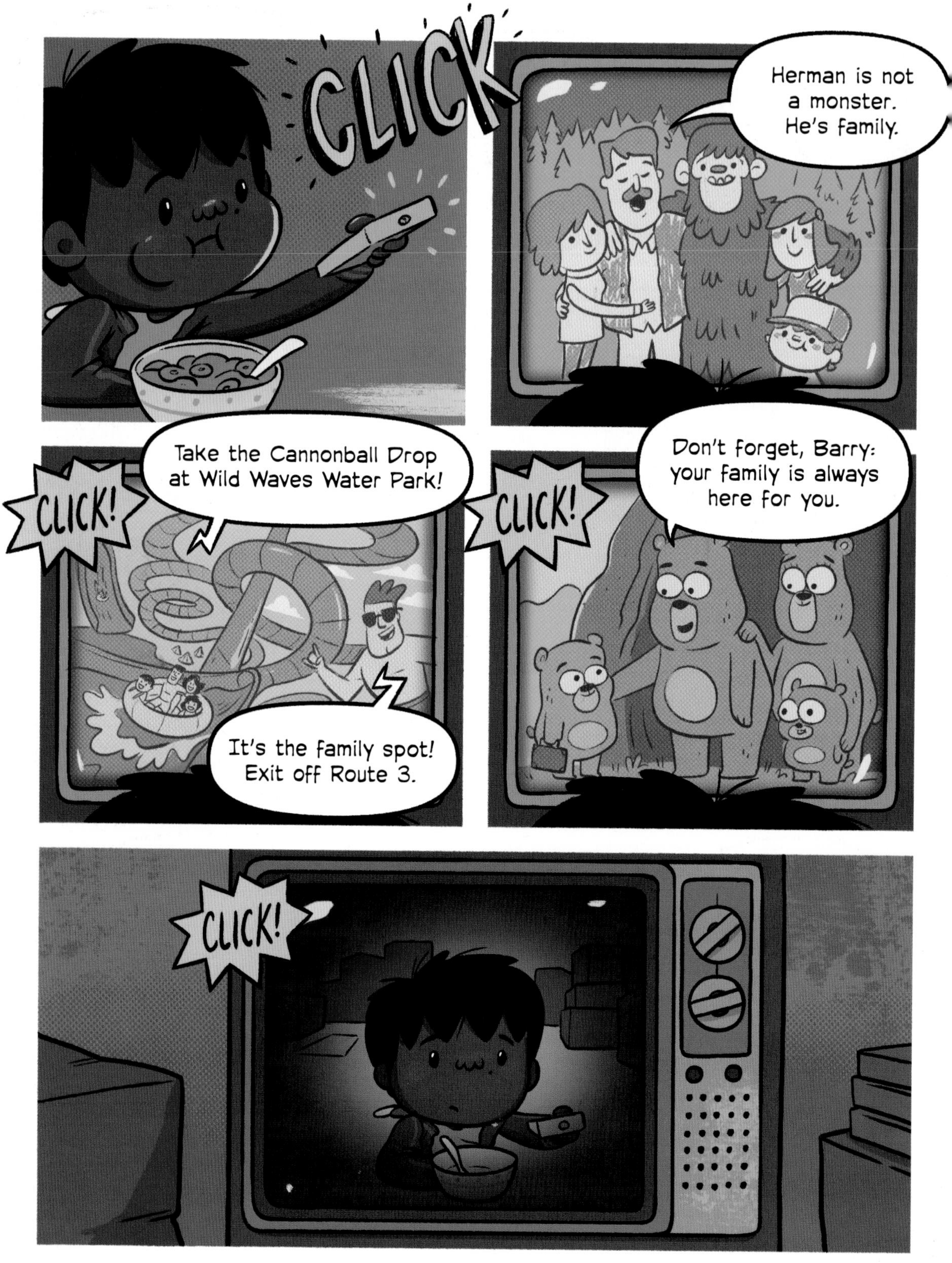
CLICK
Herman is not a monster. He's family.
CLICK!
Take the Cannonball Drop at Wild Waves Water Park!
It's the family spot! Exit off Route 3.
CLICK!
Don't forget, Barry: your family is always here for you.
CLICK!

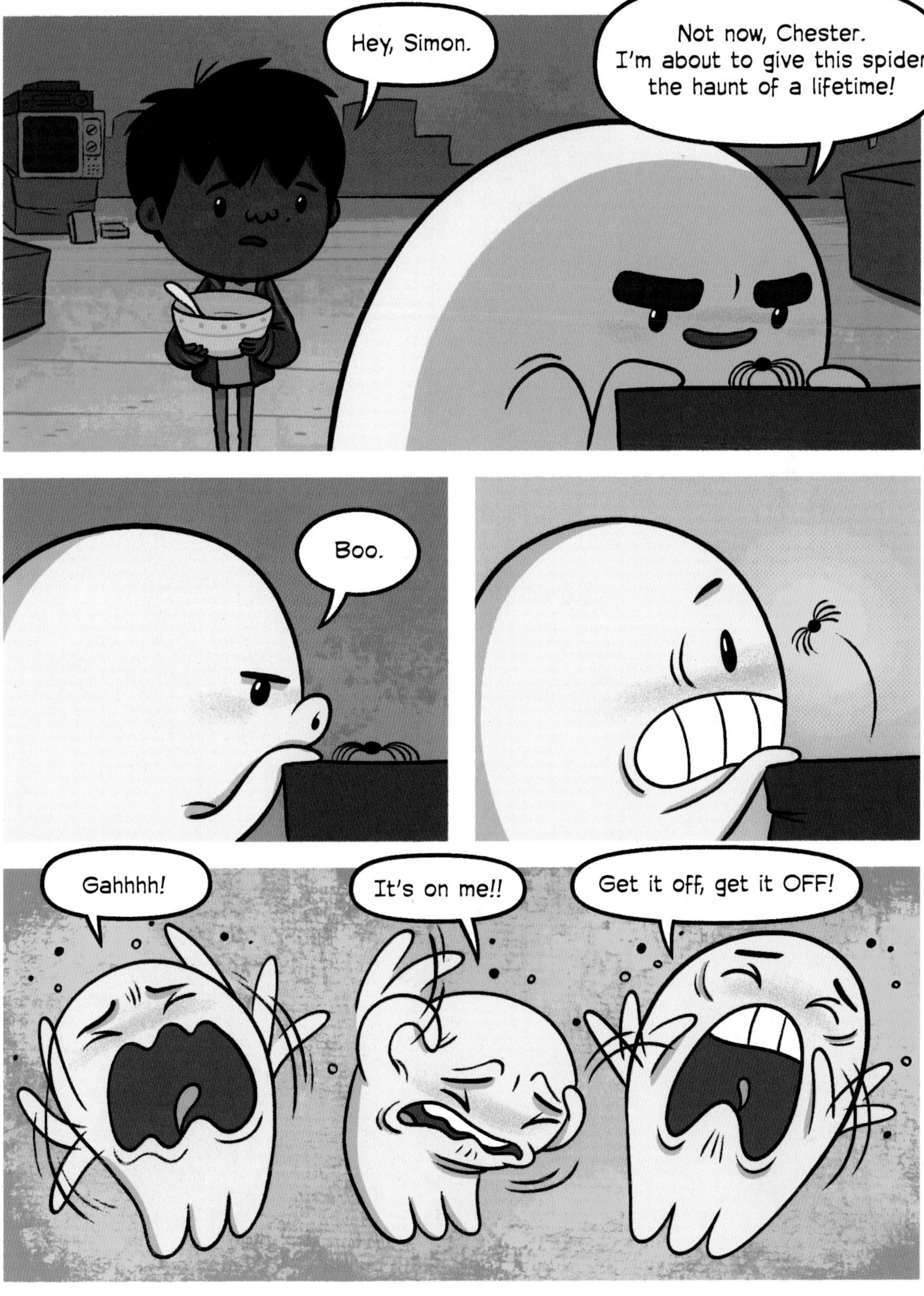
Hey, Simon.
Not now, Chester. I'm about to give this spider the haunt of a lifetime!
Boo.
Gahhhh!
It's on me!!
Get it off, get it OFF!

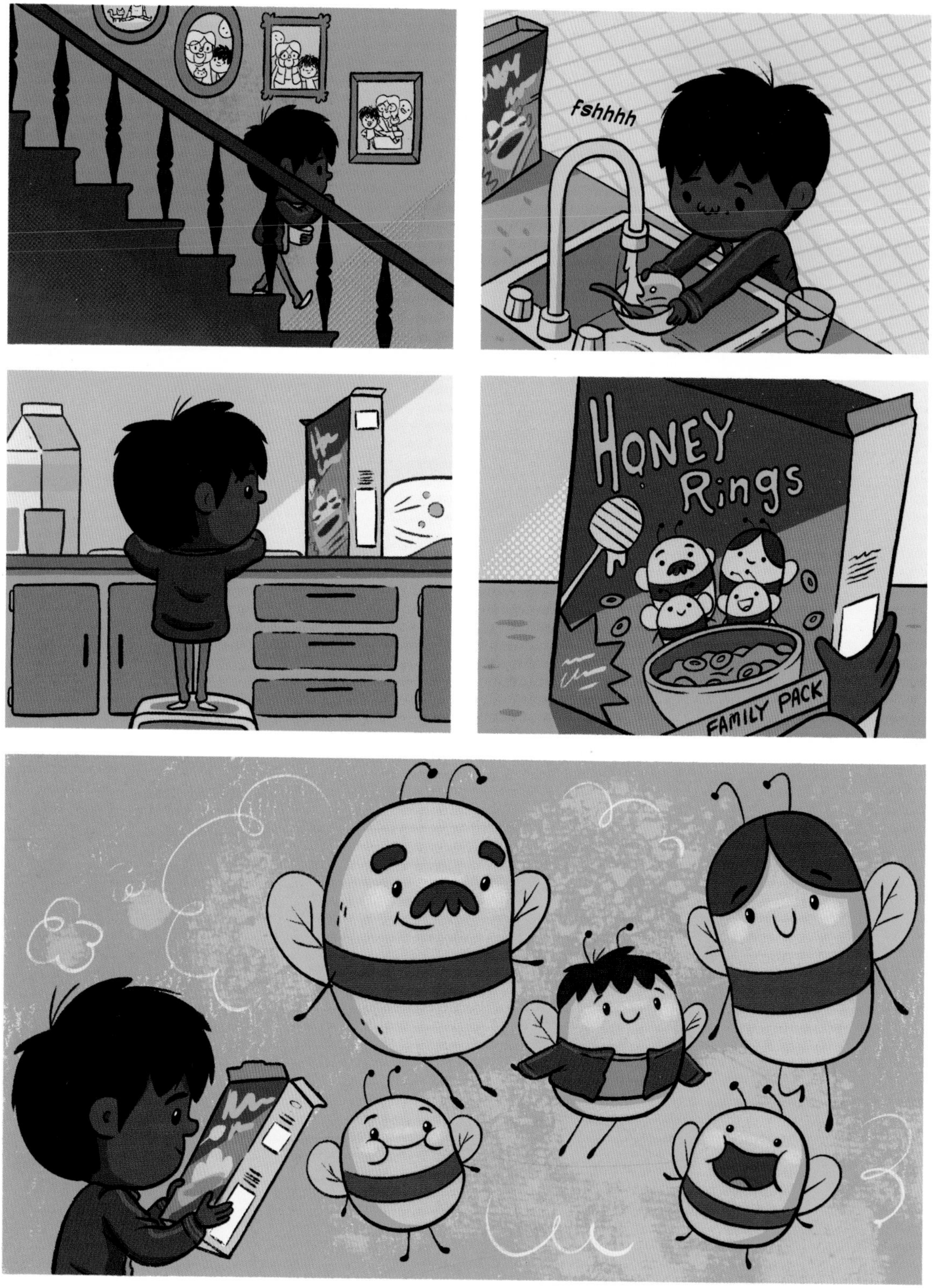
fshhhh
HONEY Rings
FAMILY PACK

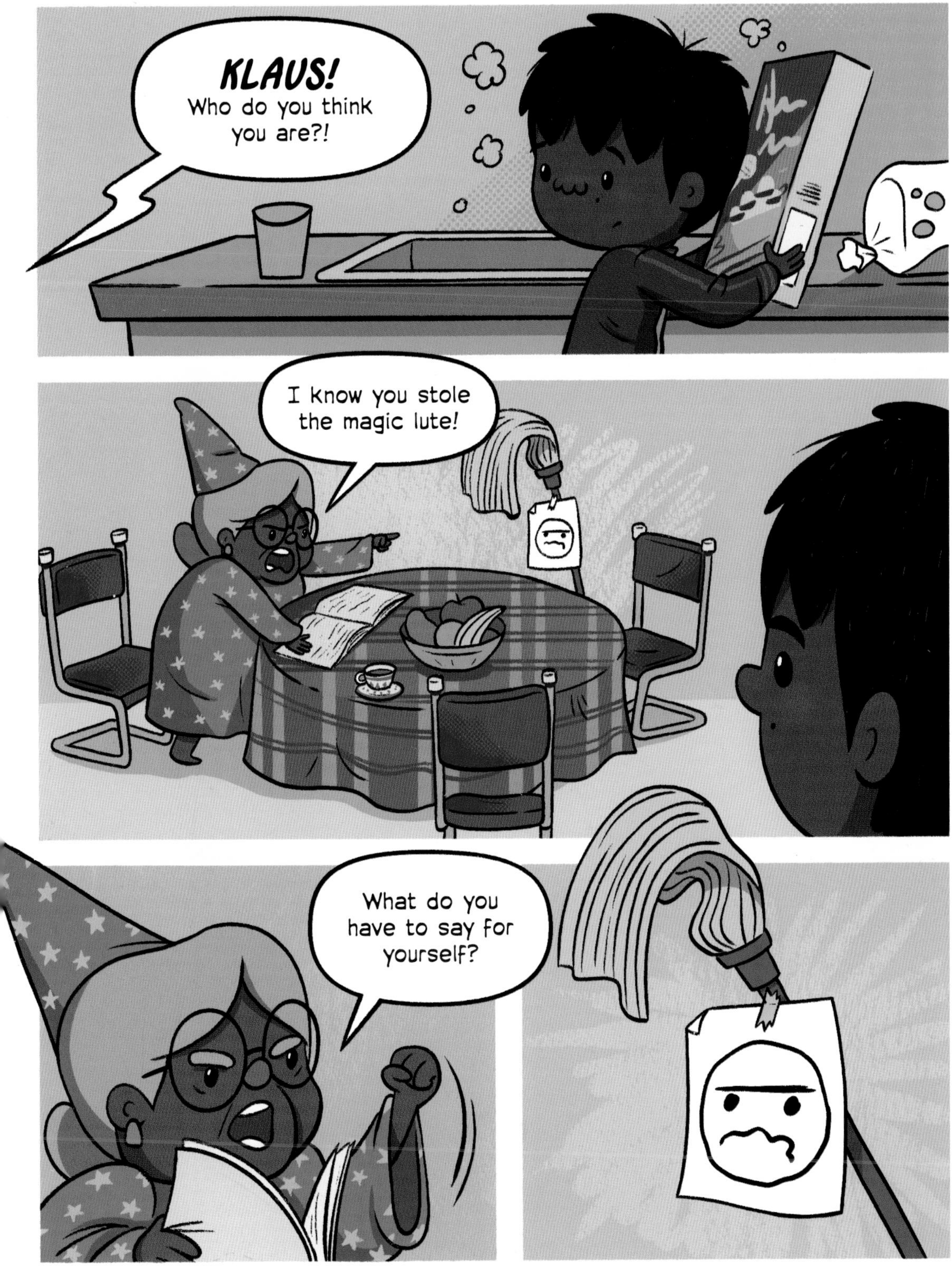
KLAUS! Who do you think you are?!
I know you stole the magic lute!
What do you have to say for yourself?

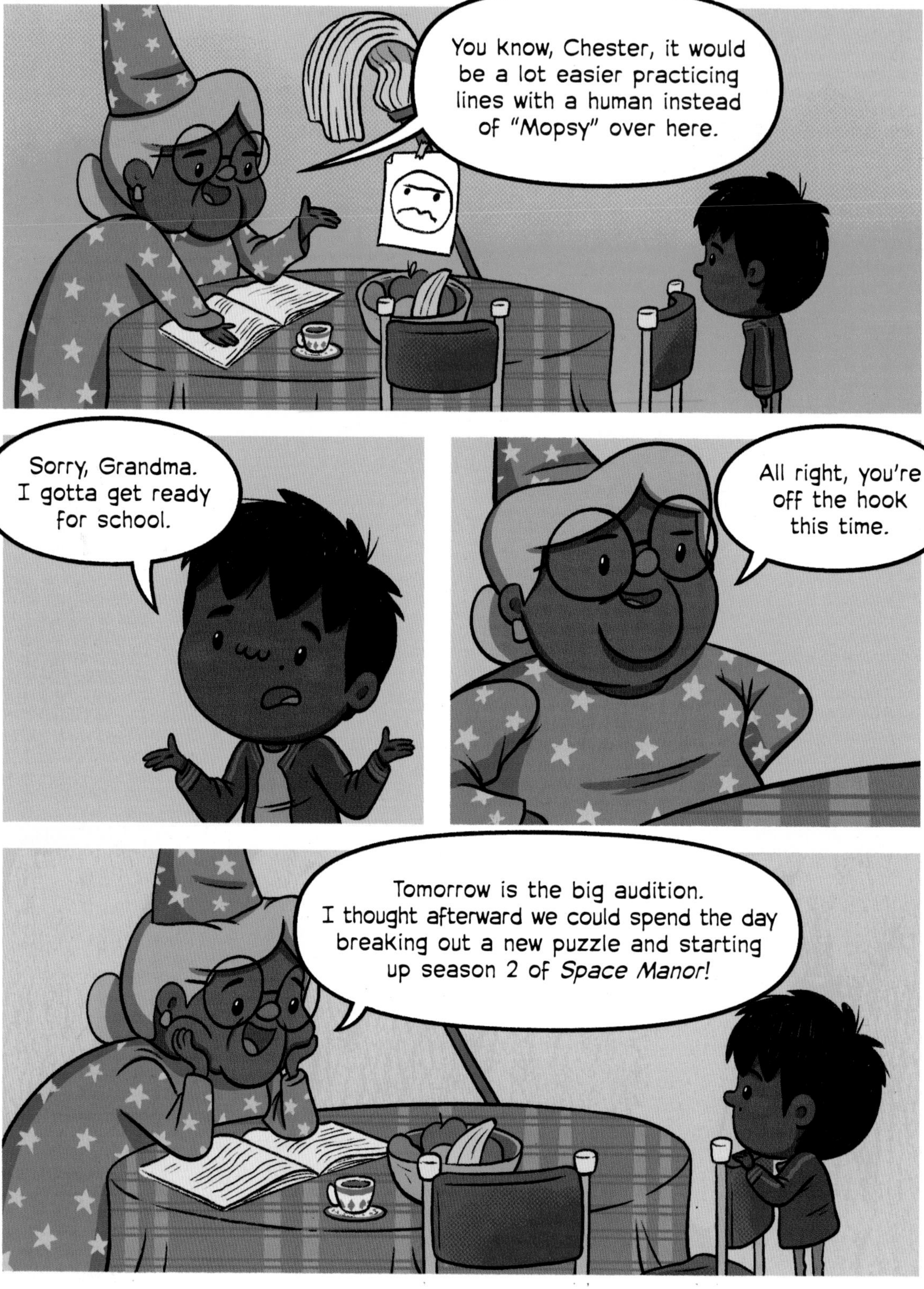
You know, Chester, it would be a lot easier practicing lines with a human instead of "Mopsy" over here.
Sorry, Grandma. I gotta get ready for school.
All right, you're off the hook this time.
Tomorrow is the big audition. I thought afterward we could spend the day breaking out a new puzzle and starting up season 2 of *Space Manor!*

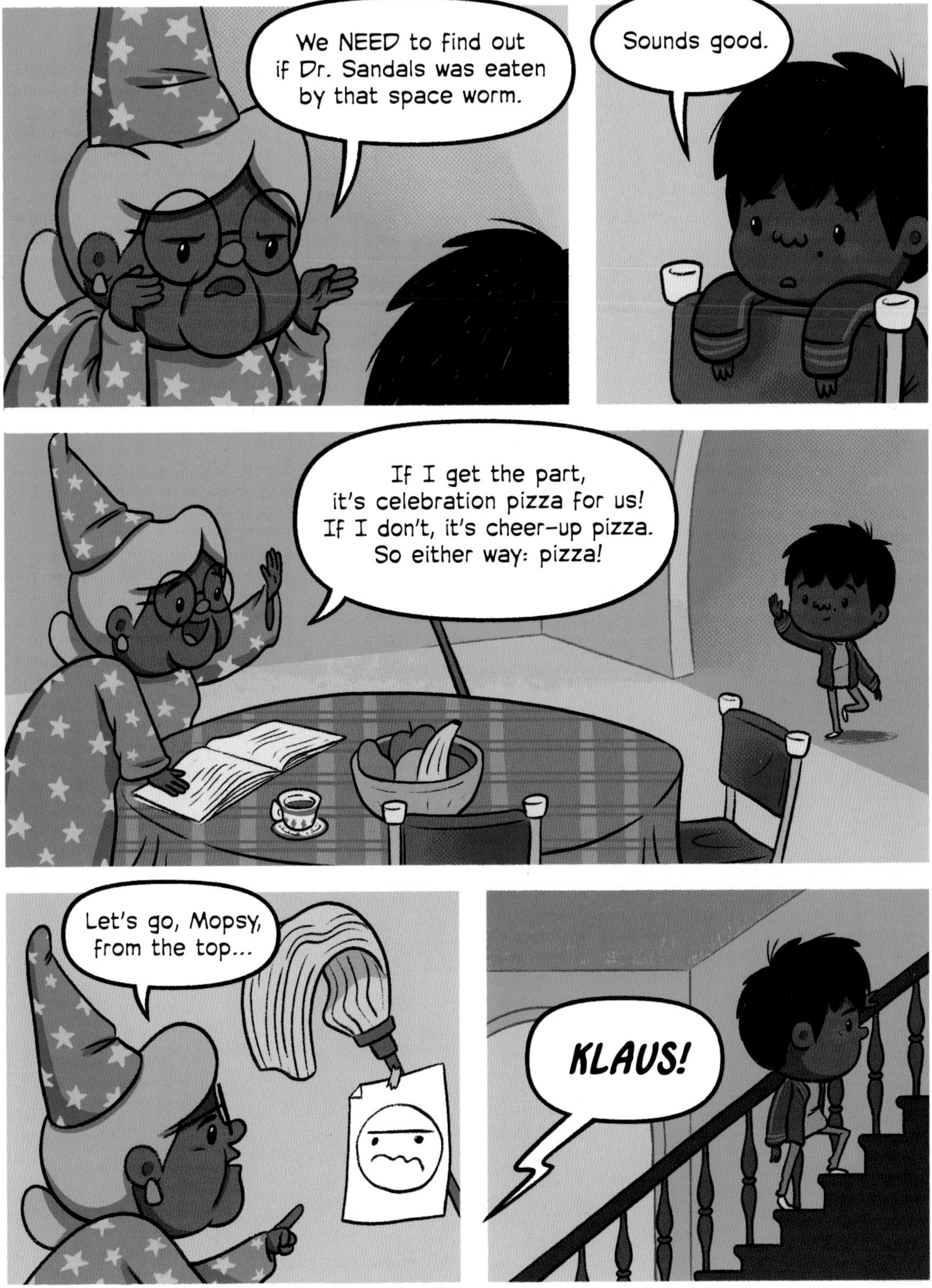
We NEED to find out if Dr. Sandals was eaten by that space worm.
Sounds good.
If I get the part, it's celebration pizza for us! If I don't, it's cheer-up pizza. So either way: pizza!
Let's go, Mopsy, from the top...
KLAUS!

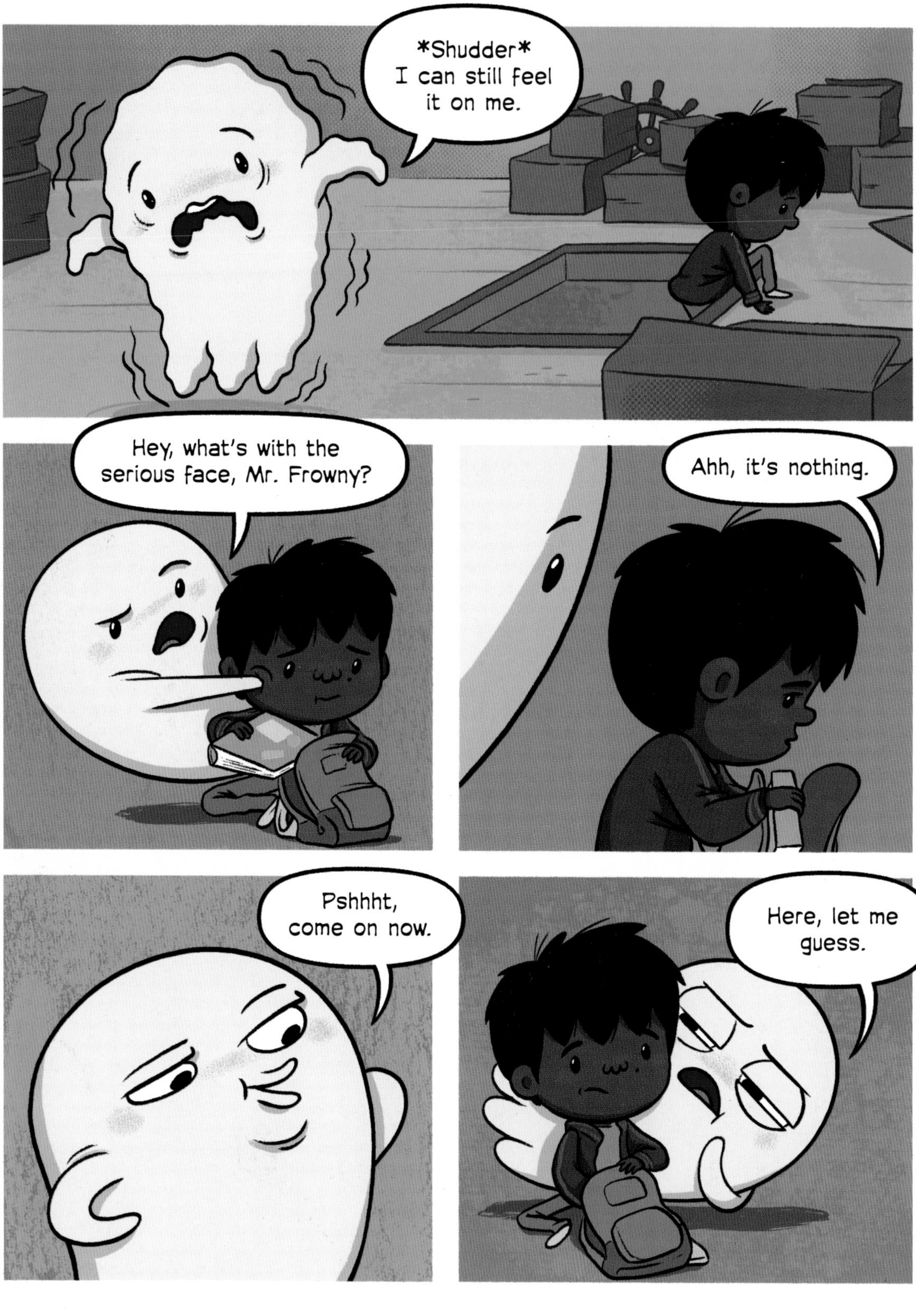
Shudder
I can still feel it on me.
Hey, what's with the serious face, Mr. Frowny?
Ahh, it's nothing.
Pshhht, come on now.
Here, let me guess.

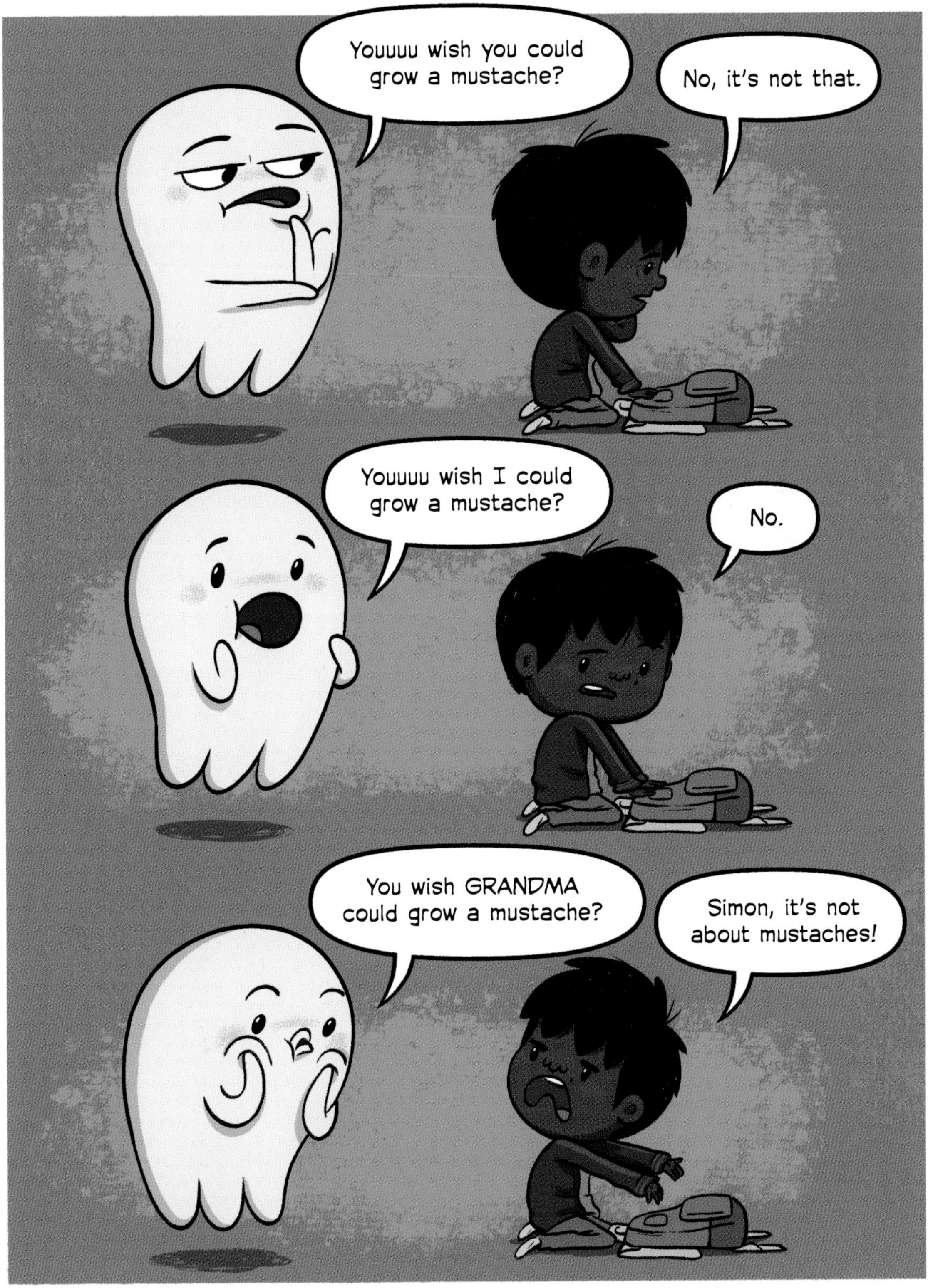
Youuuu wish you could grow a mustache?
No, it's not that.
Youuuu wish I could grow a mustache?
No.
You wish GRANDMA could grow a mustache?
Simon, it's not about mustaches!

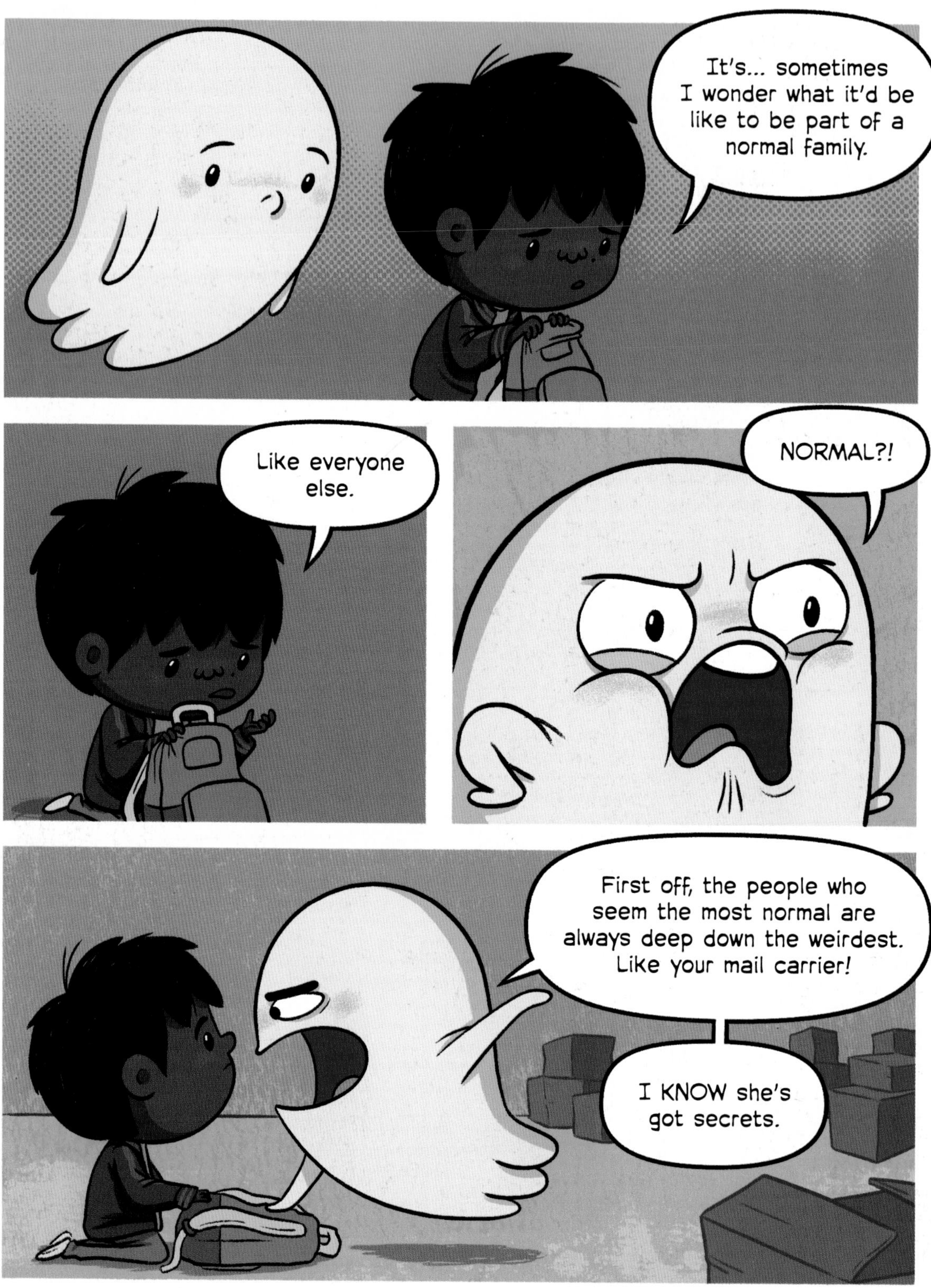

It's... sometimes I wonder what it'd be like to be part of a normal family.
Like everyone else.
NORMAL?!
First off, the people who seem the most normal are always deep down the weirdest. Like your mail carrier!
I KNOW she's got secrets.

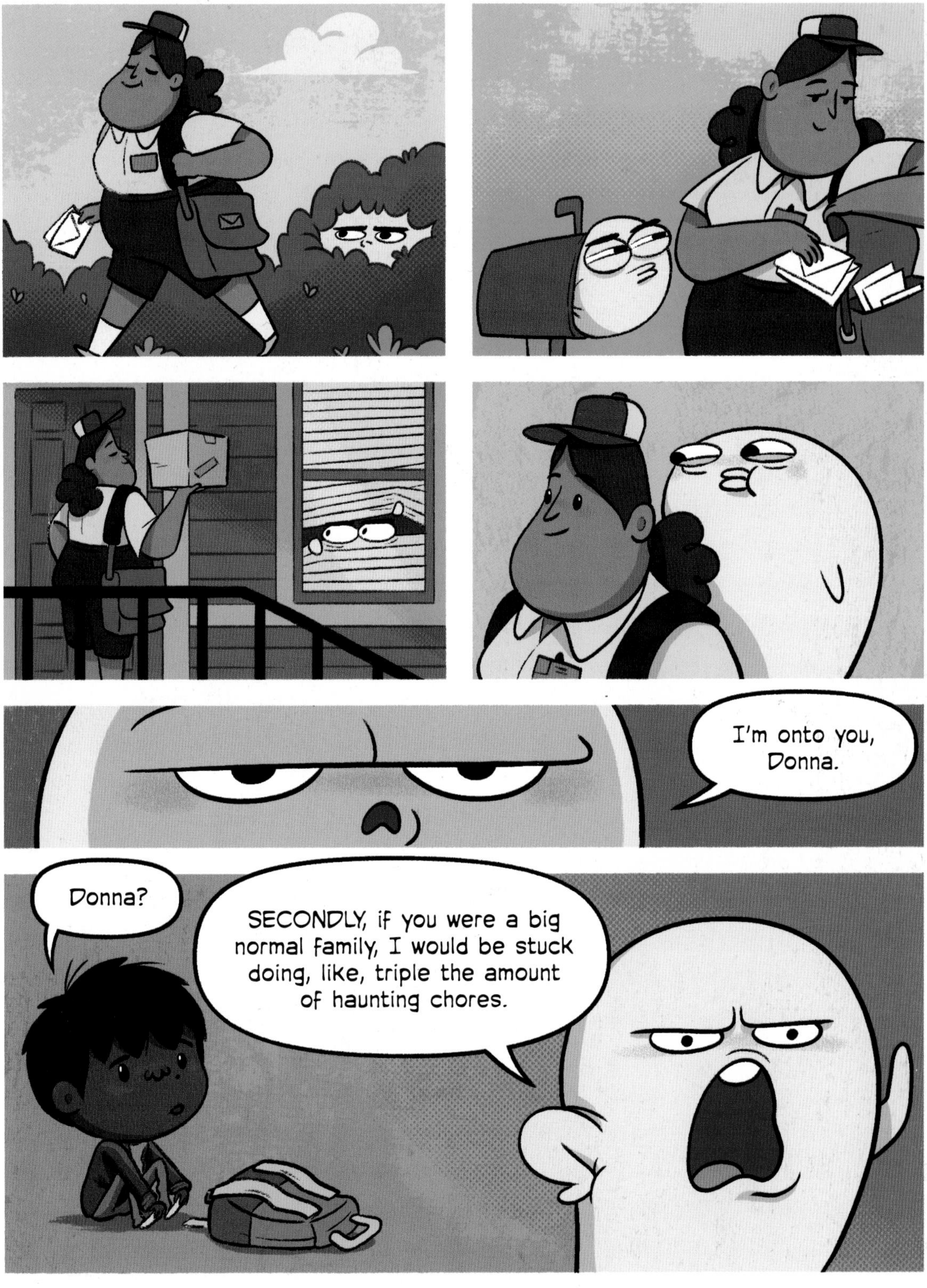
I'm onto you, Donna.
Donna?
SECONDLY, if you were a big normal family, I would be stuck doing, like, triple the amount of haunting chores.

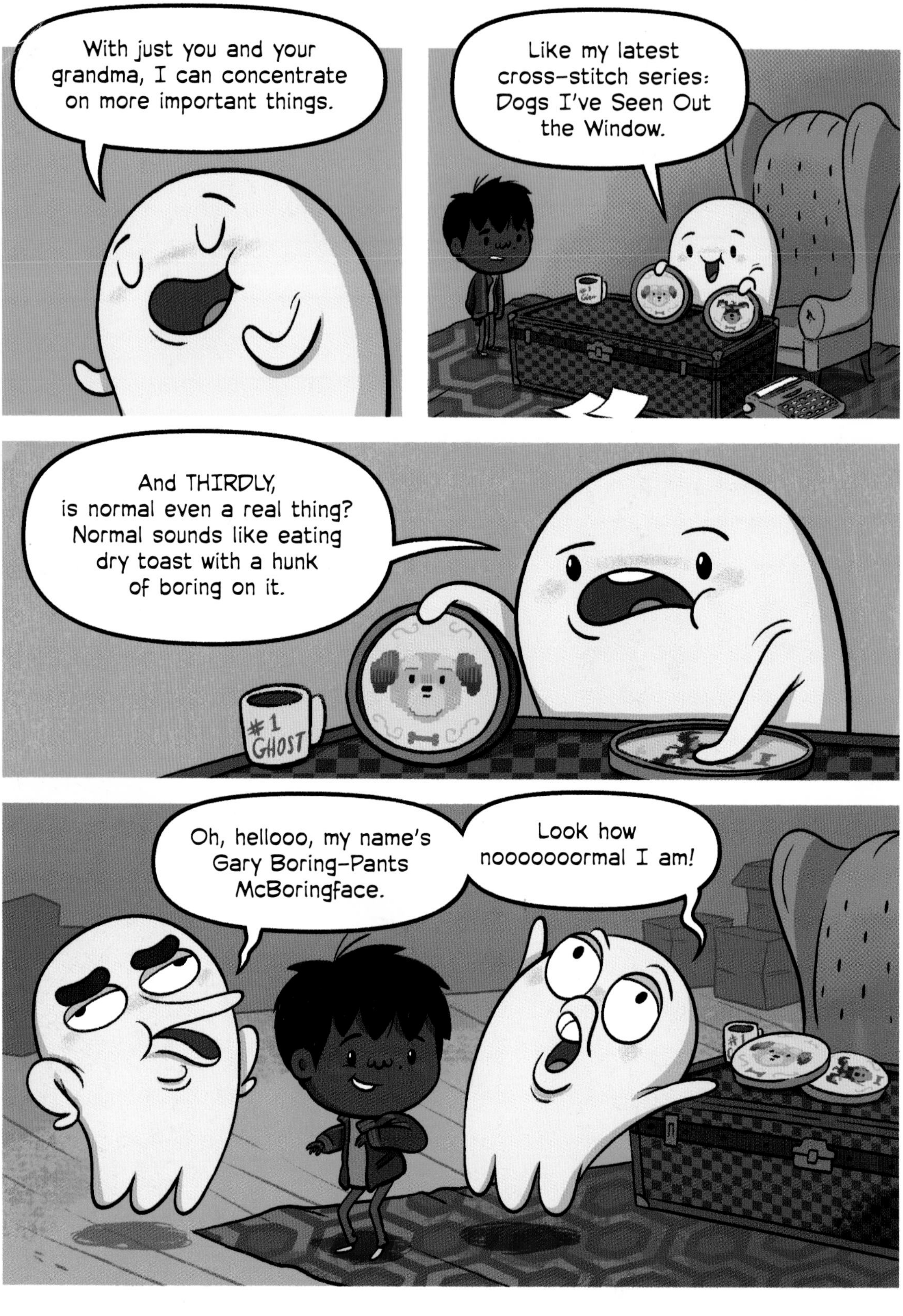
With just you and your grandma, I can concentrate on more important things.
Like my latest cross-stitch series: Dogs I've Seen Out the Window.
#1 Ghost
And THIRDLY, is normal even a real thing? Normal sounds like eating dry toast with a hunk of boring on it.
#1 GHOST
Oh, hellooo, my name's Gary Boring-Pants McBoringface.
Look how noooooooormal I am!

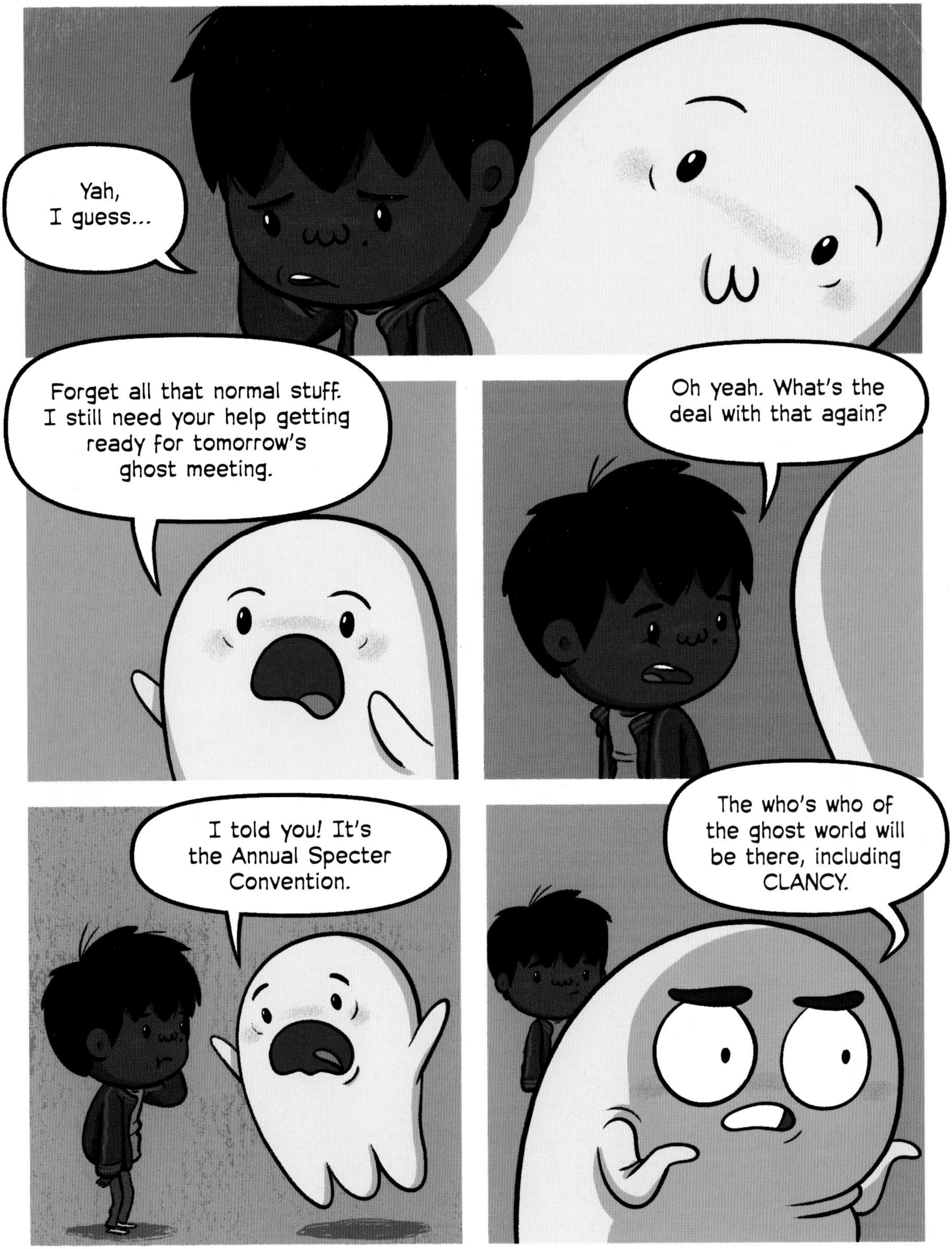
Yah, I guess...
Forget all that normal stuff. I still need your help getting ready for tomorrow's ghost meeting.
Oh yeah. What's the deal with that again?
I told you! It's the Annual Specter Convention.
The who's who of the ghost world will be there, including CLANCY.

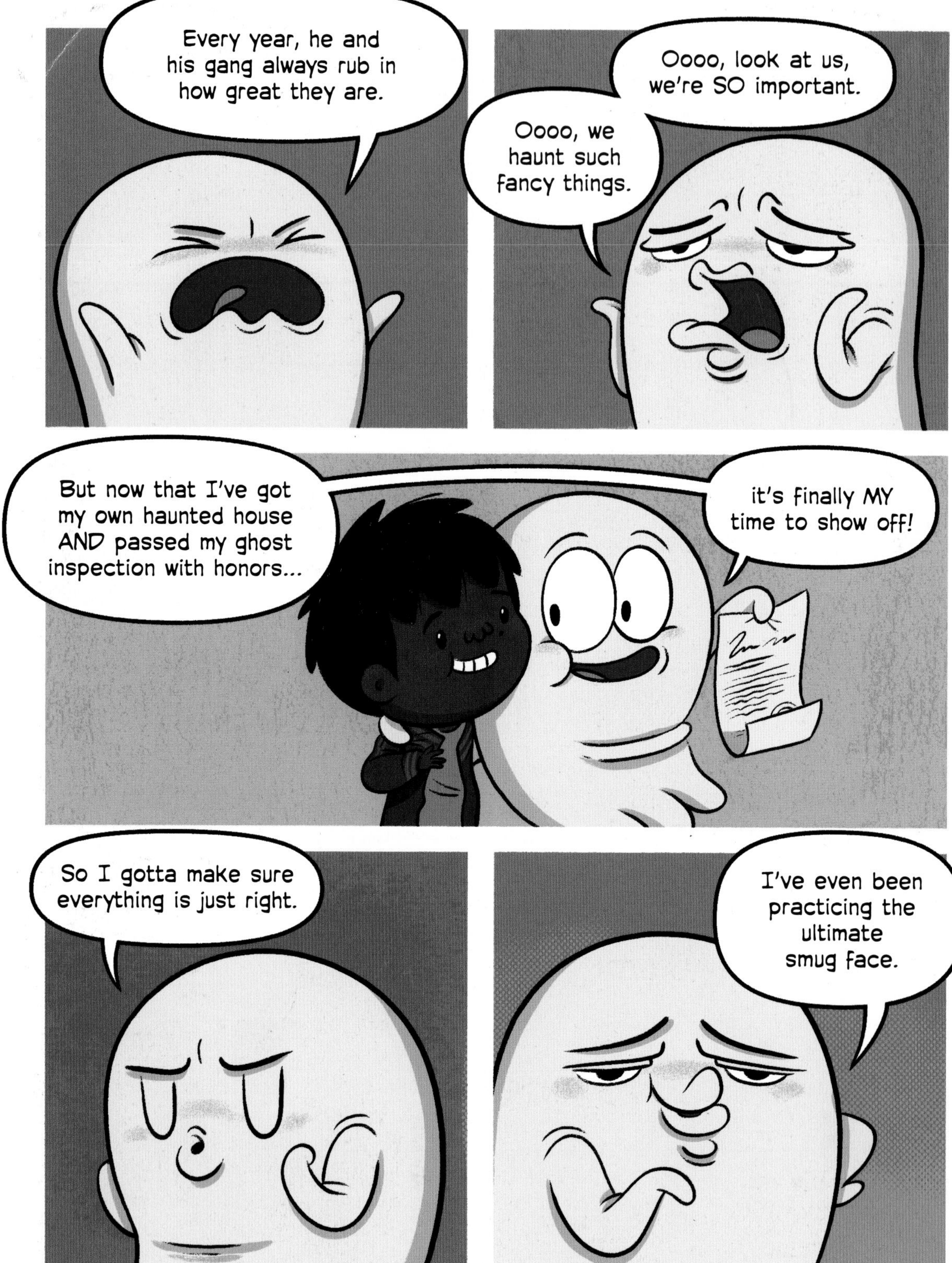
Every year, he and his gang always rub in how great they are.
Oooo, look at us, we're SO important.
Oooo, we haunt such fancy things.
But now that I've got my own haunted house AND passed my ghost inspection with honors...
it's finally MY time to show off!
So I gotta make sure everything is just right.
I've even been practicing the ultimate smug face.

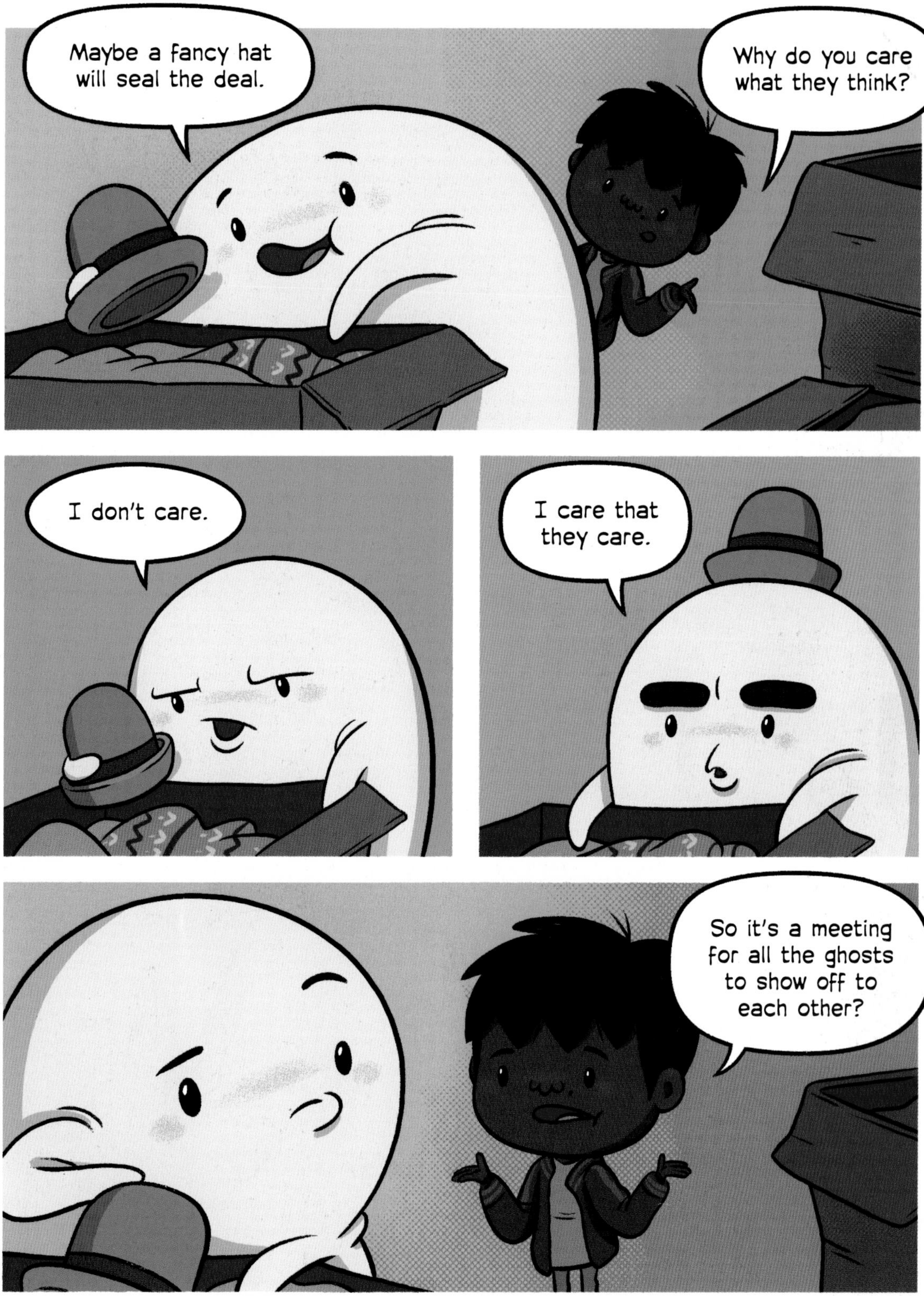
Maybe a fancy hat will seal the deal.
Why do you care what they think?
I don't care.
I care that they care.
So it's a meeting for all the ghosts to show off to each other?

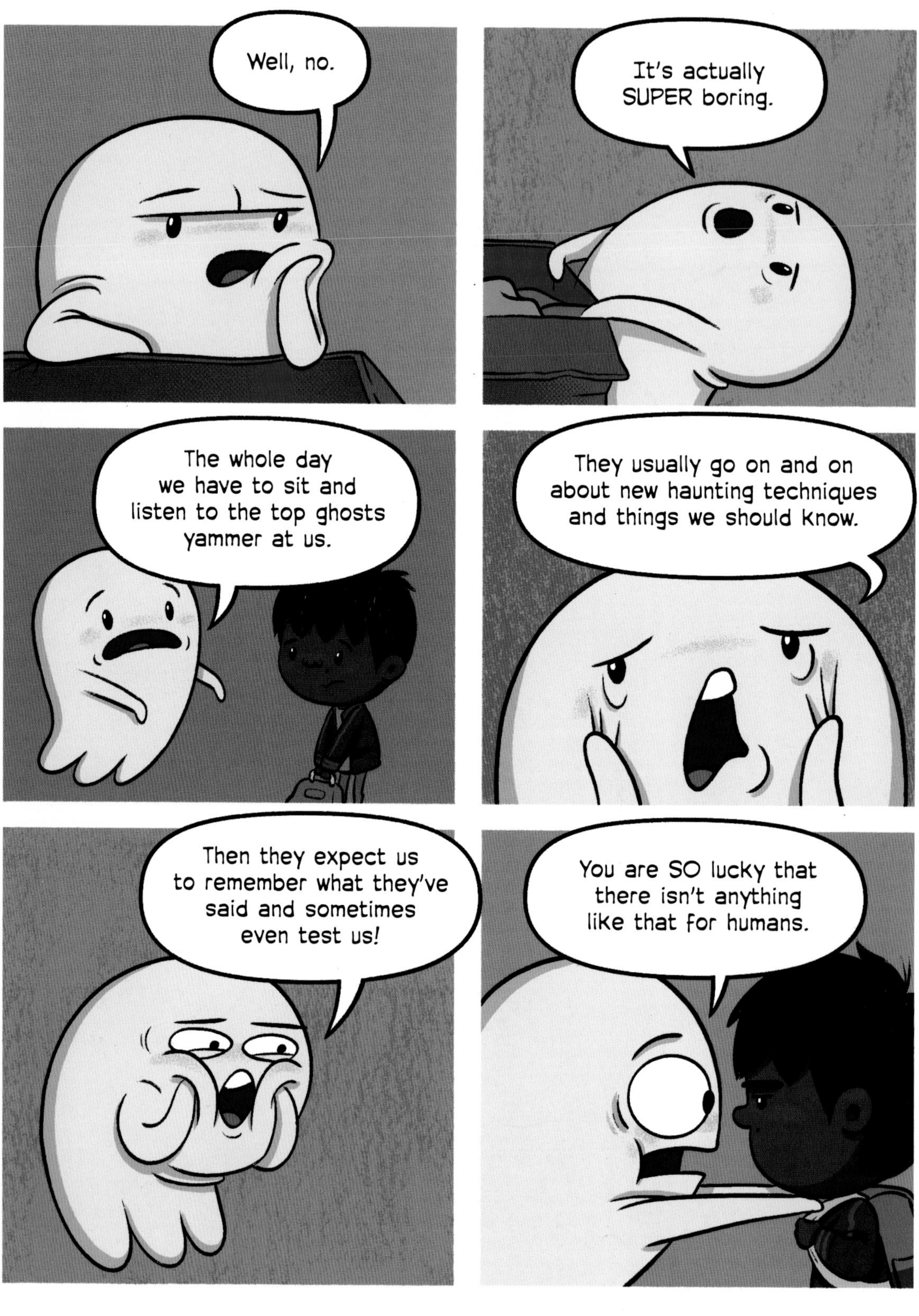
Well, no.
It's actually SUPER boring.
The whole day we have to sit and listen to the top ghosts yammer at us.
They usually go on and on about new haunting techniques and things we should know.
Then they expect us to remember what they've said and sometimes even test us!
You are SO lucky that there isn't anything like that for humans.

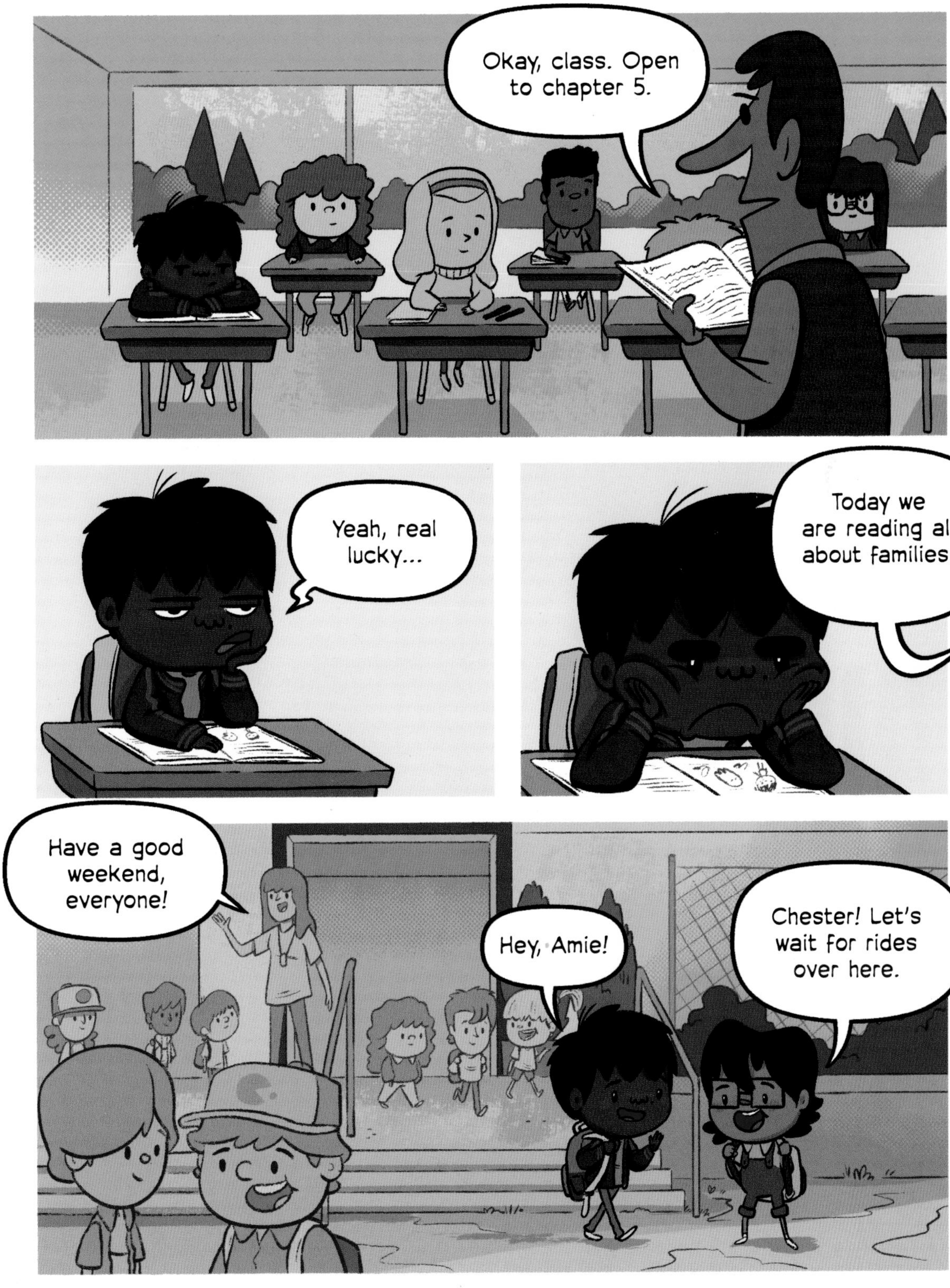
Okay, class. Open to chapter 5.
Yeah, real lucky...
Today we are reading all about families.
Have a good weekend, everyone!
Hey, Amie!
Chester! Let's wait for rides over here.

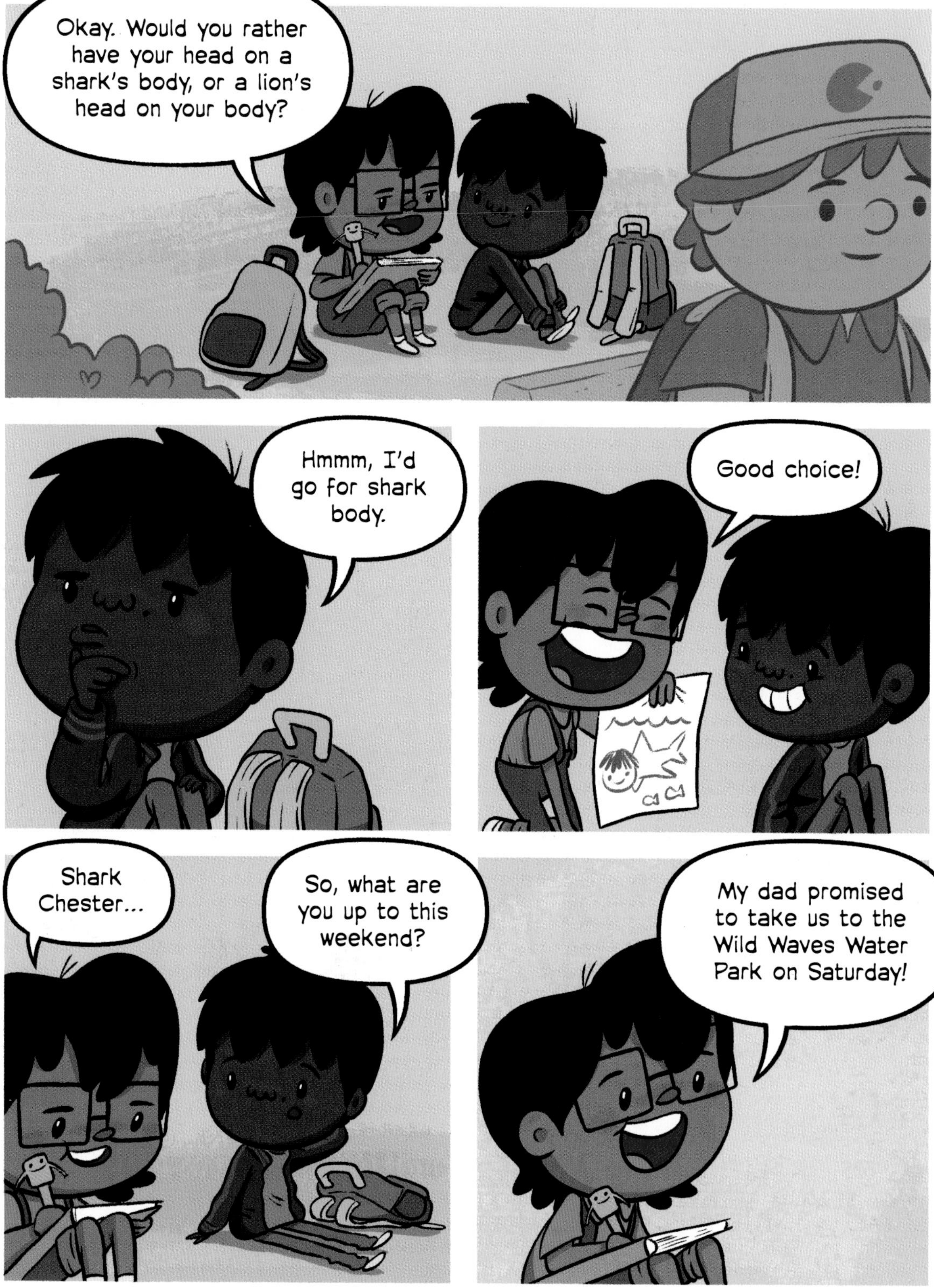
Okay. Would you rather have your head on a shark's body, or a lion's head on your body?
Hmmm, I'd go for shark body.
Good choice!
Shark Chester...
So, what are you up to this weekend?
My dad promised to take us to the Wild Waves Water Park on Saturday!

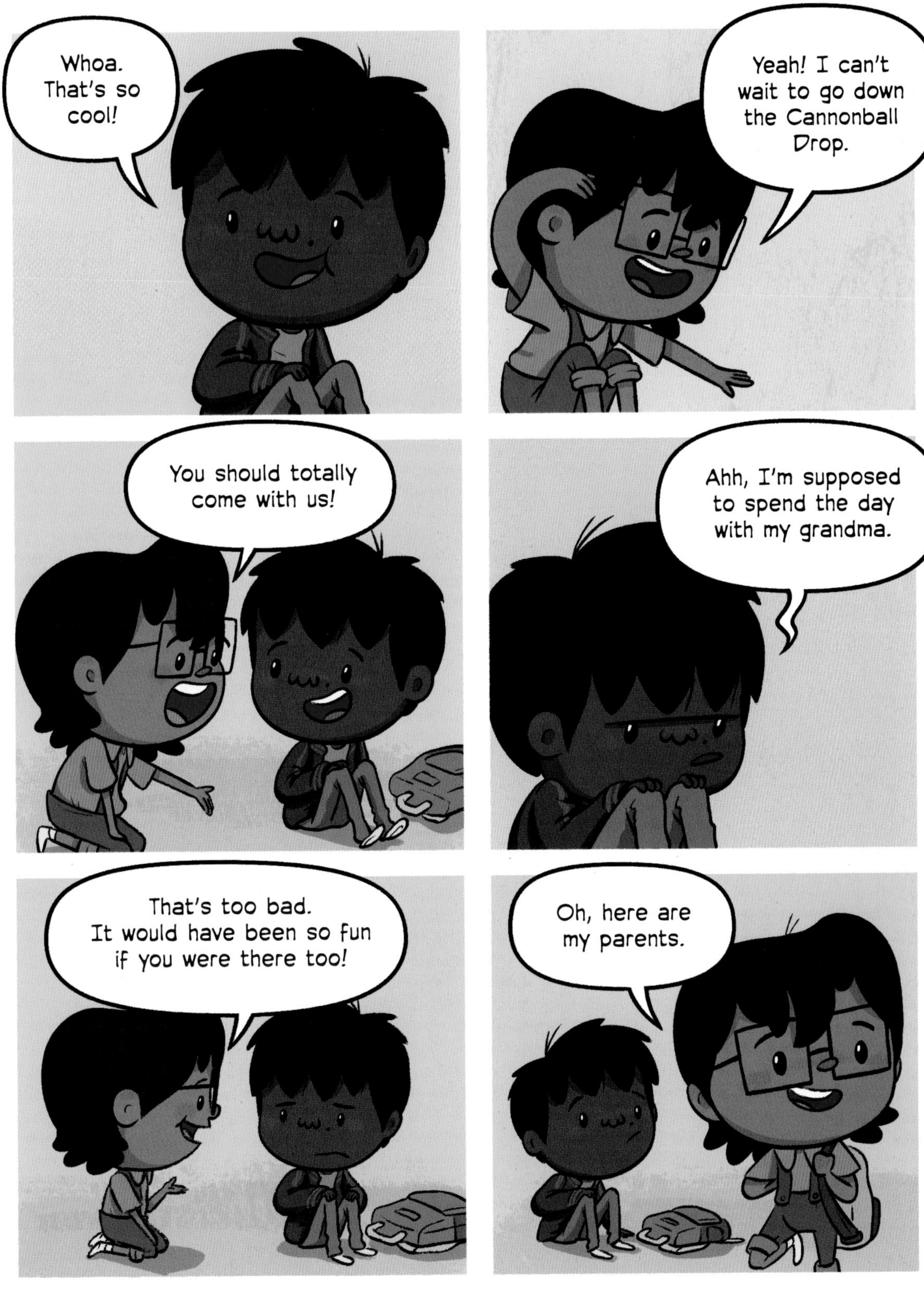
Whoa. That's so cool!
Yeah! I can't wait to go down the Cannonball Drop.
You should totally come with us!
Ahh, I'm supposed to spend the day with my grandma.
That's too bad. It would have been so fun if you were there too!
Oh, here are my parents.

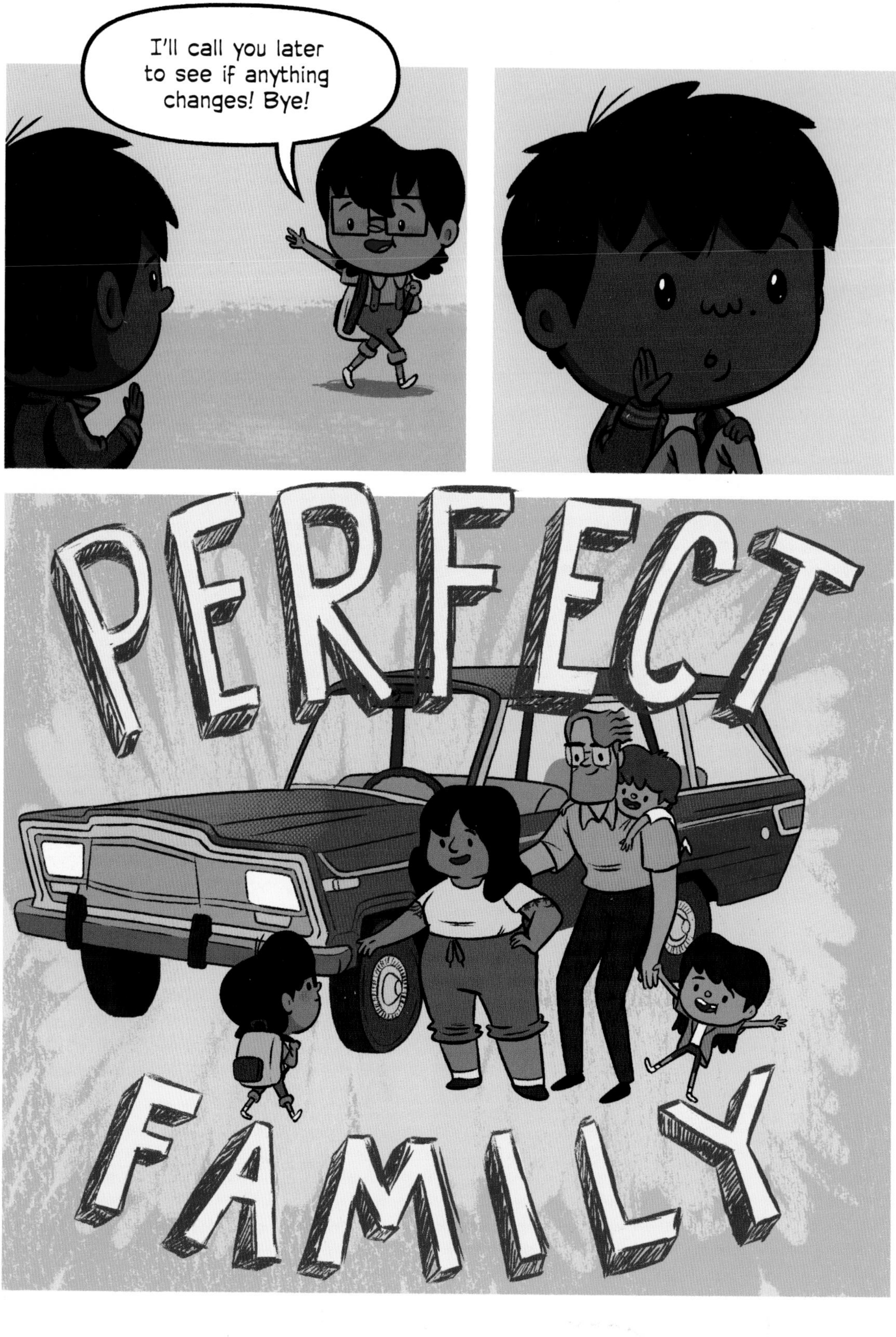
I'll call you later to see if anything changes! Bye!
PERFECT
FAMILY

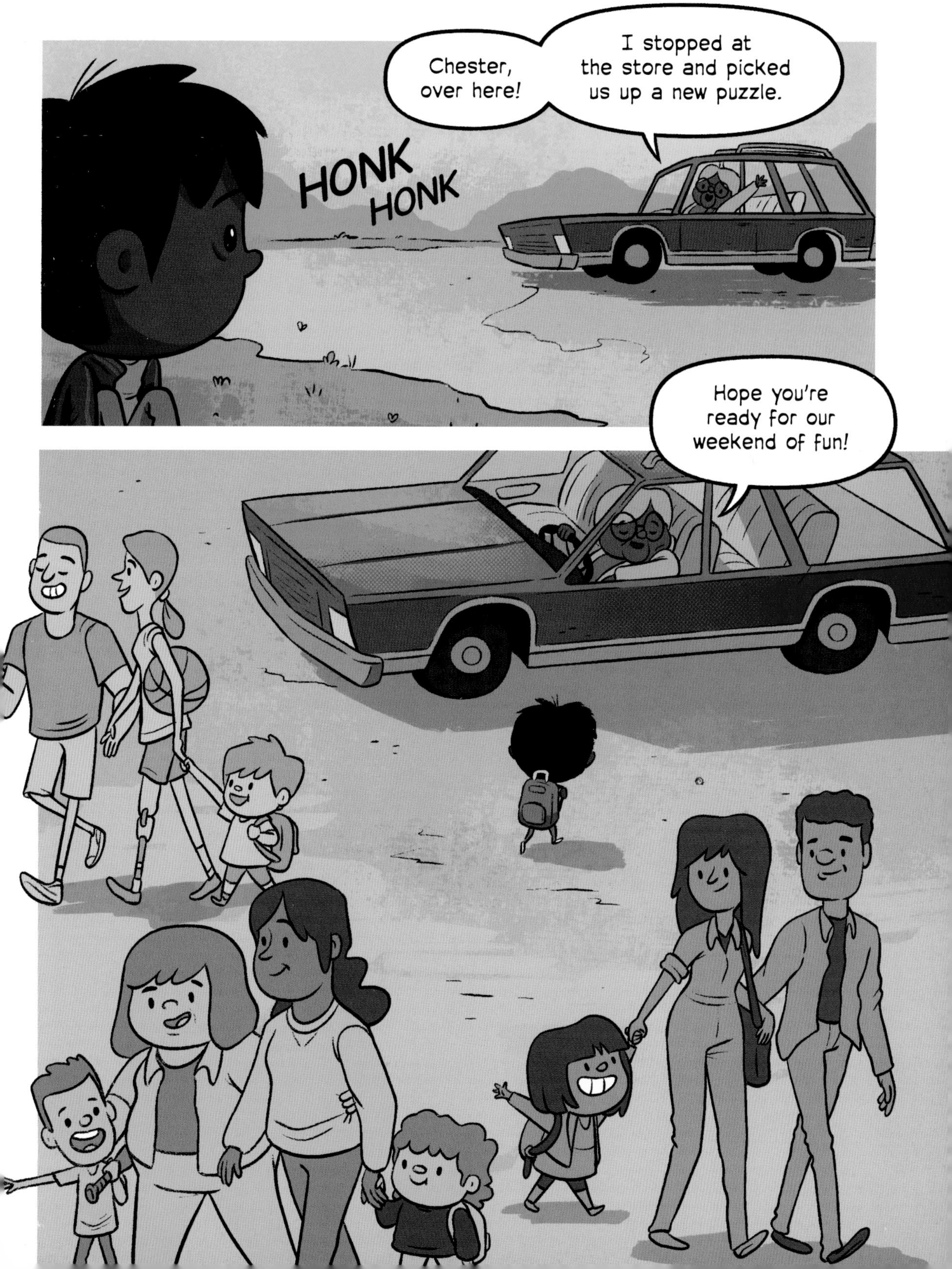
Chester, over here!
I stopped at the store and picked us up a new puzzle.
HONK HONK
Hope you're ready for our weekend of fun!

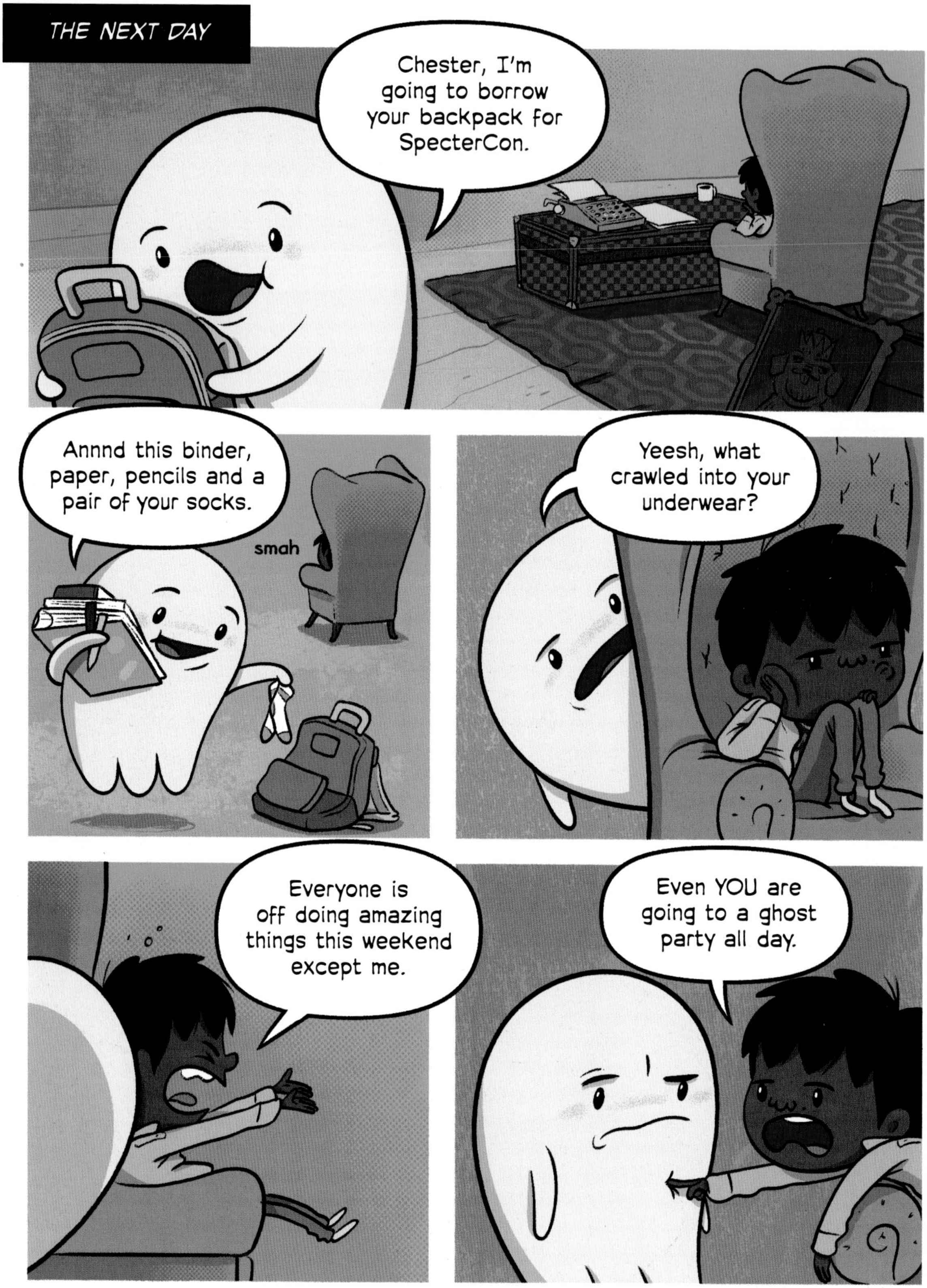
THE NEXT DAY
Chester, I'm going to borrow your backpack for SpecterCon.
Annnd this binder, paper, pencils and a pair of your socks.
smah
Yeesh, what crawled into your underwear?
Everyone is off doing amazing things this weekend except me.
Even YOU are going to a ghost party all day.

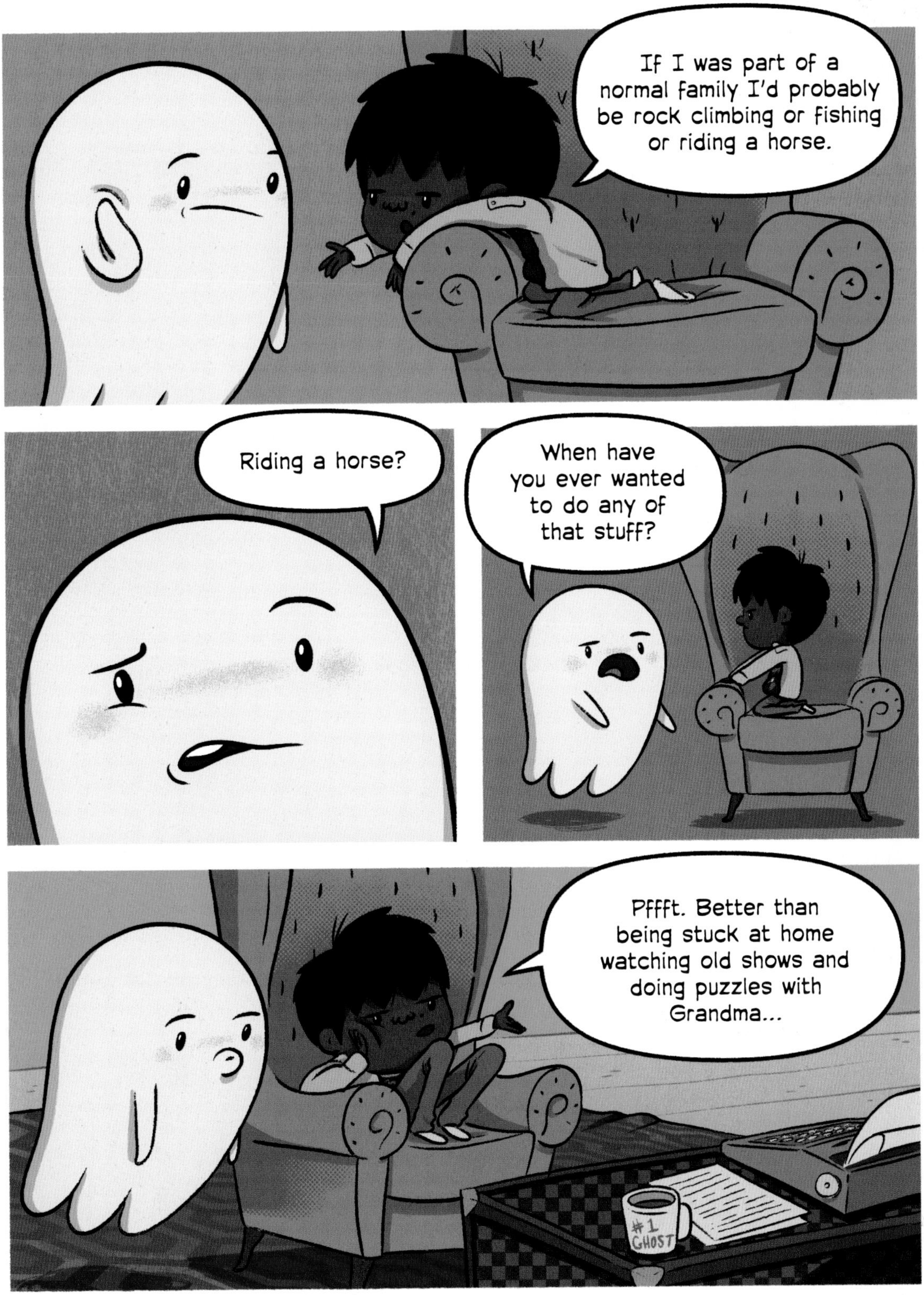
If I was part of a normal family I'd probably be rock climbing or fishing or riding a horse.
Riding a horse?
When have you ever wanted to do any of that stuff?
Pffft. Better than being stuck at home watching old shows and doing puzzles with Grandma...
#1 GHOST

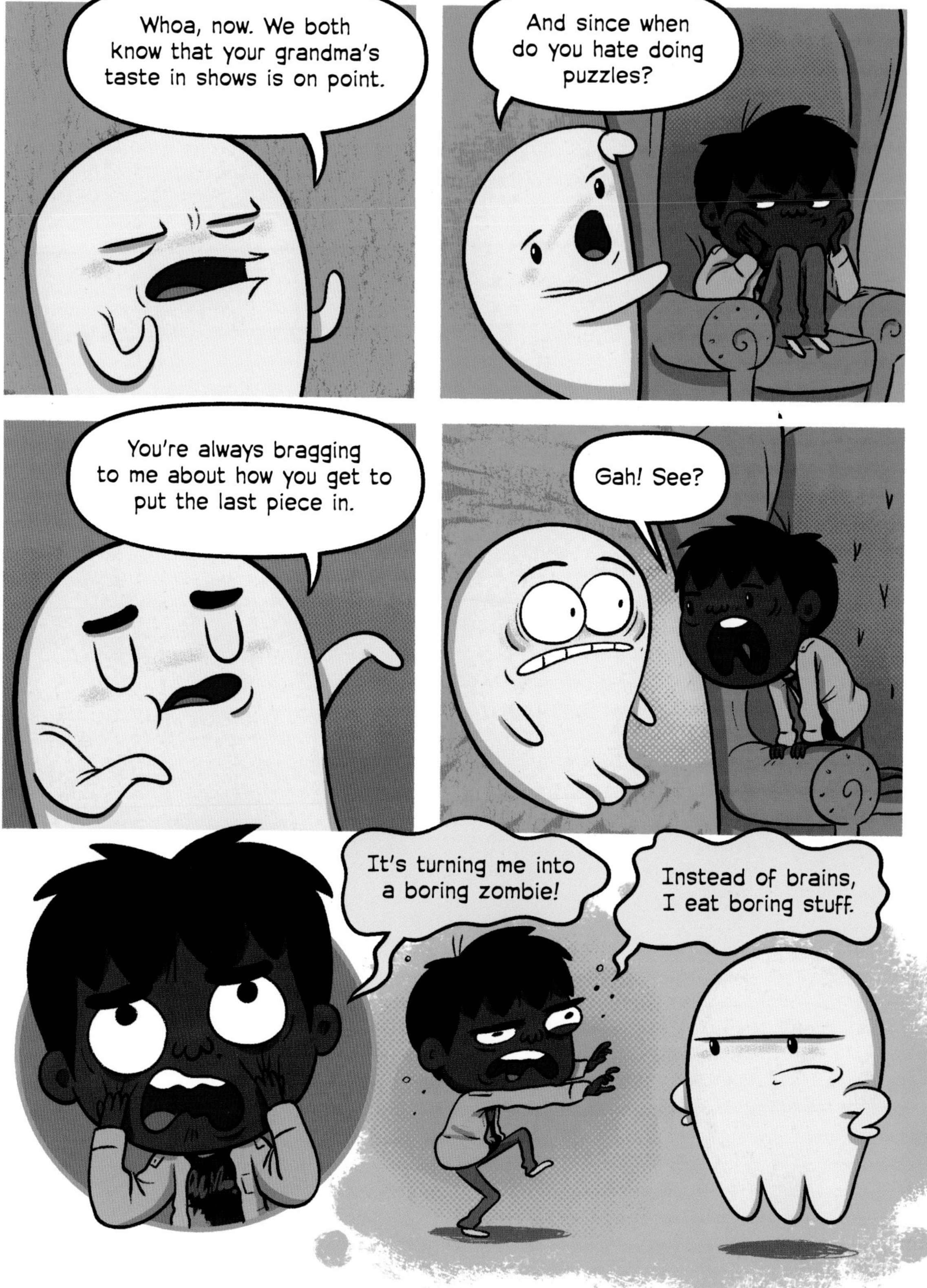
Whoa, now. We both know that your grandma's taste in shows is on point.
And since when do you hate doing puzzles?
You're always bragging to me about how you get to put the last piece in.
Gah! See?
It's turning me into a boring zombie!
Instead of brains, I eat boring stuff.

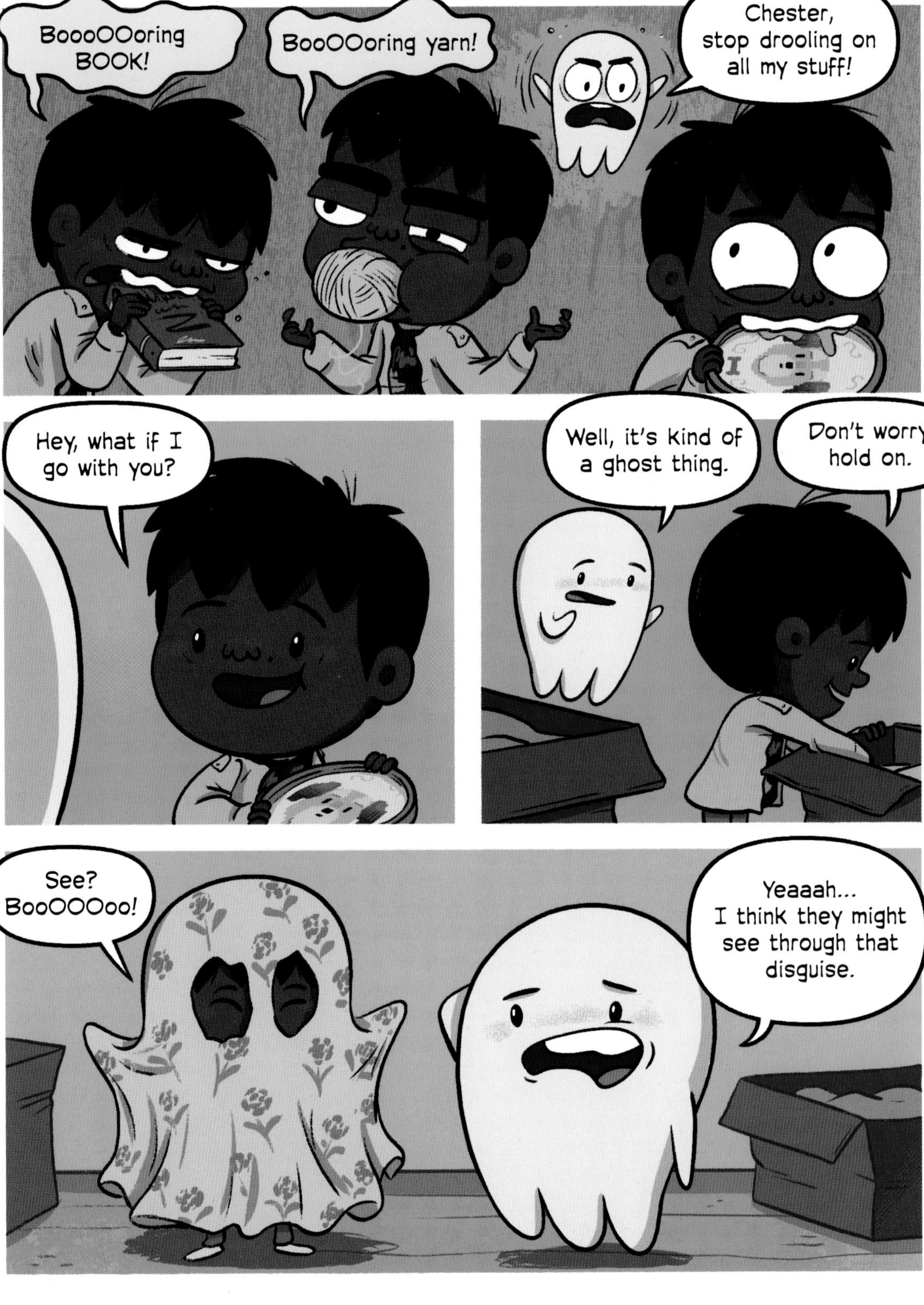
BoooOOoring BOOK!
BooOOoring yarn!
Chester, stop drooling on all my stuff!
Hey, what if I go with you?
Well, it's kind of a ghost thing.
Don't worry, hold on.
See? BooOOOoo!
Yeaaah... I think they might see through that disguise.

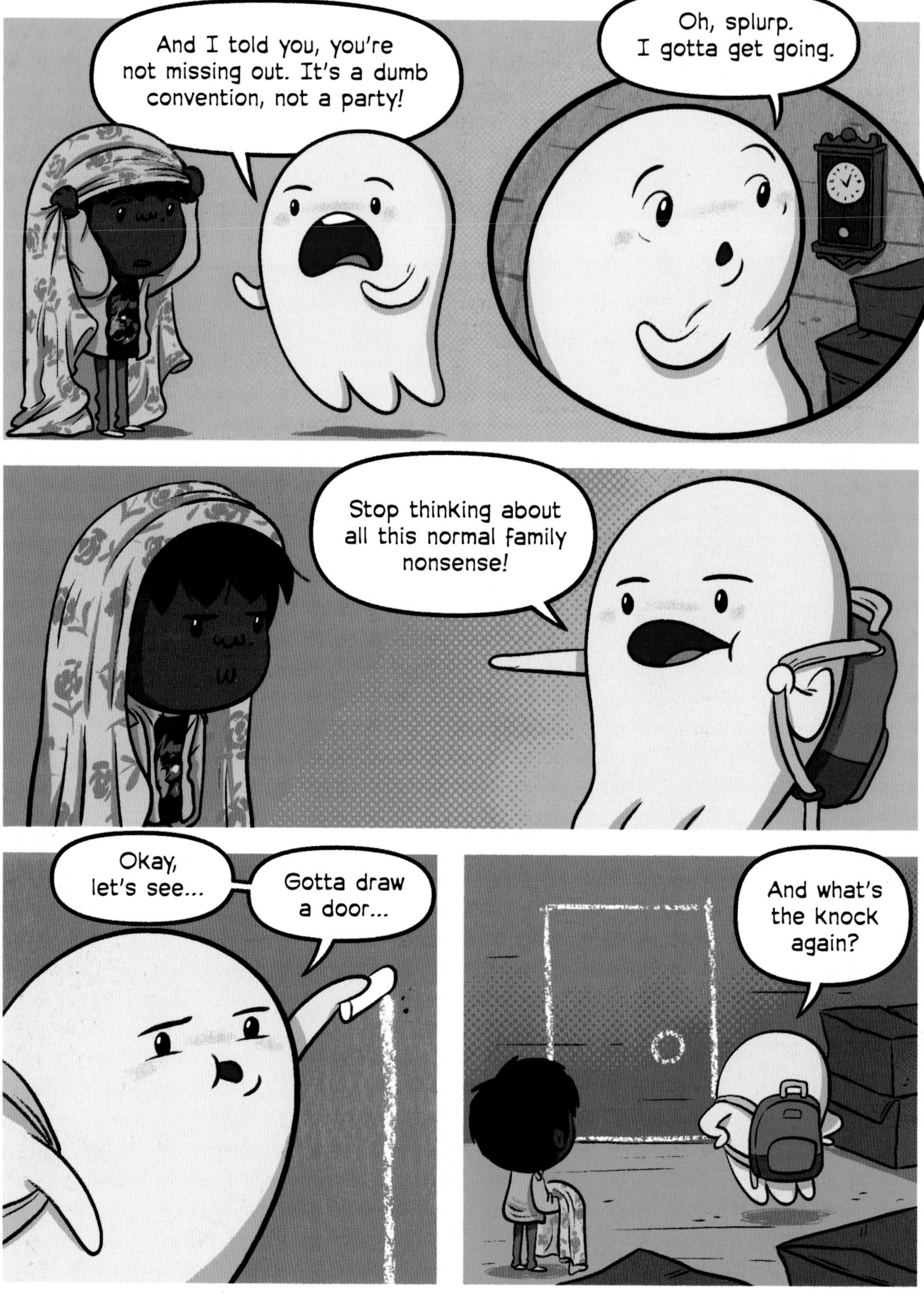
And I told you, you're not missing out. It's a dumb convention, not a party!
Oh, splurp. I gotta get going.
Stop thinking about all this normal family nonsense!
Okay, let's see...
Gotta draw a door...
And what's the knock again?

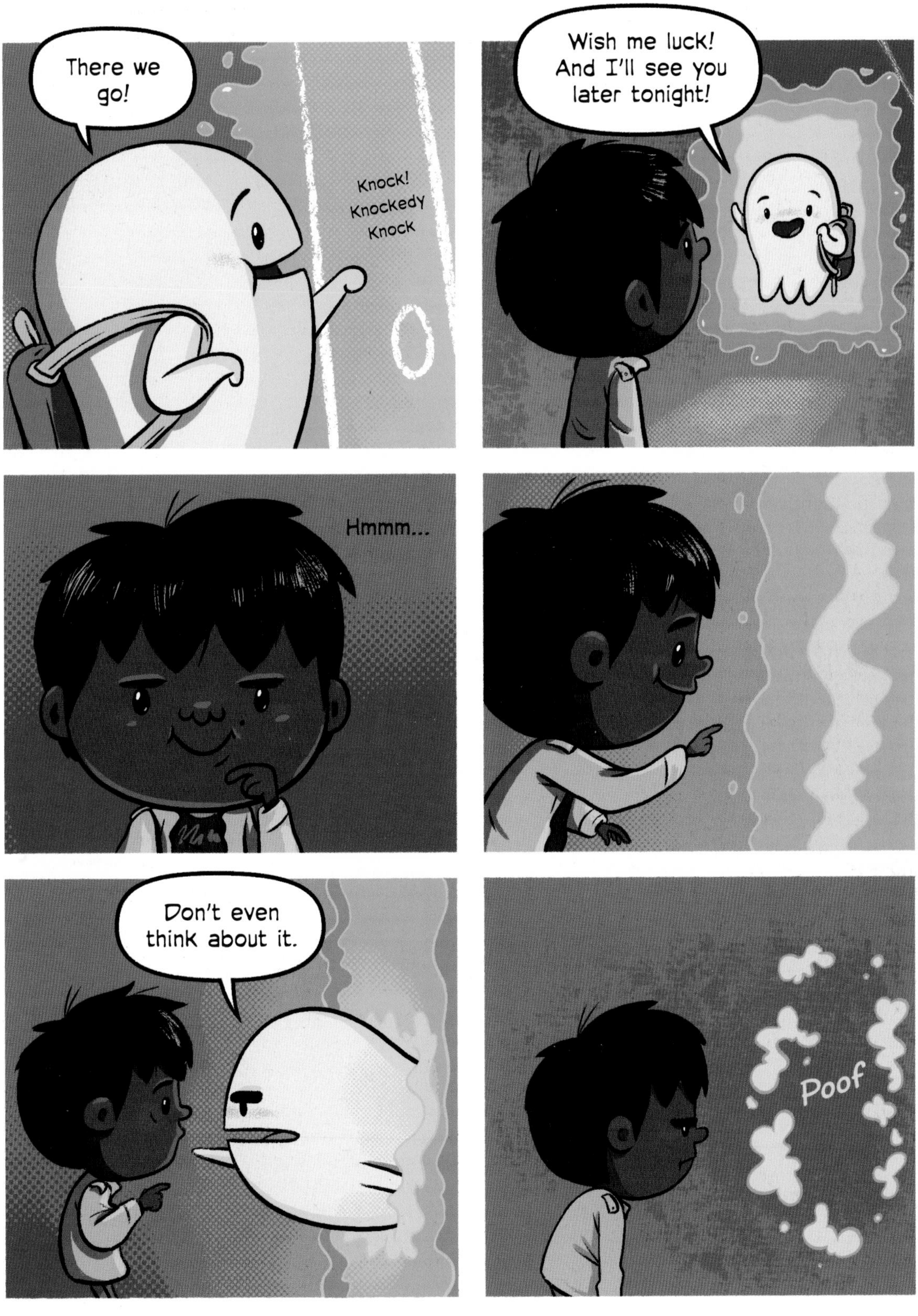
There we go!
Knock! Knockedy Knock
Wish me luck! And I'll see you later tonight!
Hmmm...
Don't even think about it.
Poof

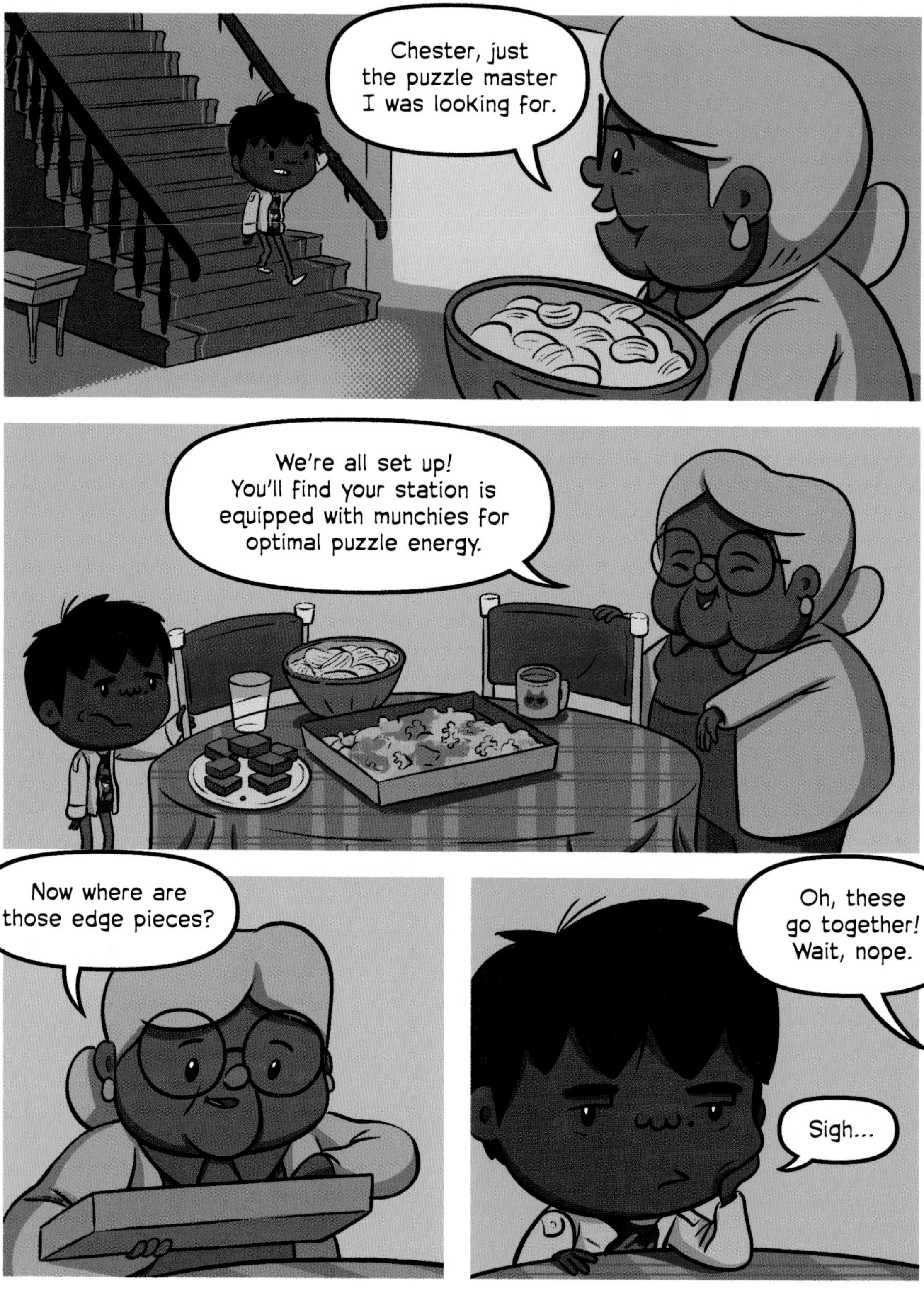
Chester, just the puzzle master I was looking for.
We're all set up! You'll find your station is equipped with munchies for optimal puzzle energy.
Now where are those edge pieces?
Oh, these go together! Wait, nope.
Sigh...

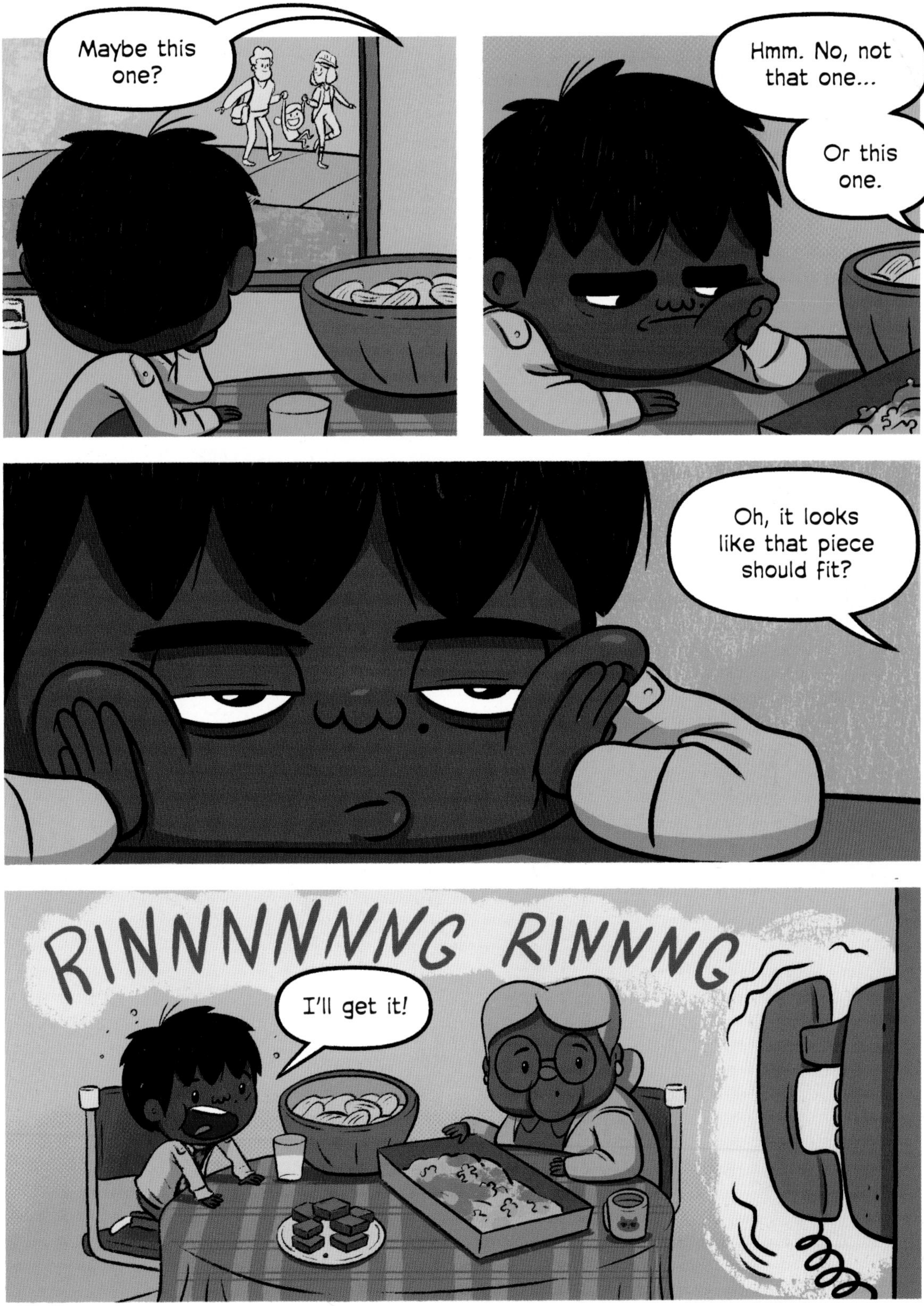
Maybe this one?
Hmm. No, not that one...
Or this one.
Oh, it looks like that piece should fit?
RINNNNNNG RINNNG
I'll get it!

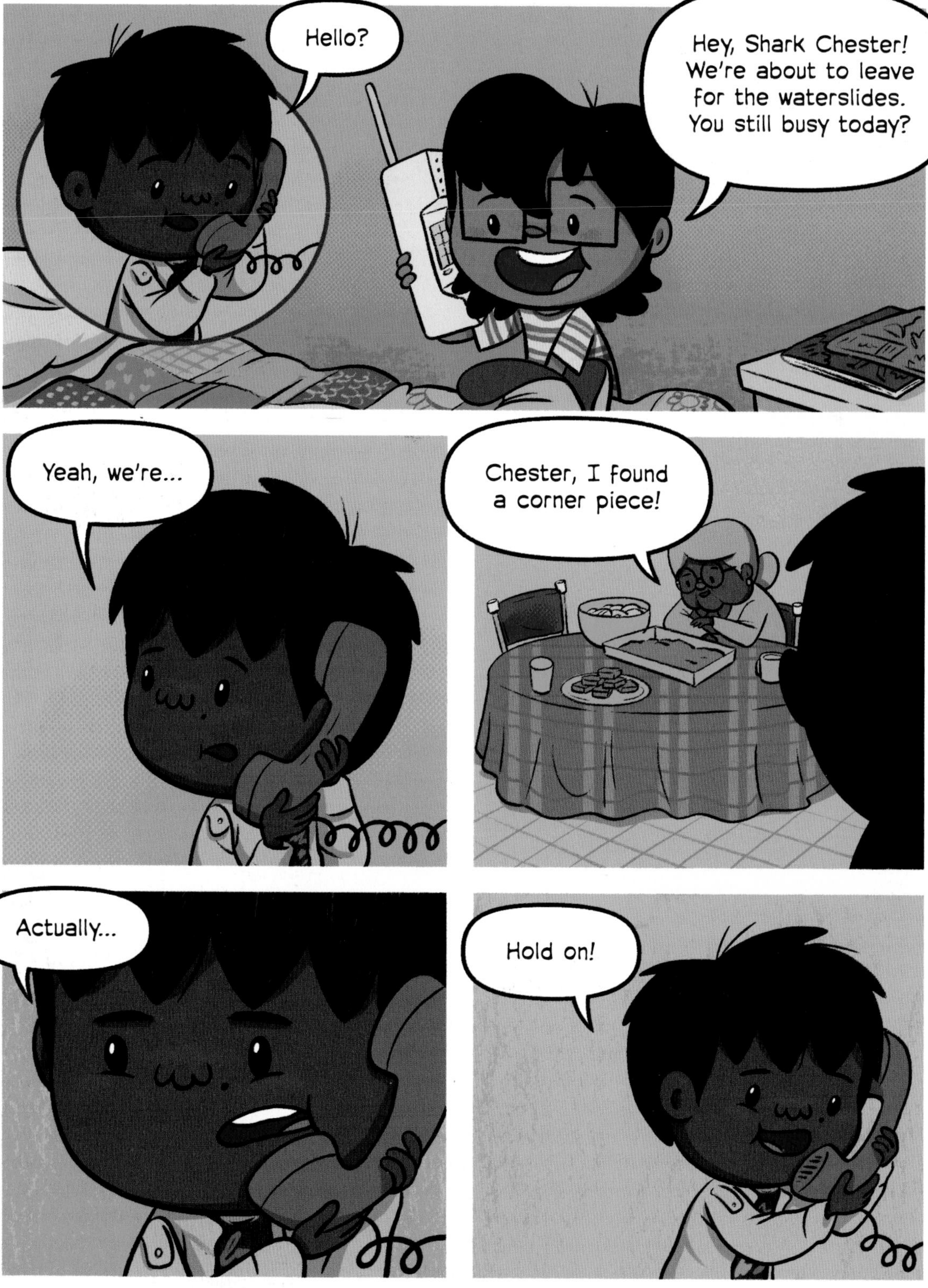
Hello?
Hey, Shark Chester! We're about to leave for the waterslides. You still busy today?
Yeah, we're...
Chester, I found a corner piece!
Actually...
Hold on!

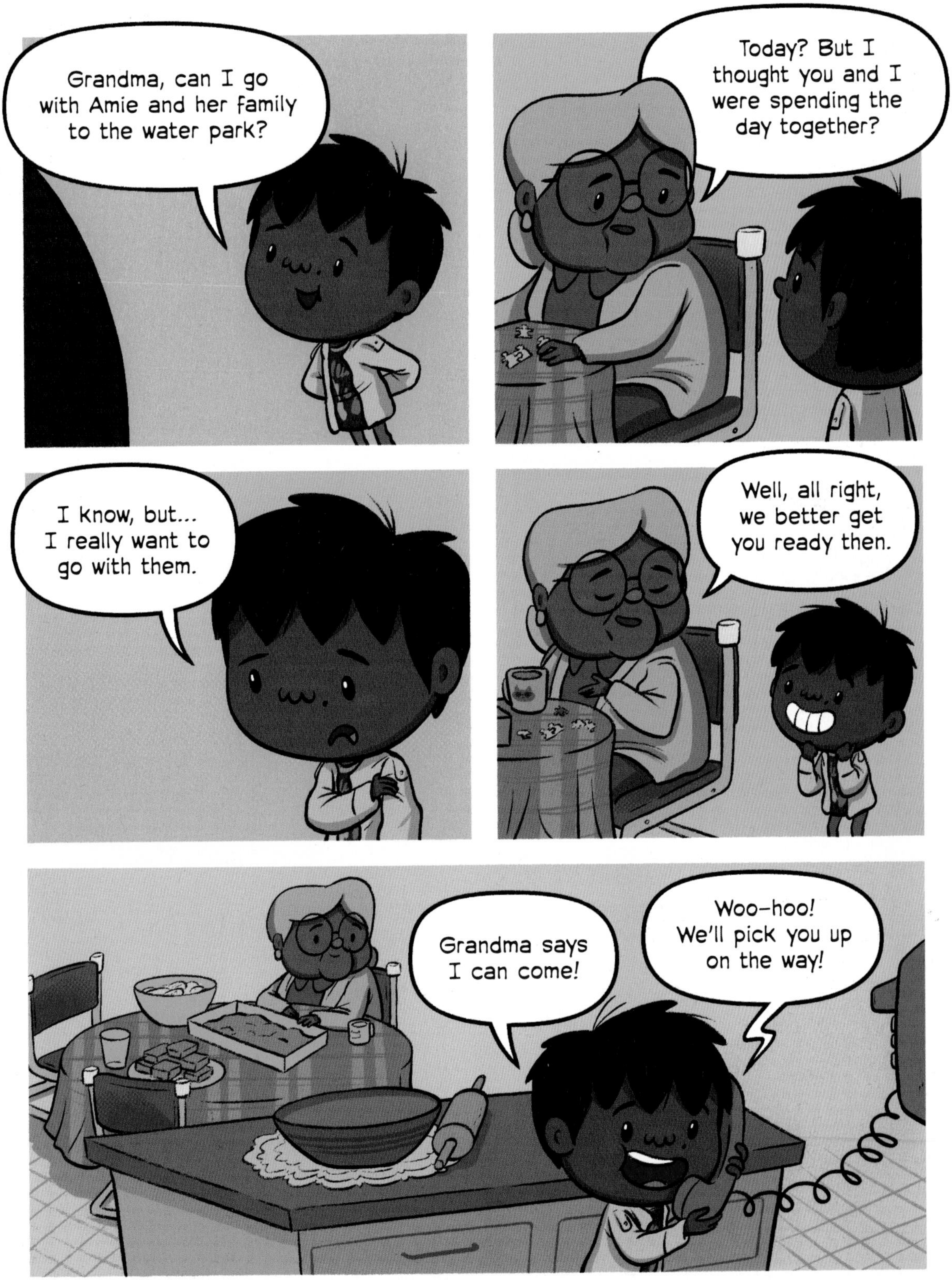
Grandma, can I go with Amie and her family to the water park?
Today? But I thought you and I were spending the day together?
I know, but... I really want to go with them.
Well, all right, we better get you ready then.
Grandma says I can come!
Woo-hoo! We'll pick you up on the way!

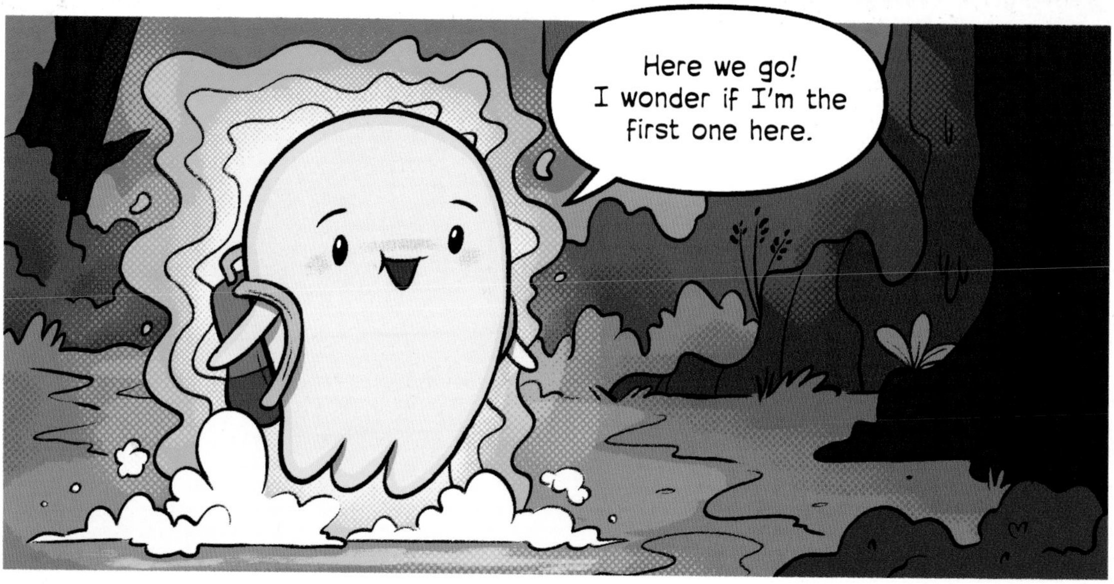
Here we go!
I wonder if I'm the first one here.

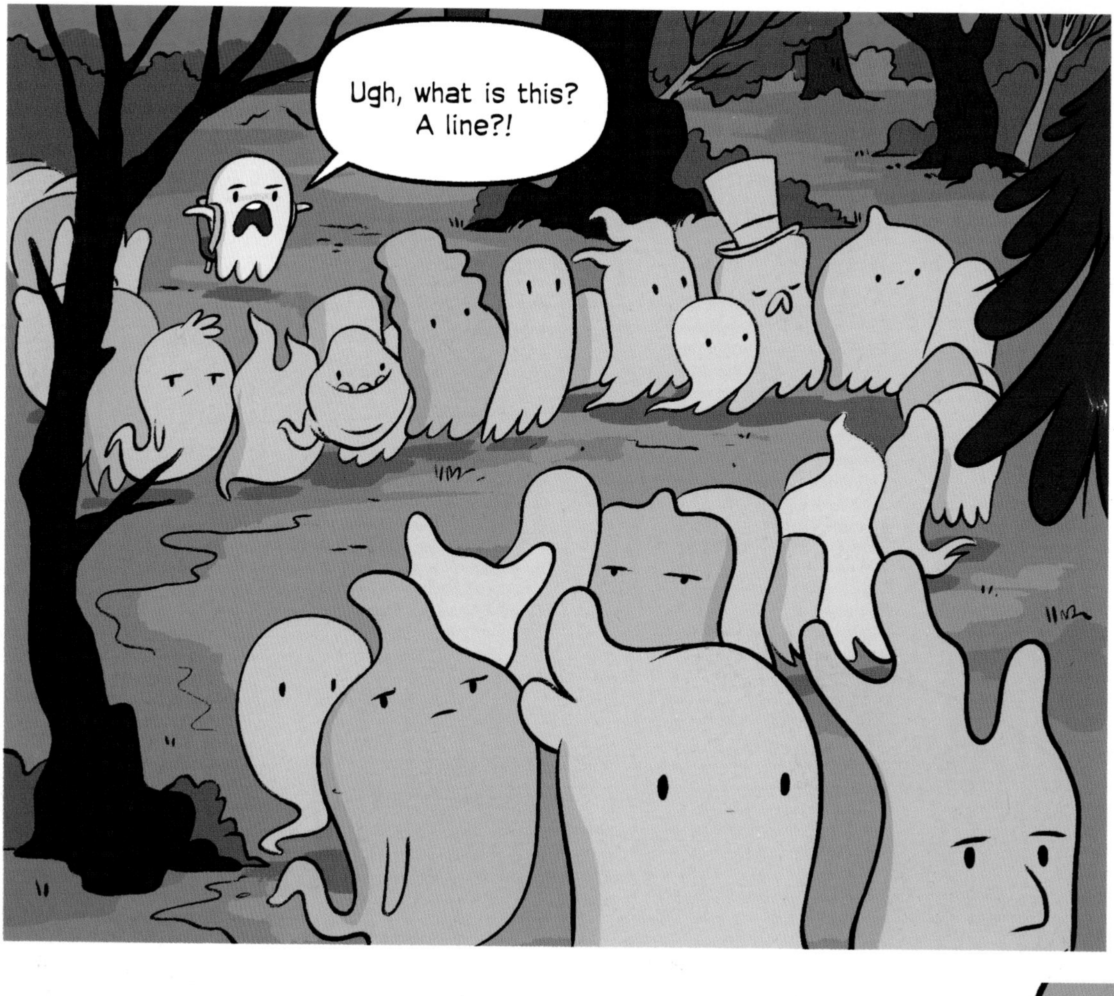
Ugh, what is this? A line?!

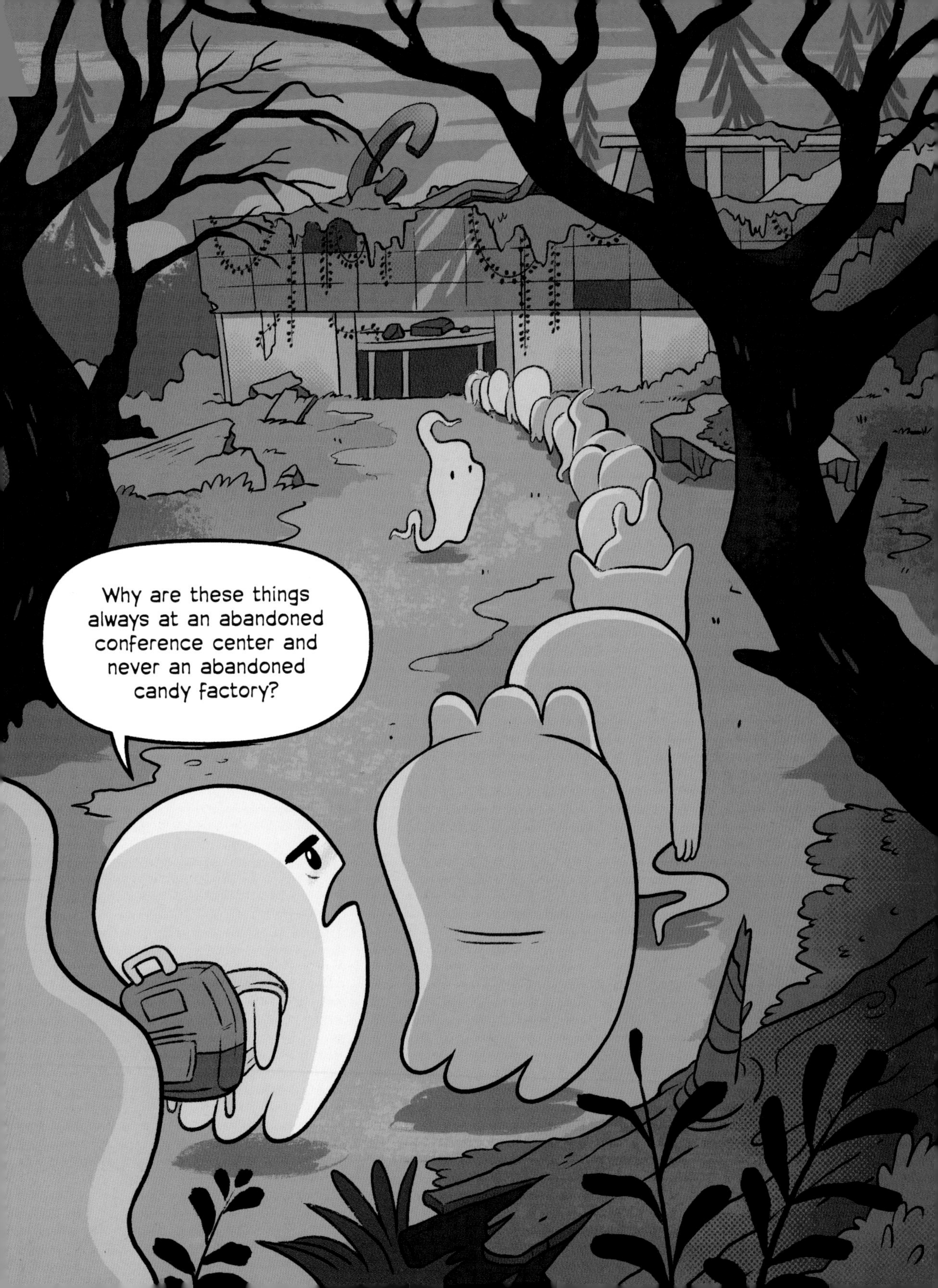
Why are these things always at an abandoned conference center and never an abandoned candy factory?

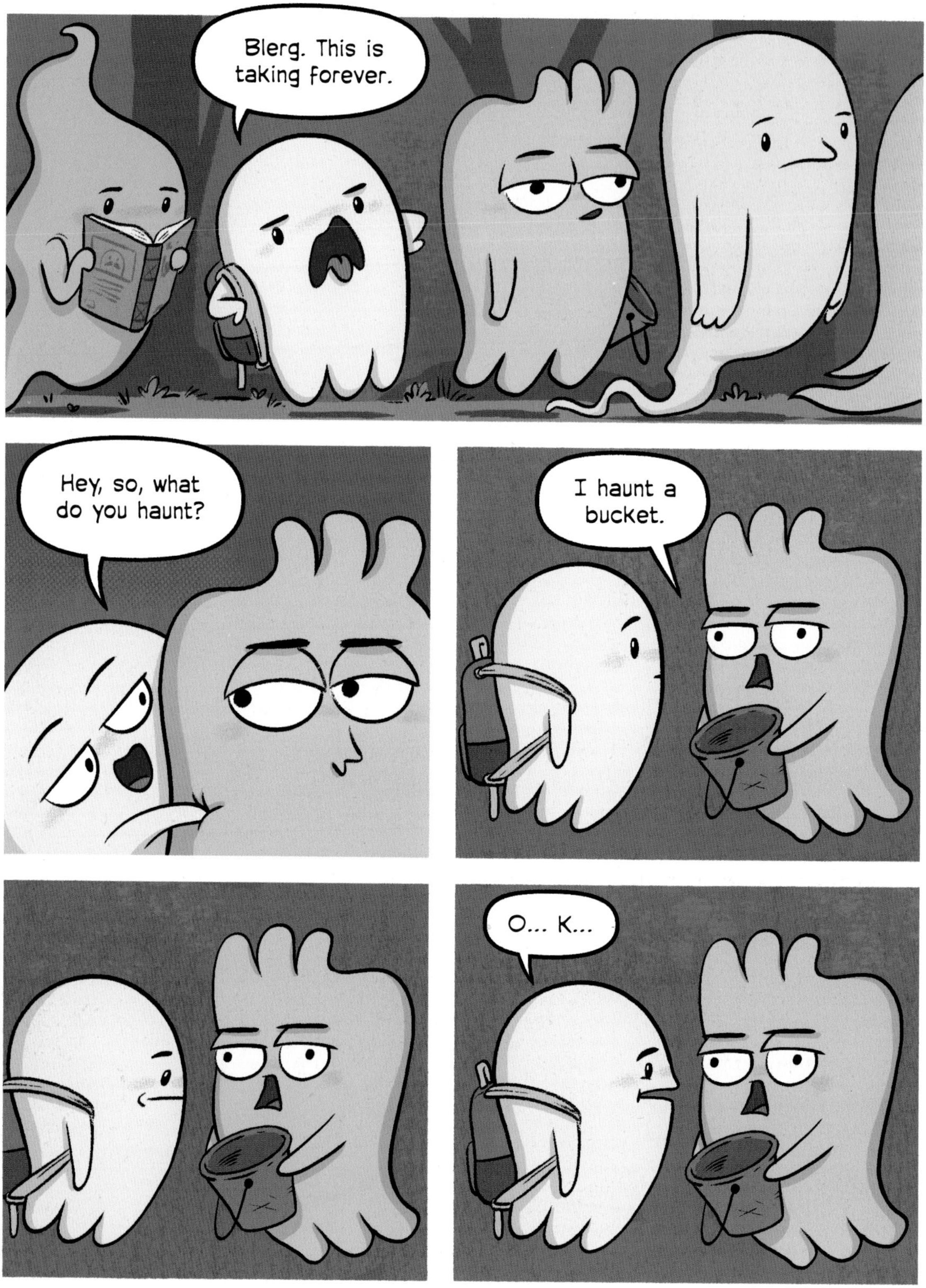
Blerg. This is taking forever.
Hey, so, what do you haunt?
I haunt a bucket.
O... K...

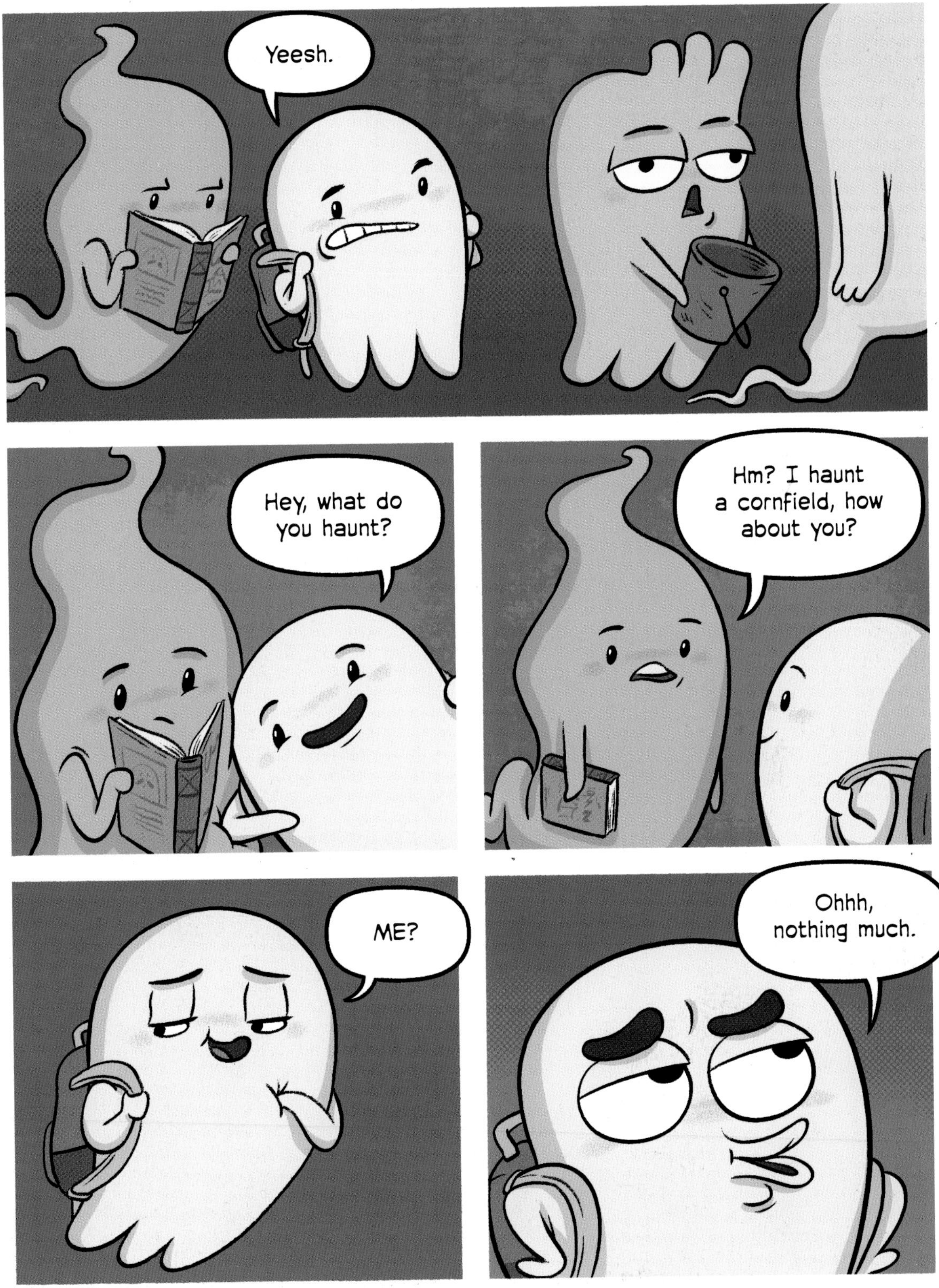
Yeesh.
Hey, what do you haunt?
Hm? I haunt a cornfield, how about you?
ME?
Ohhh, nothing much.

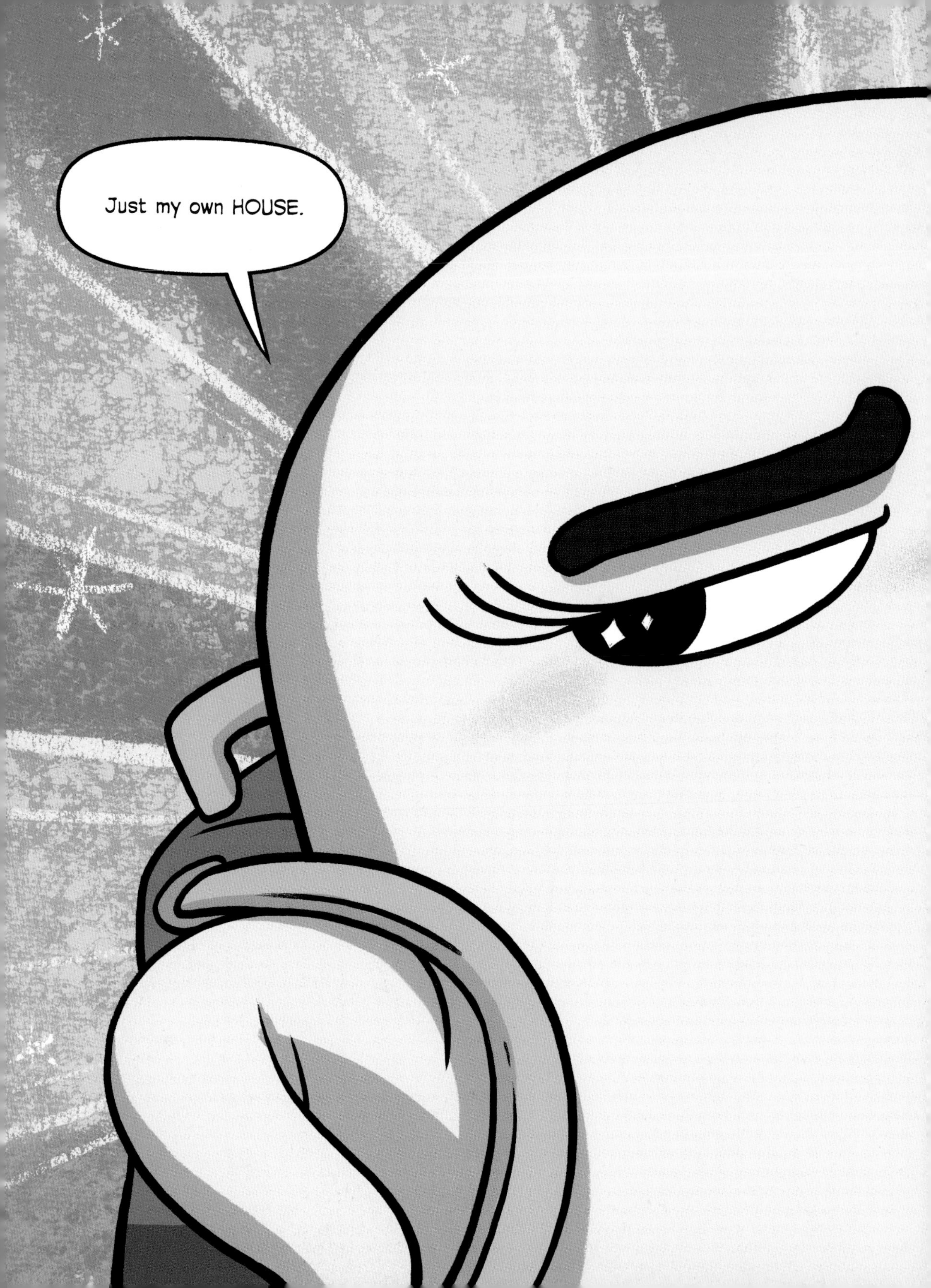
Just my own HOUSE.

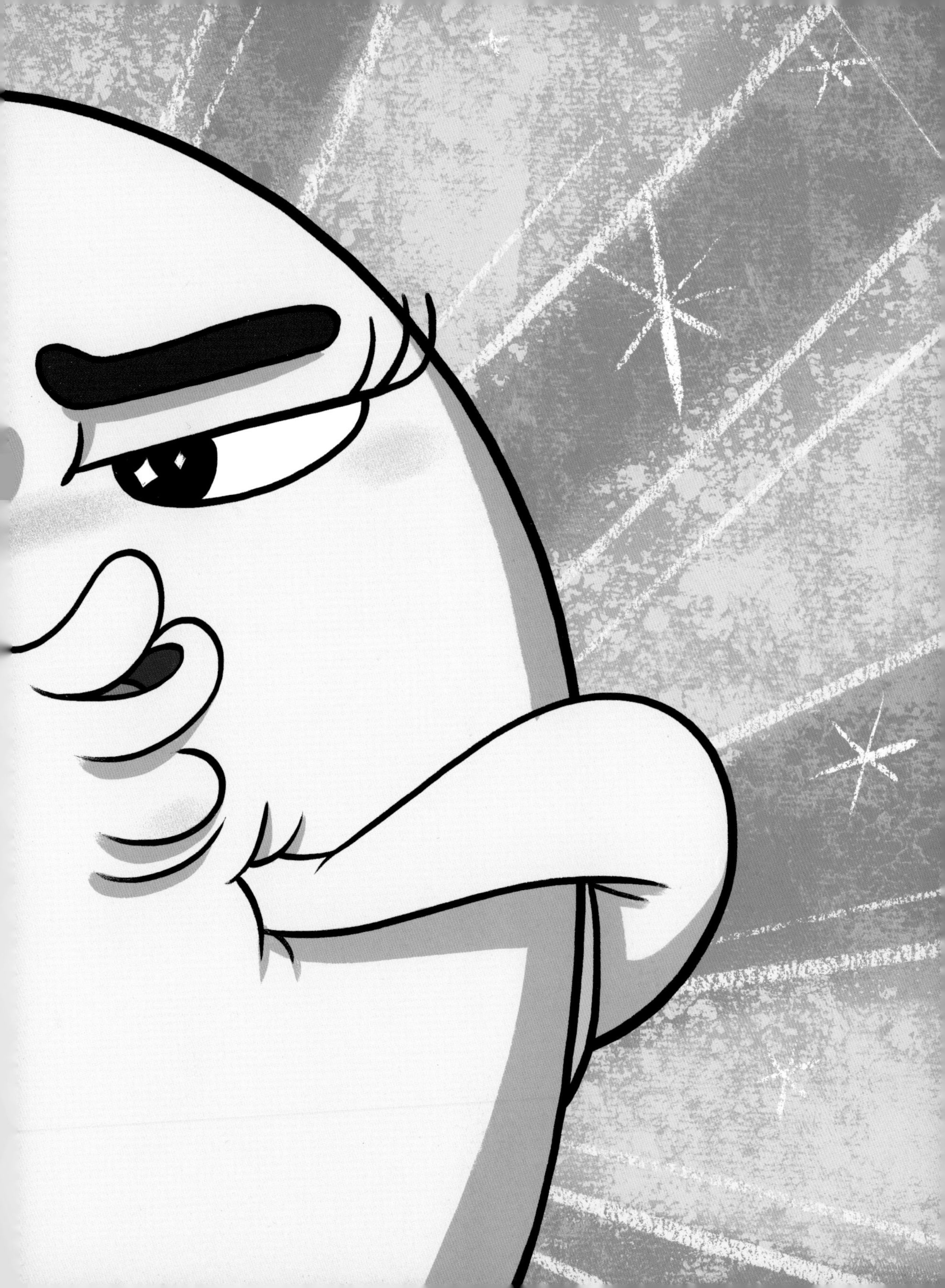

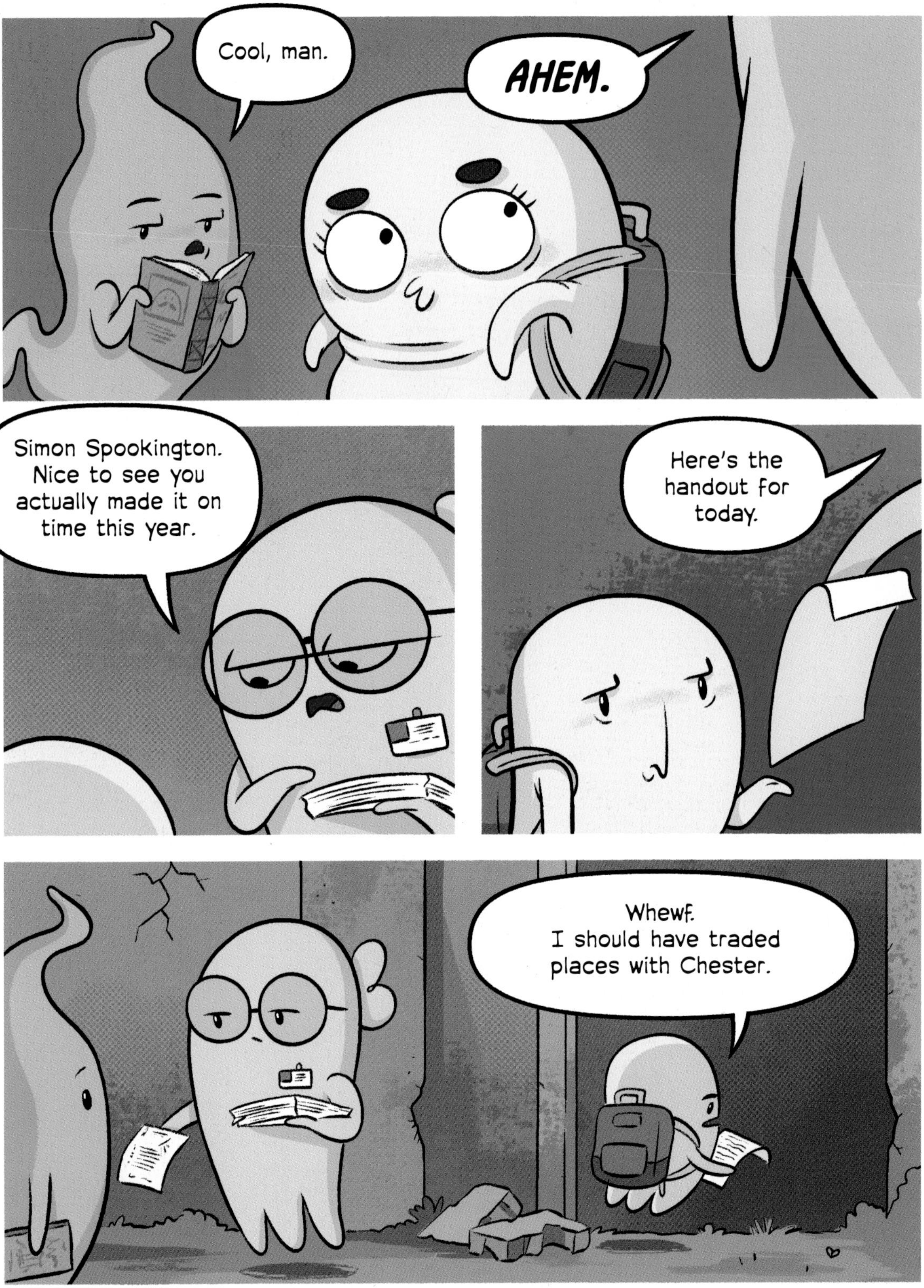
Cool, man.
AHEM.
Simon Spookington. Nice to see you actually made it on time this year.
Here's the handout for today.
Whewf. I should have traded places with Chester.

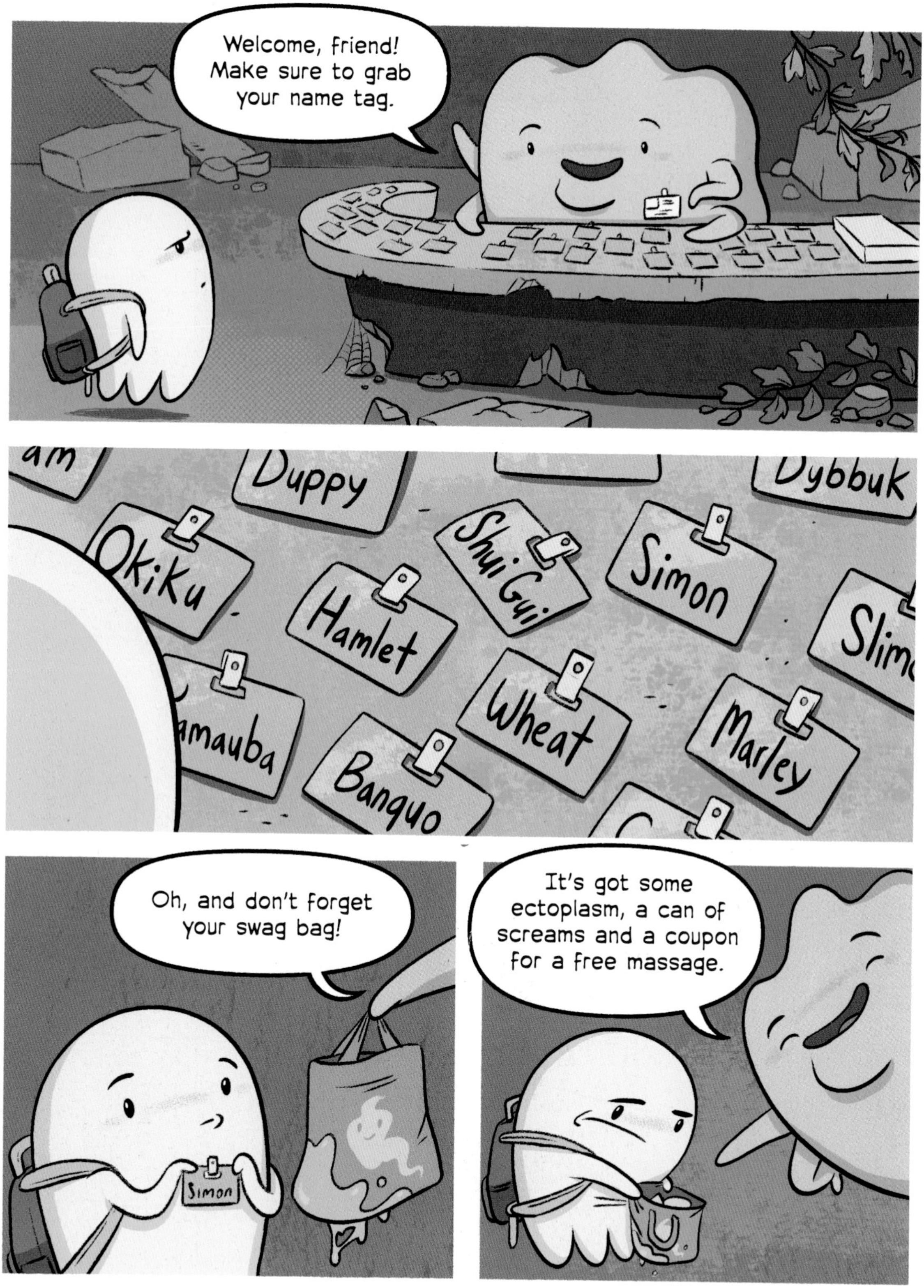
Welcome, friend! Make sure to grab your name tag.
Duppy
Dybbuk
Okiku
Shui Gui
Simon
Hamlet
Wheat
Marley
Banquo
Oh, and don't forget your swag bag!
Simon
It's got some ectoplasm, a can of screams and a coupon for a free massage.

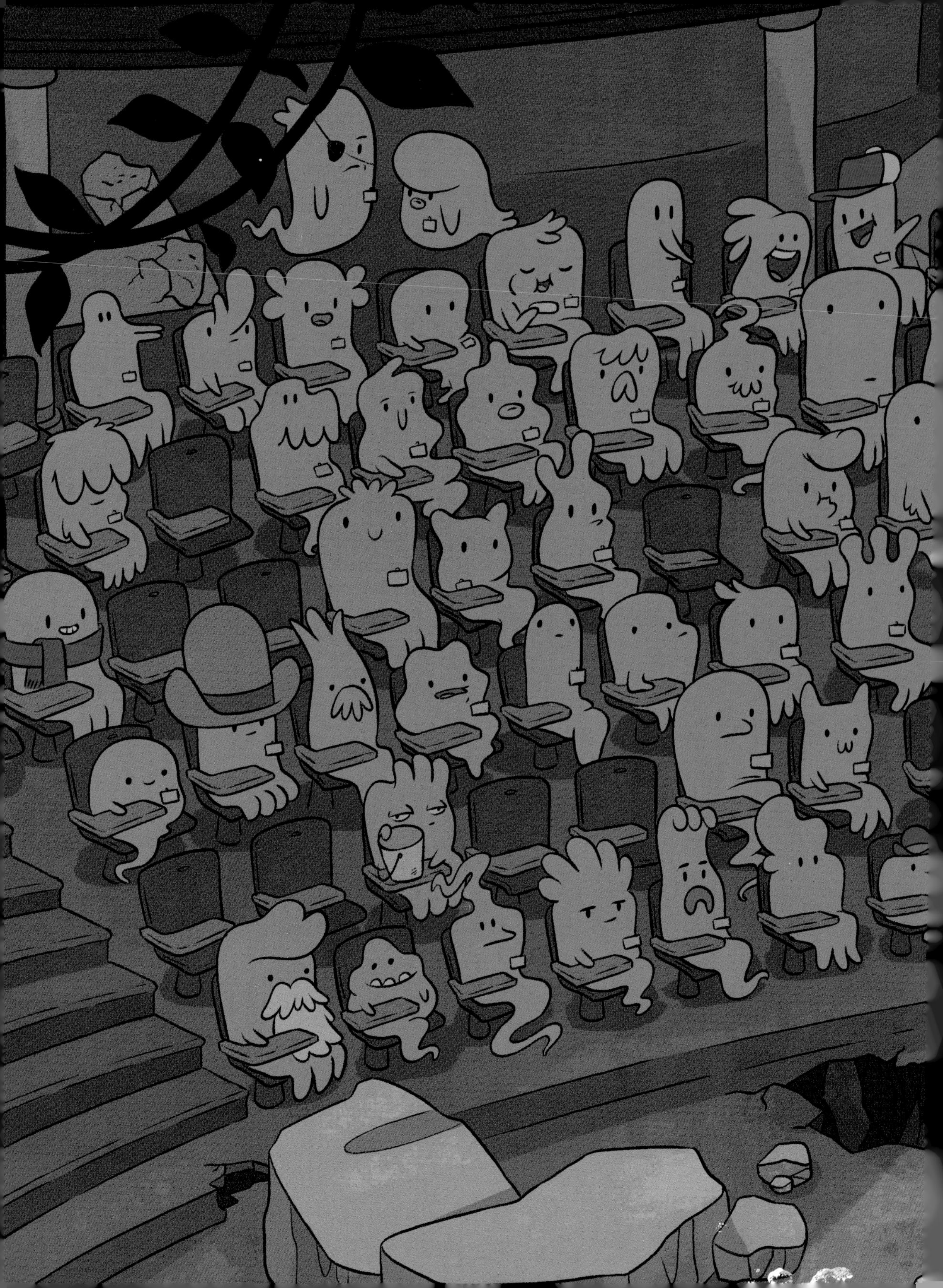

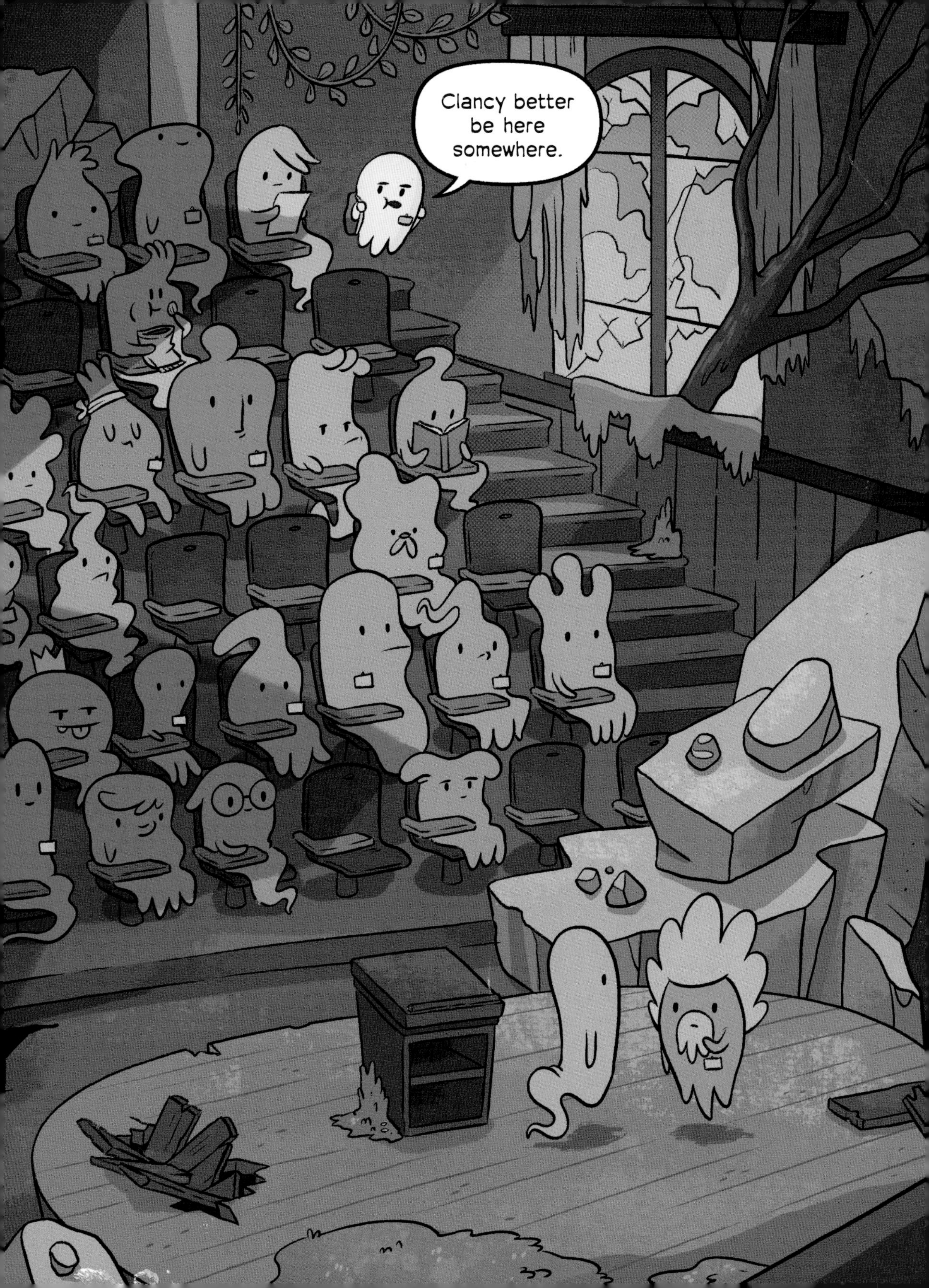
Clancy better be here somewhere.

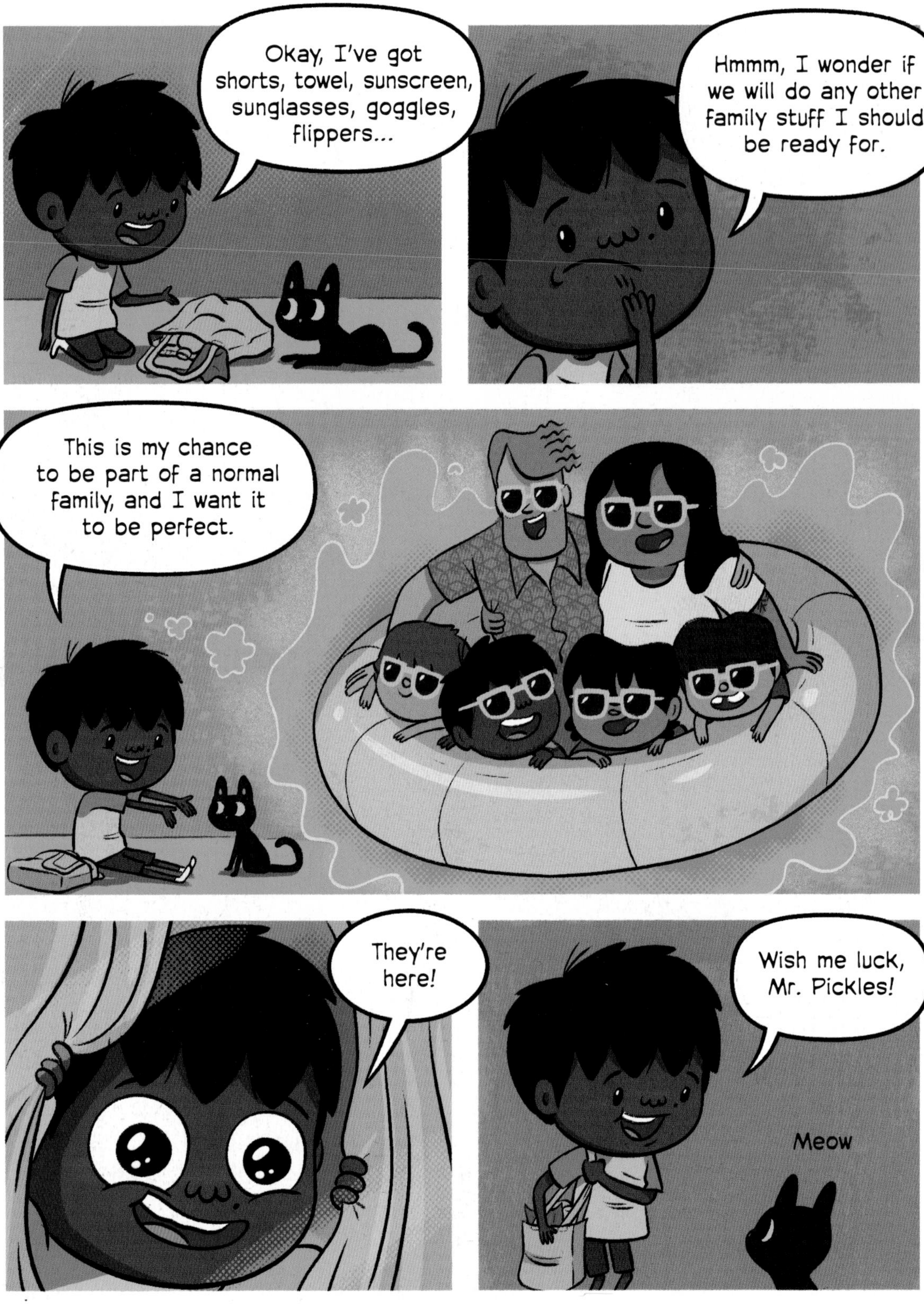
Okay, I've got shorts, towel, sunscreen, sunglasses, goggles, flippers...
Hmmm, I wonder if we will do any other family stuff I should be ready for.
This is my chance to be part of a normal family, and I want it to be perfect.
They're here!
Wish me luck, Mr. Pickles!
Meow

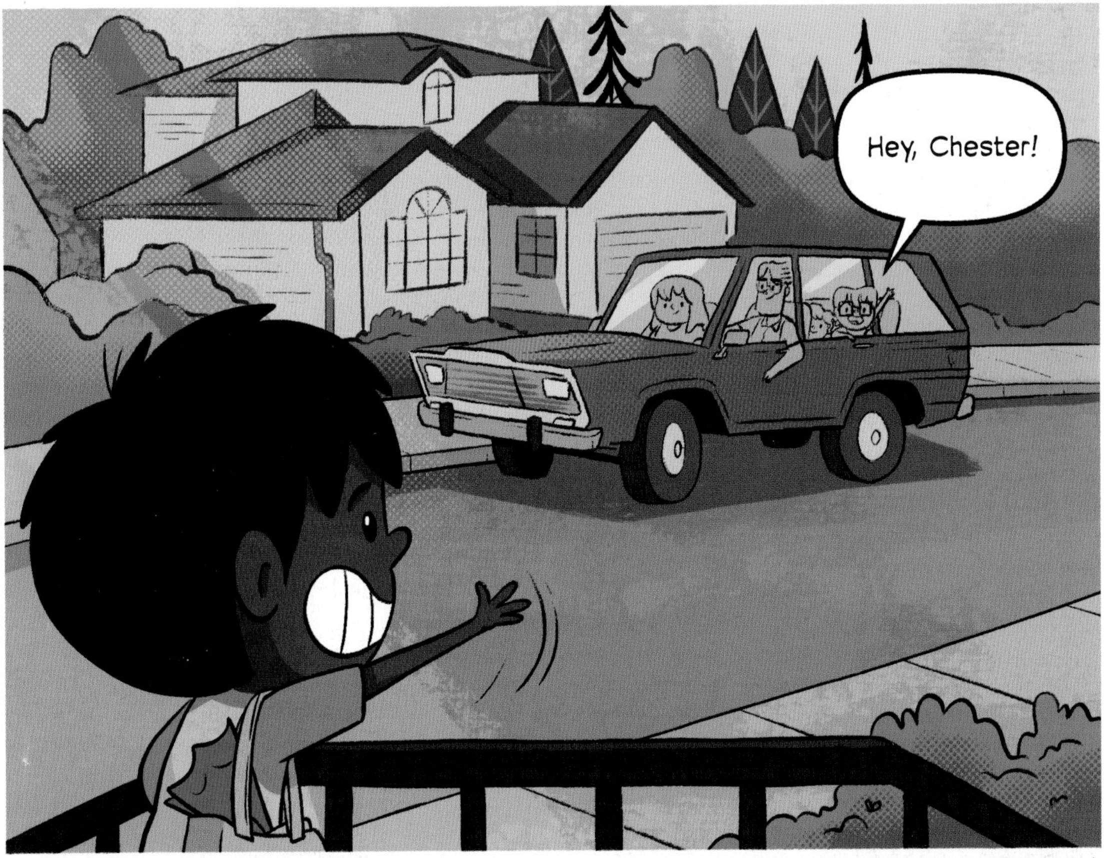
Hey, Chester!

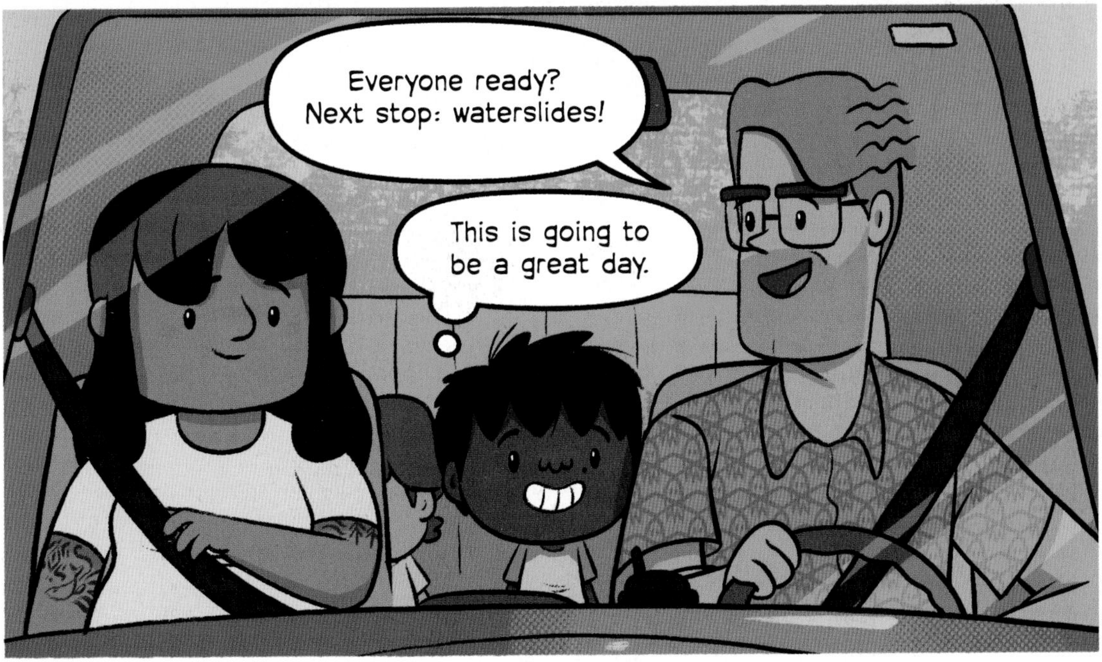
Everyone ready?
Next stop: waterslides!
This is going to be a great day.

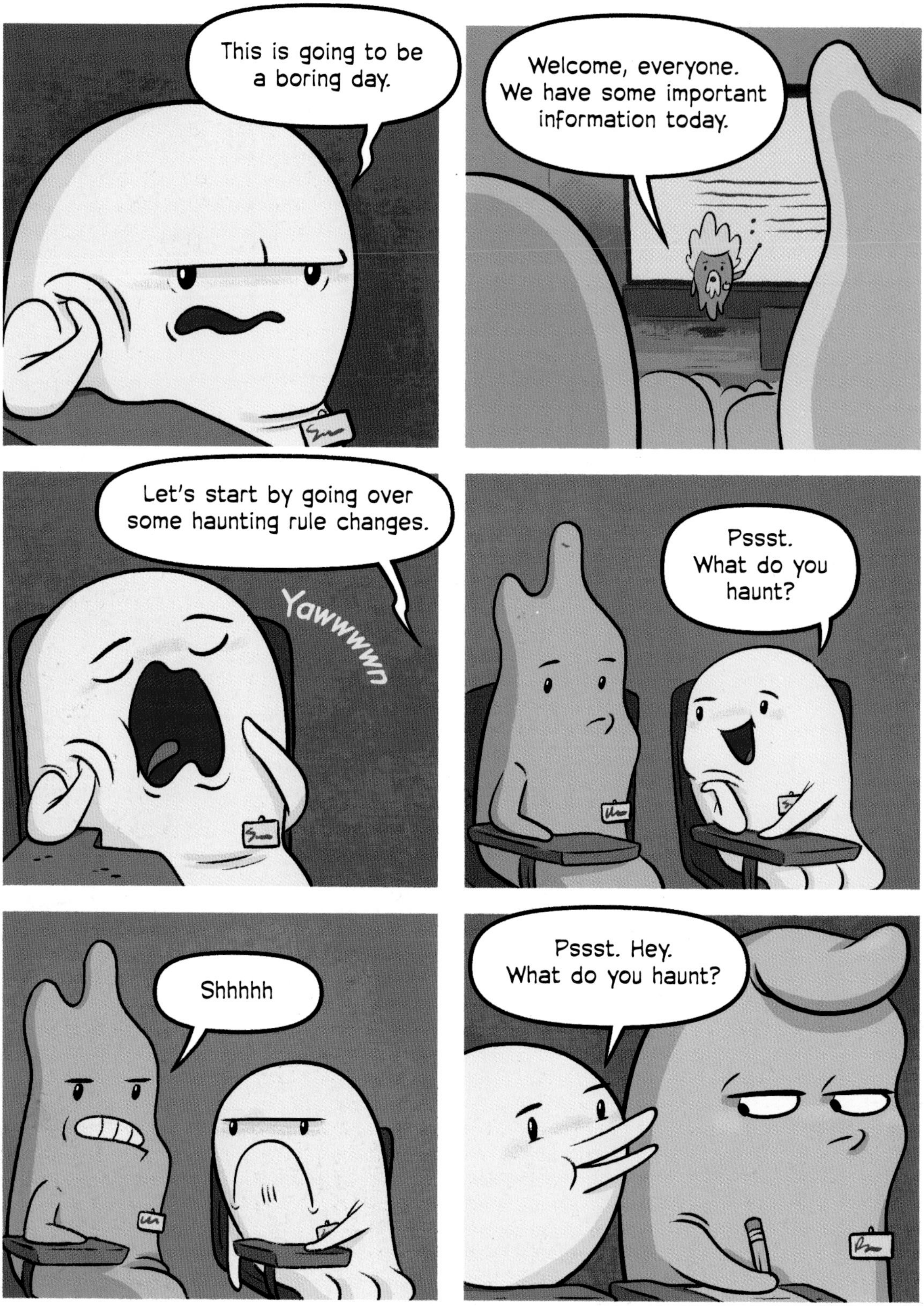
This is going to be a boring day.
Welcome, everyone. We have some important information today.
Let's start by going over some haunting rule changes.
Yawwwwn
Pssst. What do you haunt?
Shhhhh
Pssst. Hey. What do you haunt?

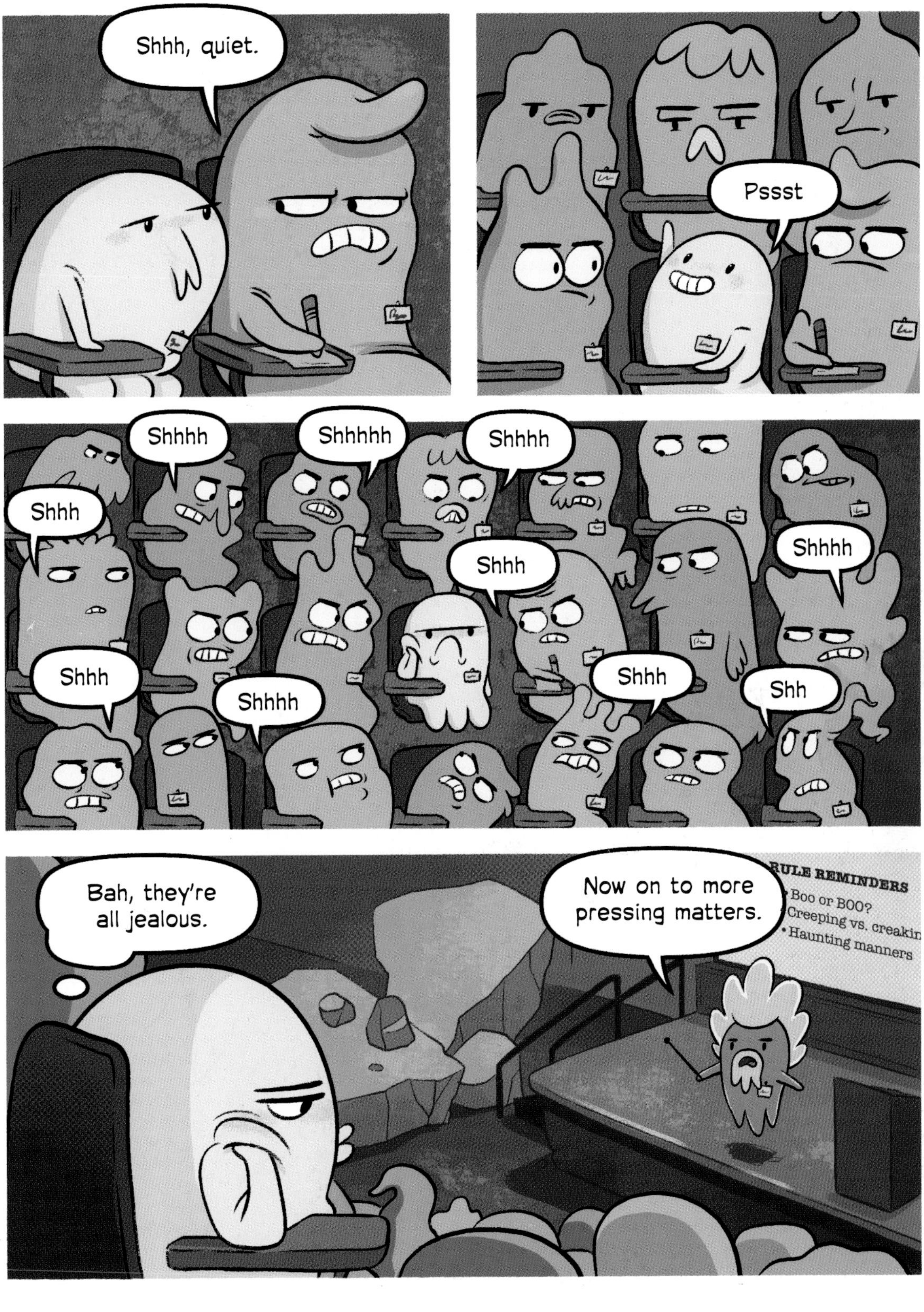
Shhh, quiet.
Pssst
Shhhh
Shhhhh
Shhhh
Shhh
Shhh
Shhhh
Shhh
Shhhh
Shhh
Shh
Bah, they're all jealous.
Now on to more pressing matters.
RULE REMINDERS
• Boo or BOO?
• Creeping vs. creakin
• Haunting manners

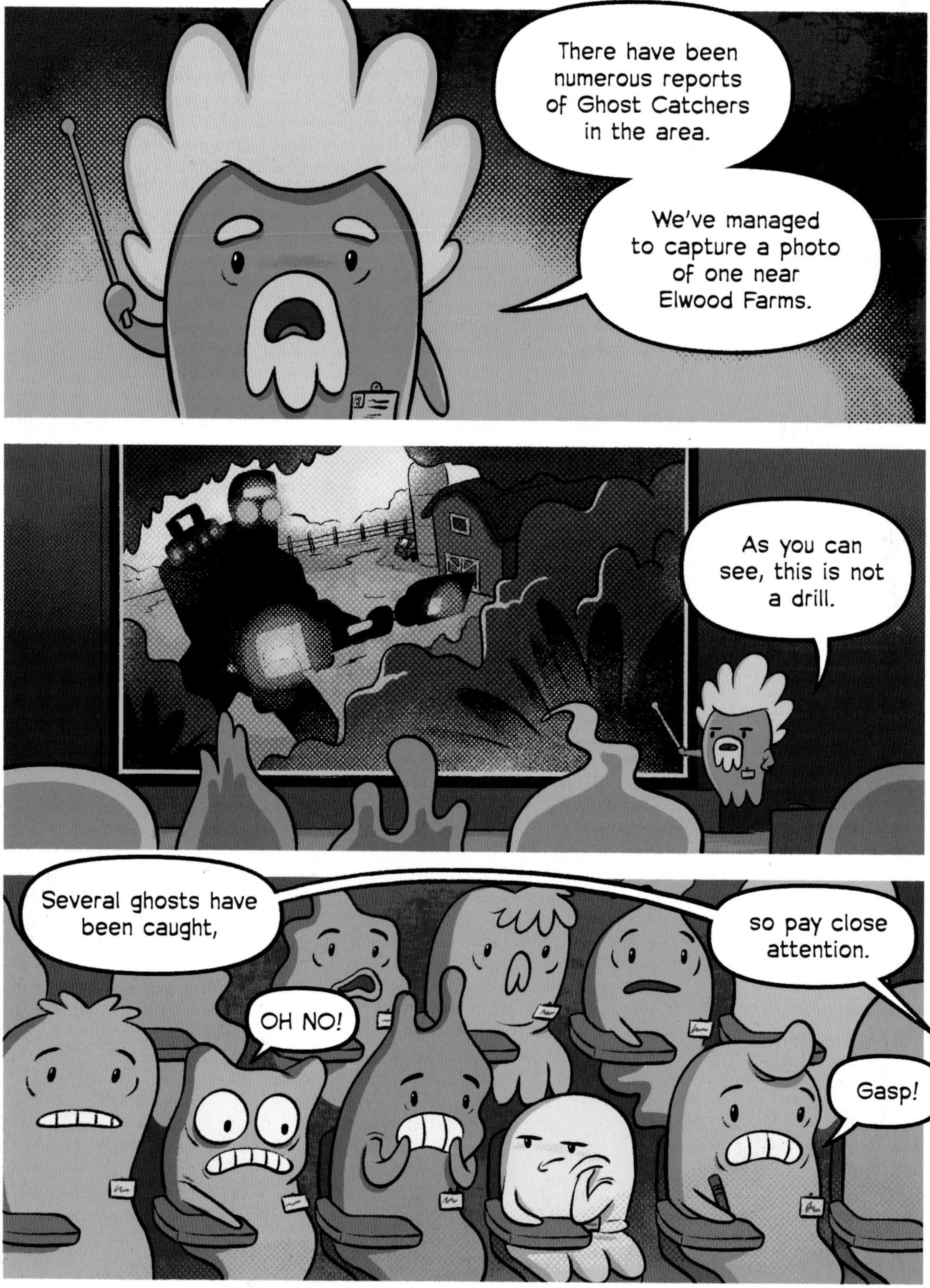
There have been numerous reports of Ghost Catchers in the area.
We've managed to capture a photo of one near Elwood Farms.
As you can see, this is not a drill.
Several ghosts have been caught,
so pay close attention.
OH NO!
Gasp!

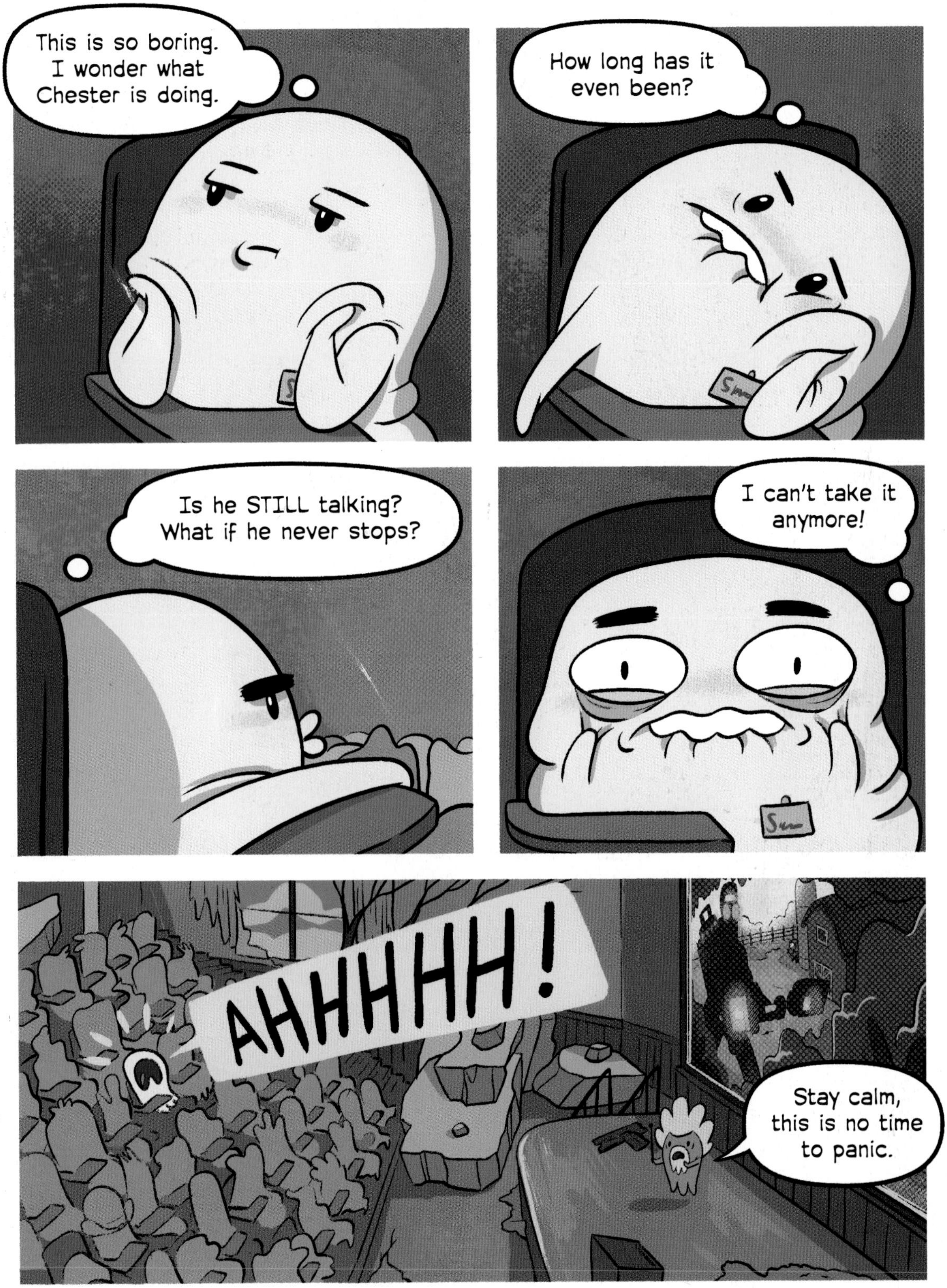
This is so boring. I wonder what Chester is doing.
How long has it even been?
Is he STILL talking? What if he never stops?
I can't take it anymore!
AHHHHH!
Stay calm, this is no time to panic.

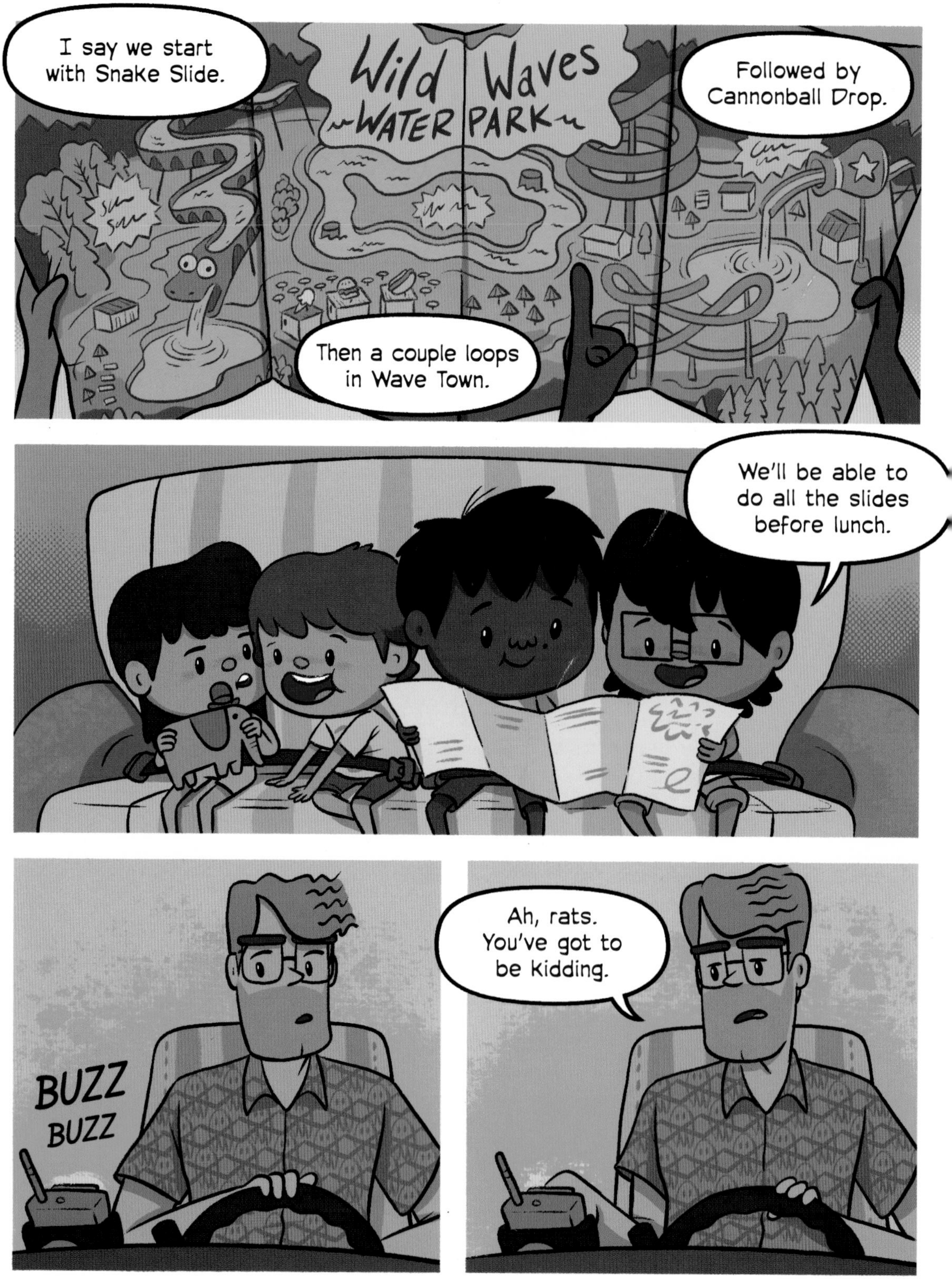
I say we start with Snake Slide.
Wild Waves
WATER PARK
Followed by Cannonball Drop.
Then a couple loops in Wave Town.
We'll be able to do all the slides before lunch.
BUZZ
BUZZ
Ah, rats. You've got to be kidding.

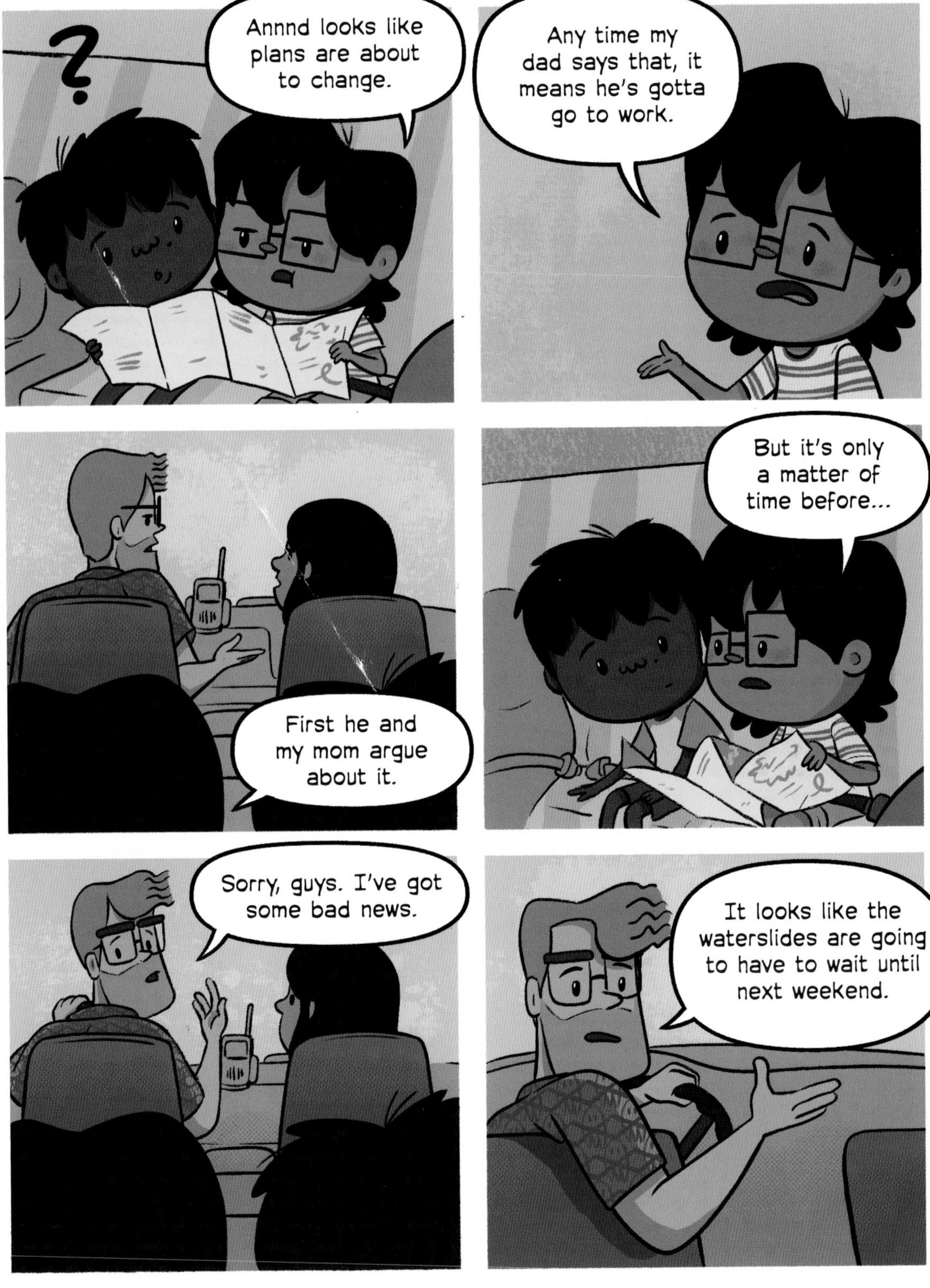
?
Annnd looks like plans are about to change.
Any time my dad says that, it means he's gotta go to work.
First he and my mom argue about it.
But it's only a matter of time before...
Sorry, guys. I've got some bad news.
It looks like the waterslides are going to have to wait until next weekend.

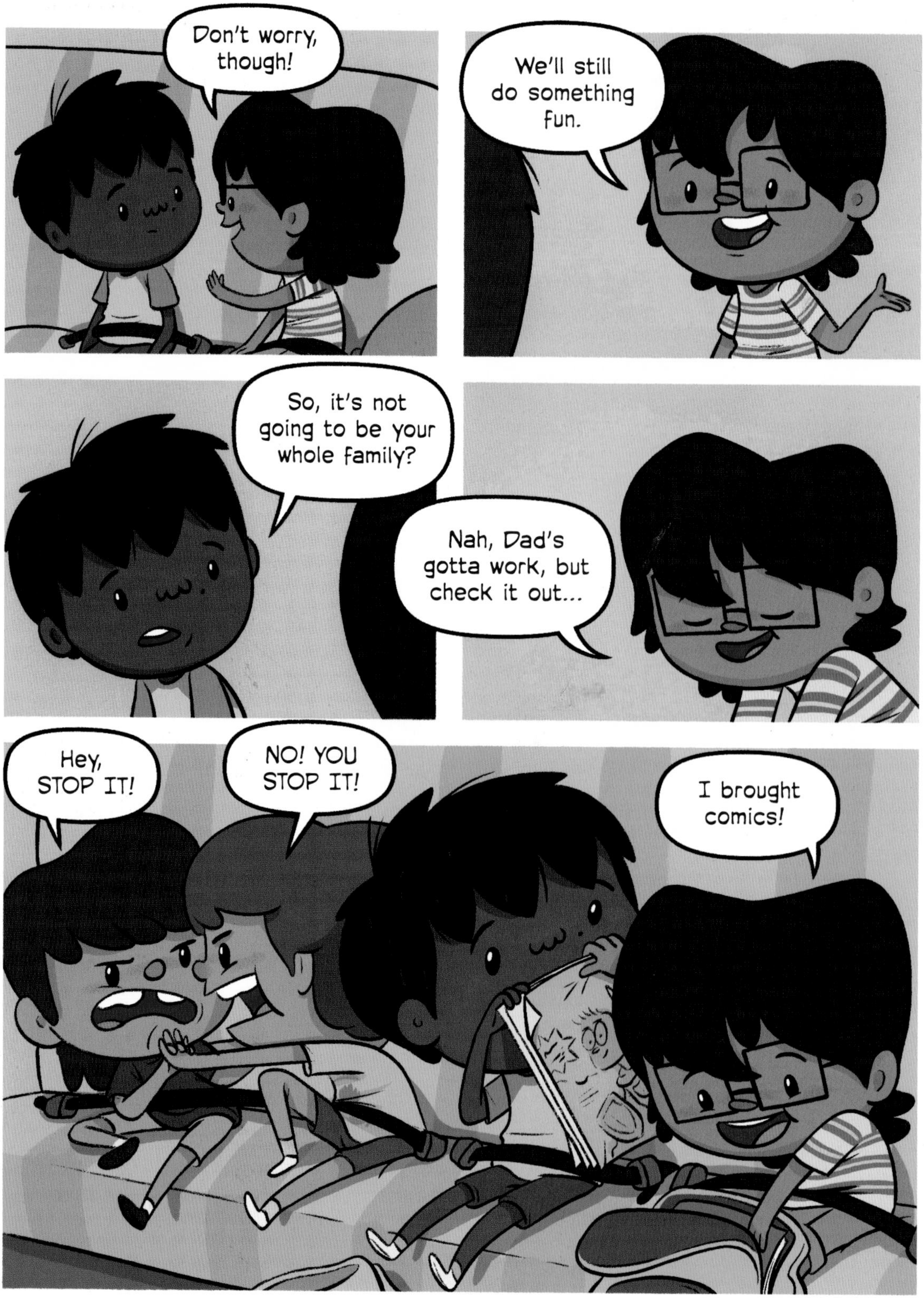
Don't worry, though!
We'll still do something fun.
So, it's not going to be your whole family?
Nah, Dad's gotta work, but check it out...
Hey, STOP IT!
NO! YOU STOP IT!
I brought comics!

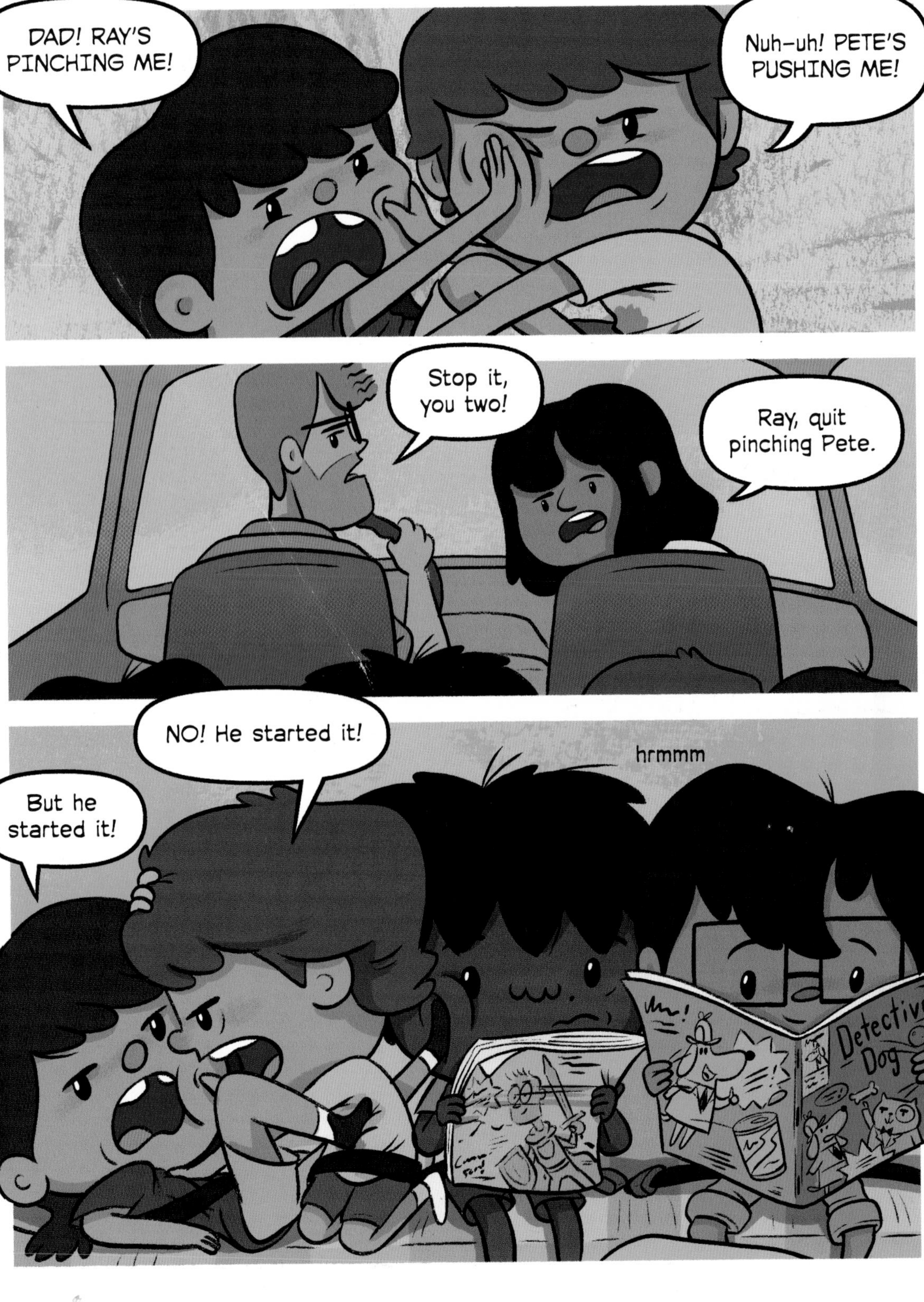
DAD! RAY'S PINCHING ME!
Nuh-uh! PETE'S PUSHING ME!
Stop it, you two!
Ray, quit pinching Pete.
NO! He started it!
But he started it!
hrmmm
Detective Dog

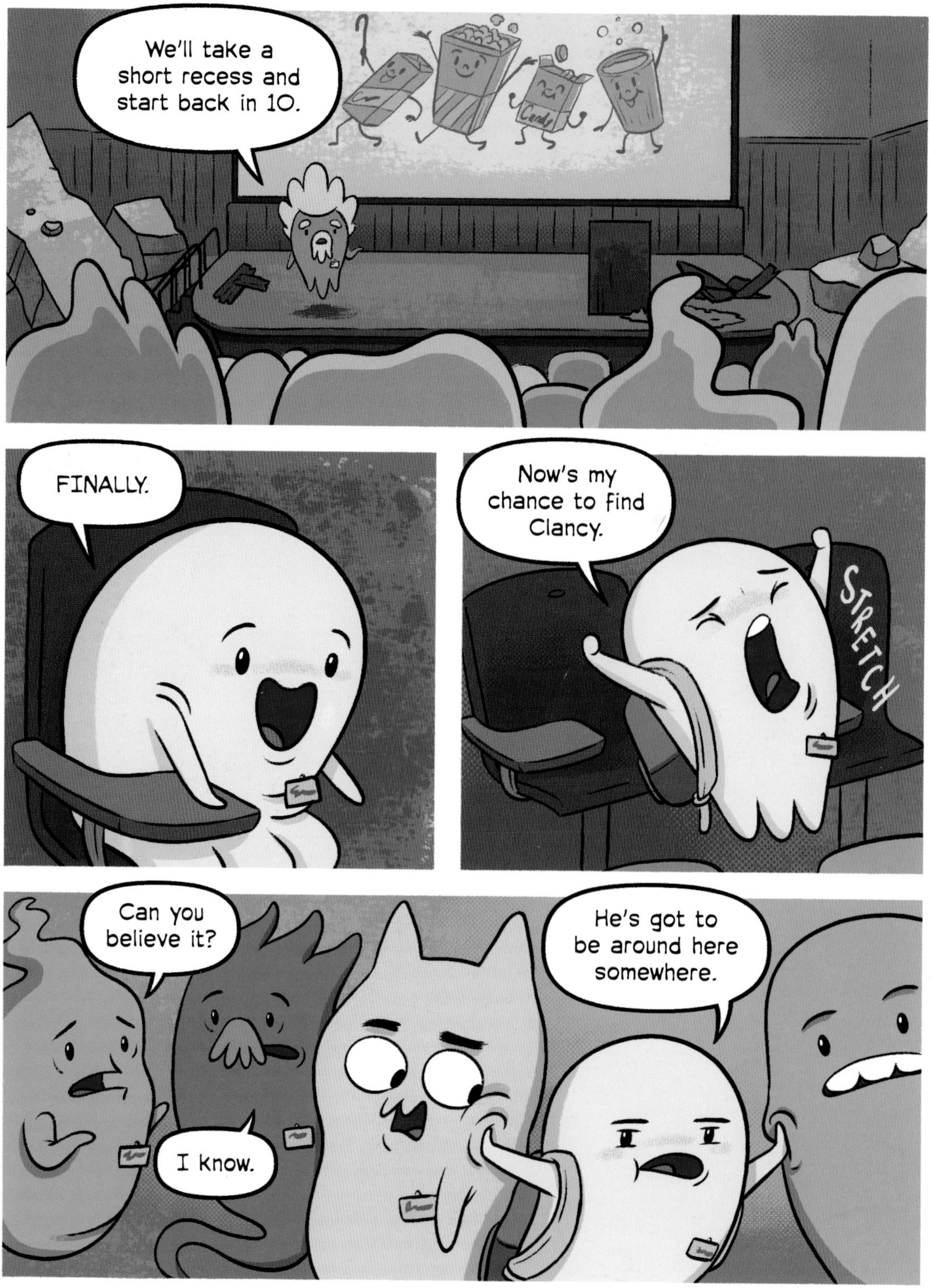
We'll take a short recess and start back in 10.
FINALLY.
Now's my chance to find Clancy.
STRETCH
Can you believe it?
I know.
He's got to be around here somewhere.

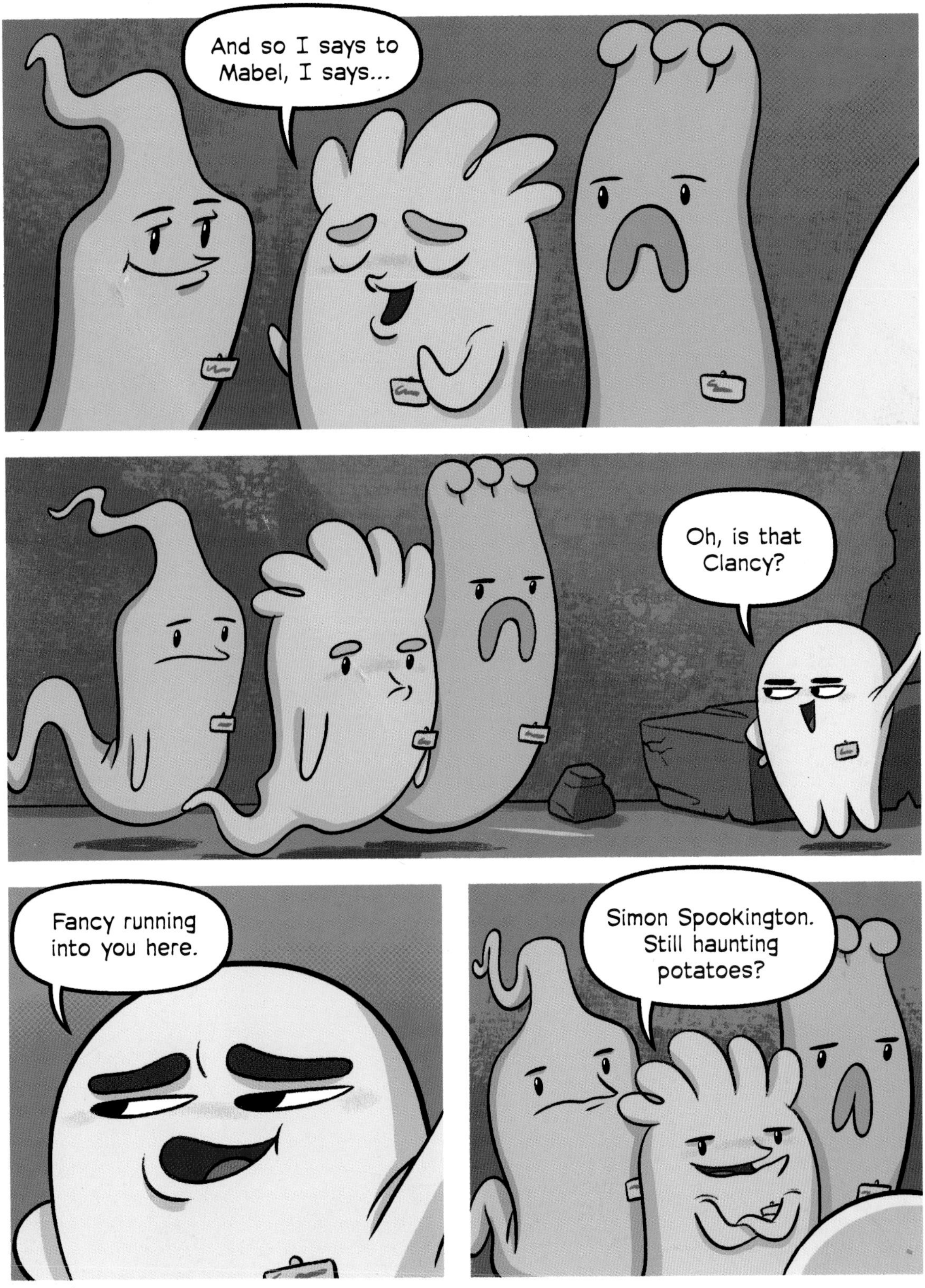
And so I says to Mabel, I says...
Oh, is that Clancy?
Fancy running into you here.
Simon Spookington. Still haunting potatoes?

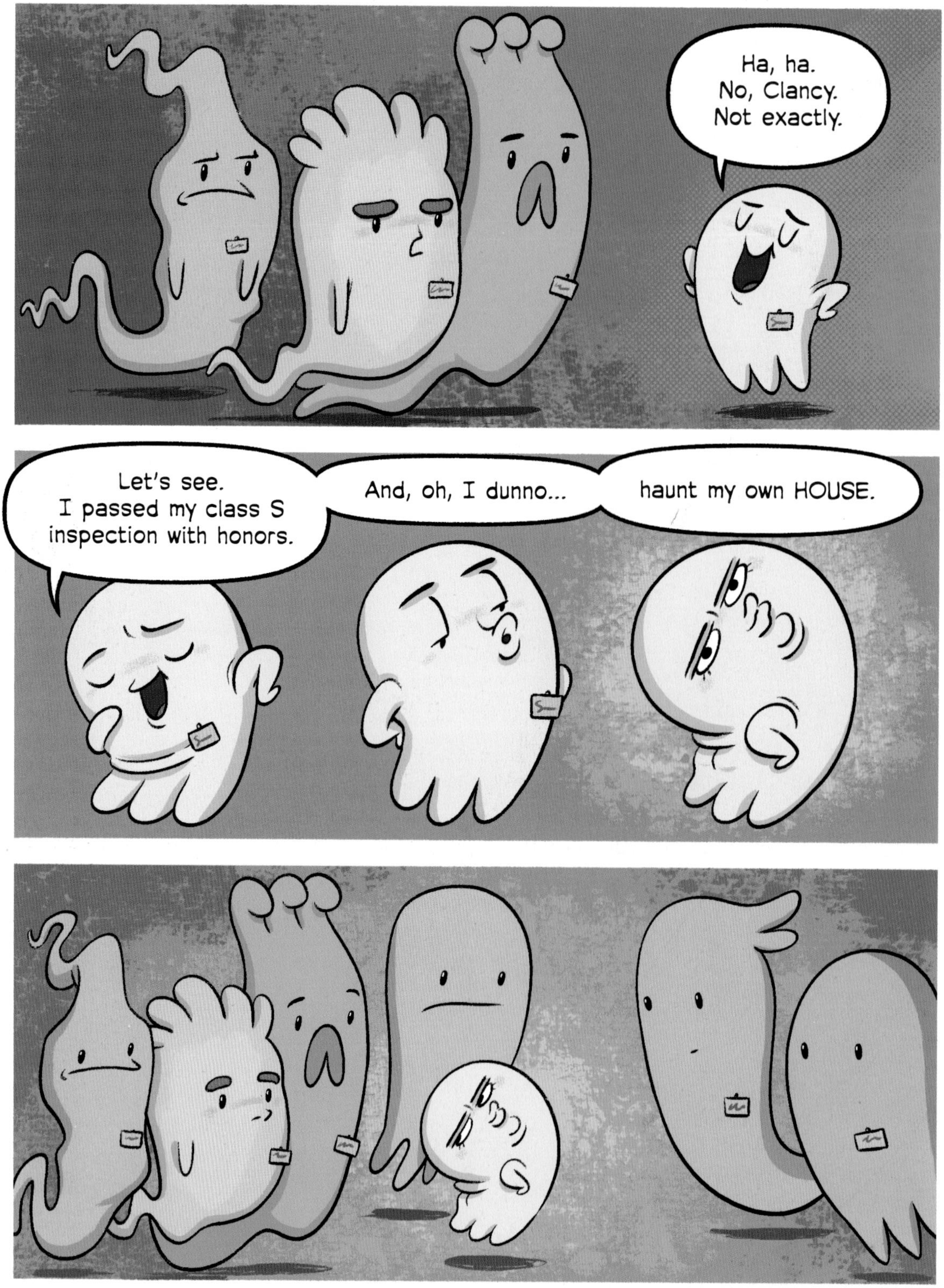
Ha, ha.
No, Clancy.
Not exactly.
Let's see.
I passed my class S
inspection with honors.
And, oh, I dunno...
haunt my own HOUSE.

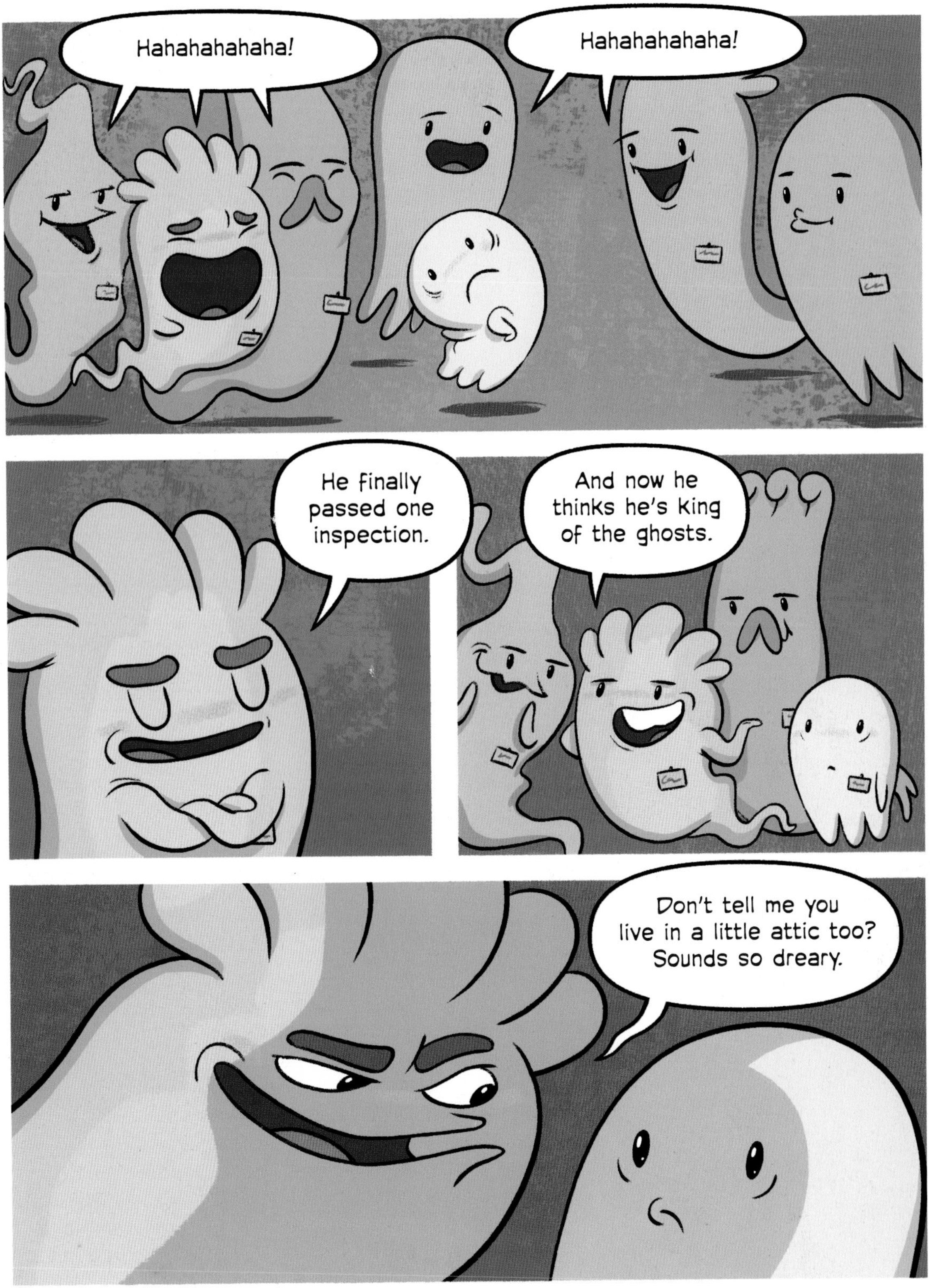
Hahahahahaha!
Hahahahahaha!
He finally passed one inspection.
And now he thinks he's king of the ghosts.
Don't tell me you live in a little attic too? Sounds so dreary.

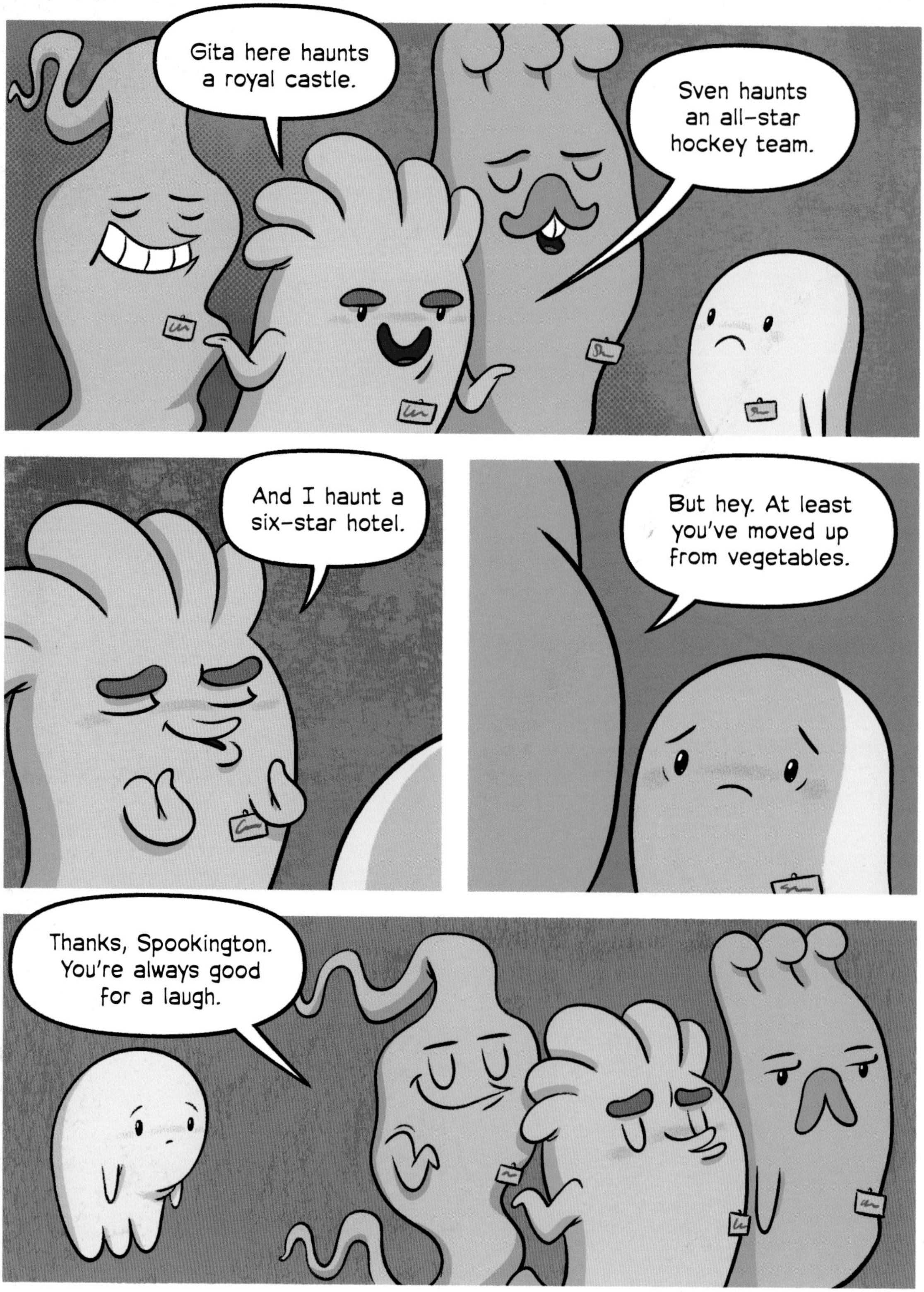
Gita here haunts a royal castle.
Sven haunts an all-star hockey team.
And I haunt a six-star hotel.
But hey. At least you've moved up from vegetables.
Thanks, Spookington. You're always good for a laugh.

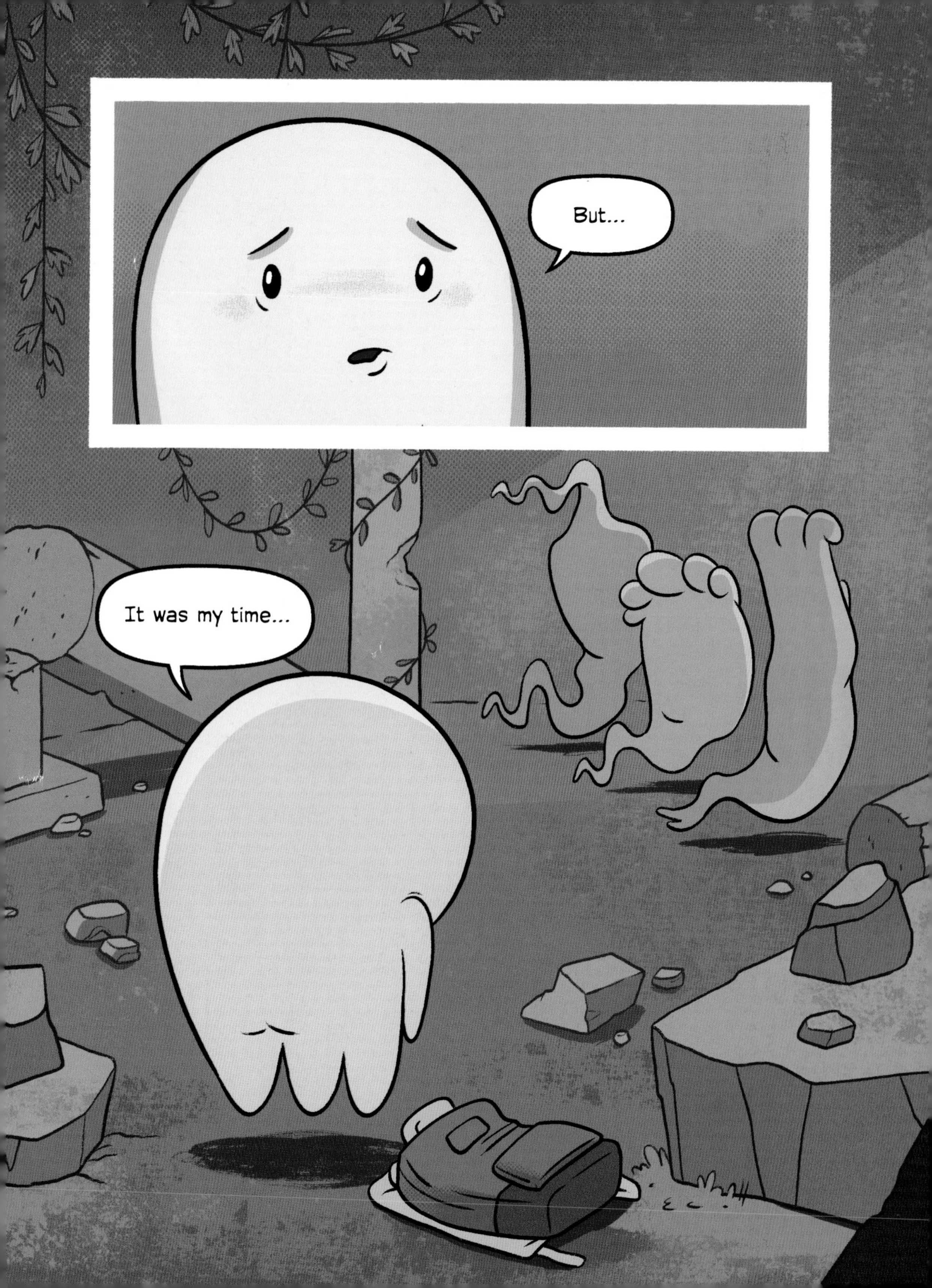
But...
It was my time...

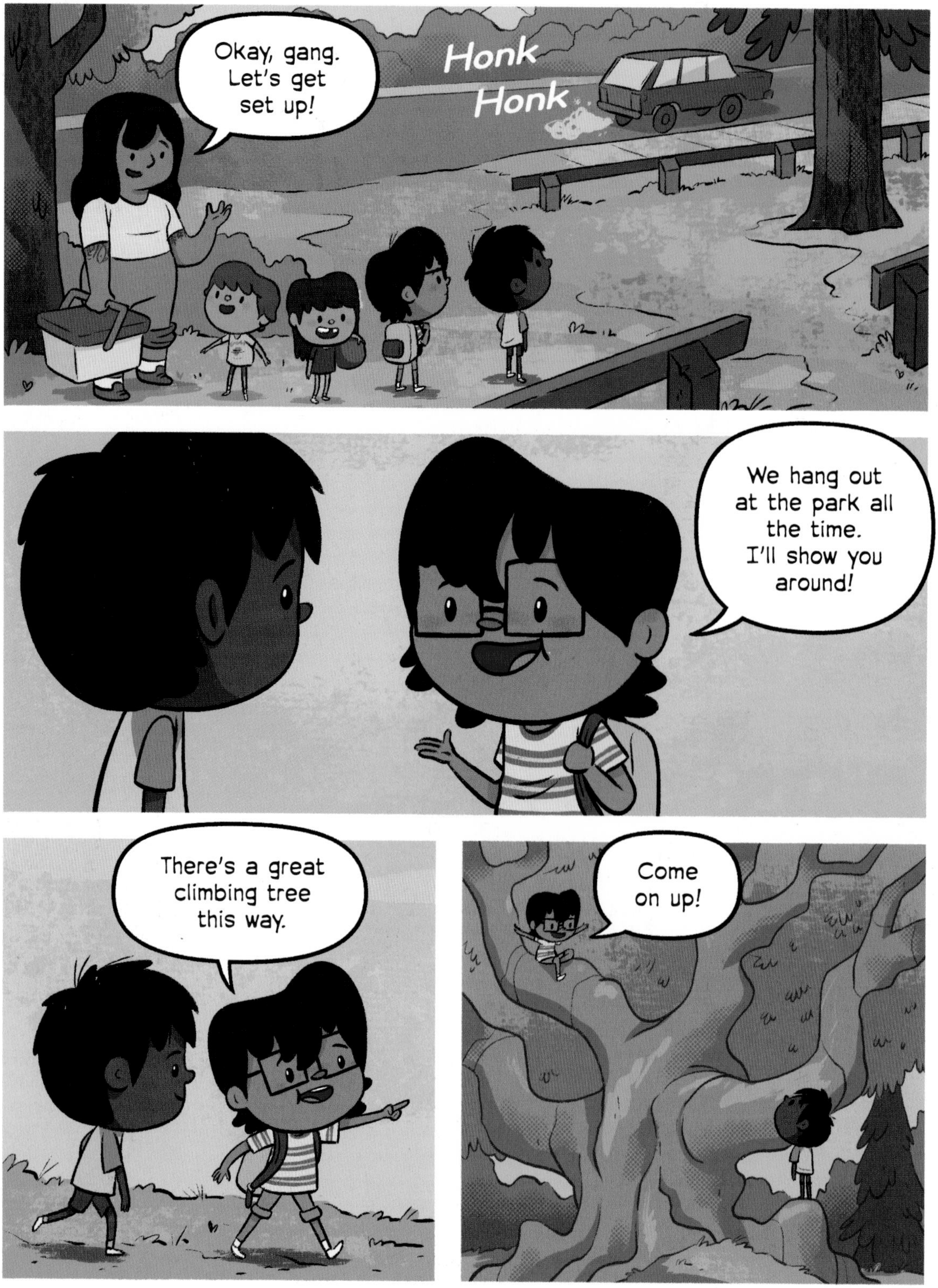
Okay, gang. Let's get set up!
Honk
Honk
We hang out at the park all the time. I'll show you around!
There's a great climbing tree this way.
Come on up!

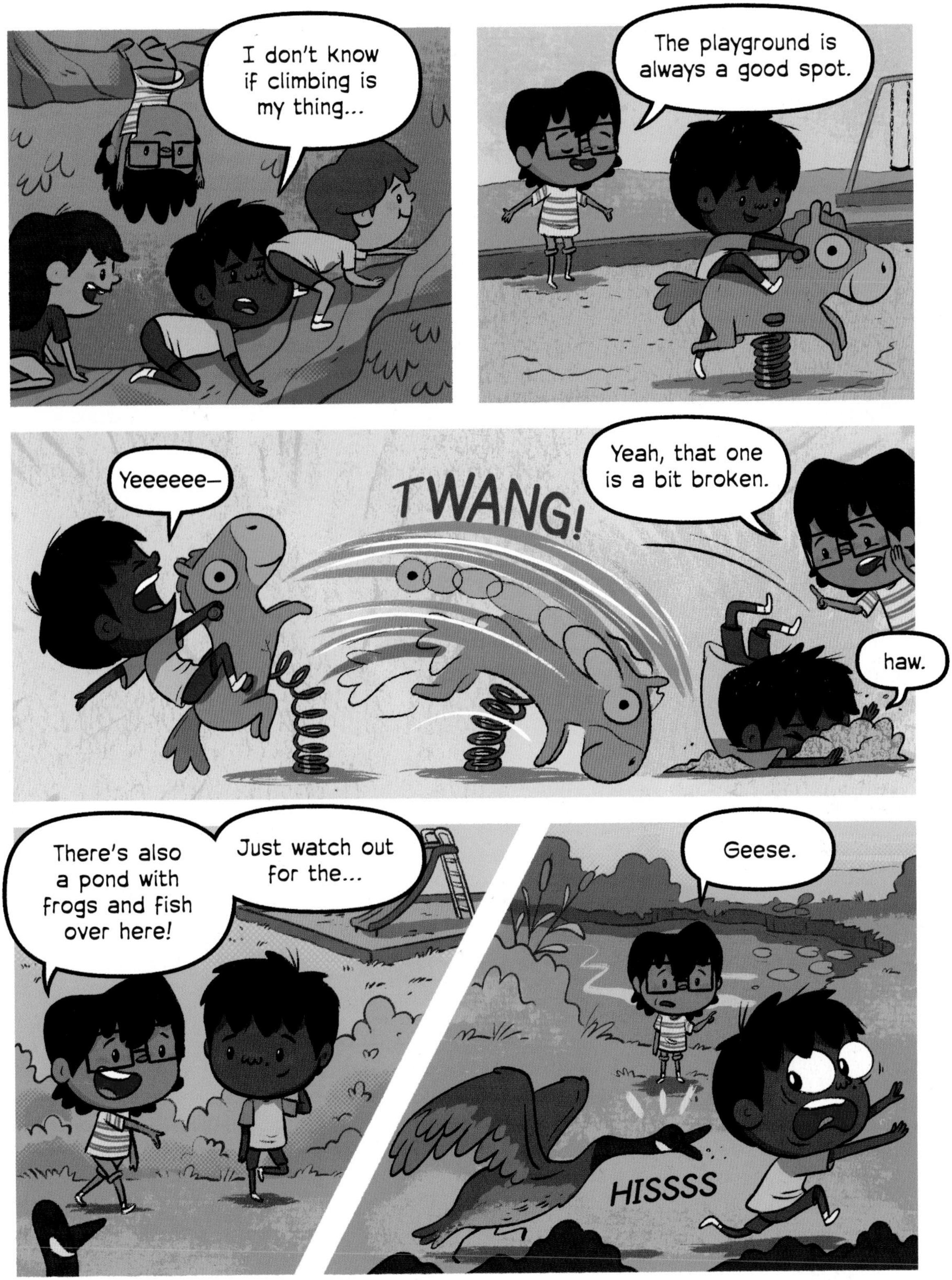
I don't know if climbing is my thing...
The playground is always a good spot.
Yeeeeee–
TWANG!
Yeah, that one is a bit broken.
haw.
There's also a pond with frogs and fish over here!
Just watch out for the...
Geese.
HISSSS

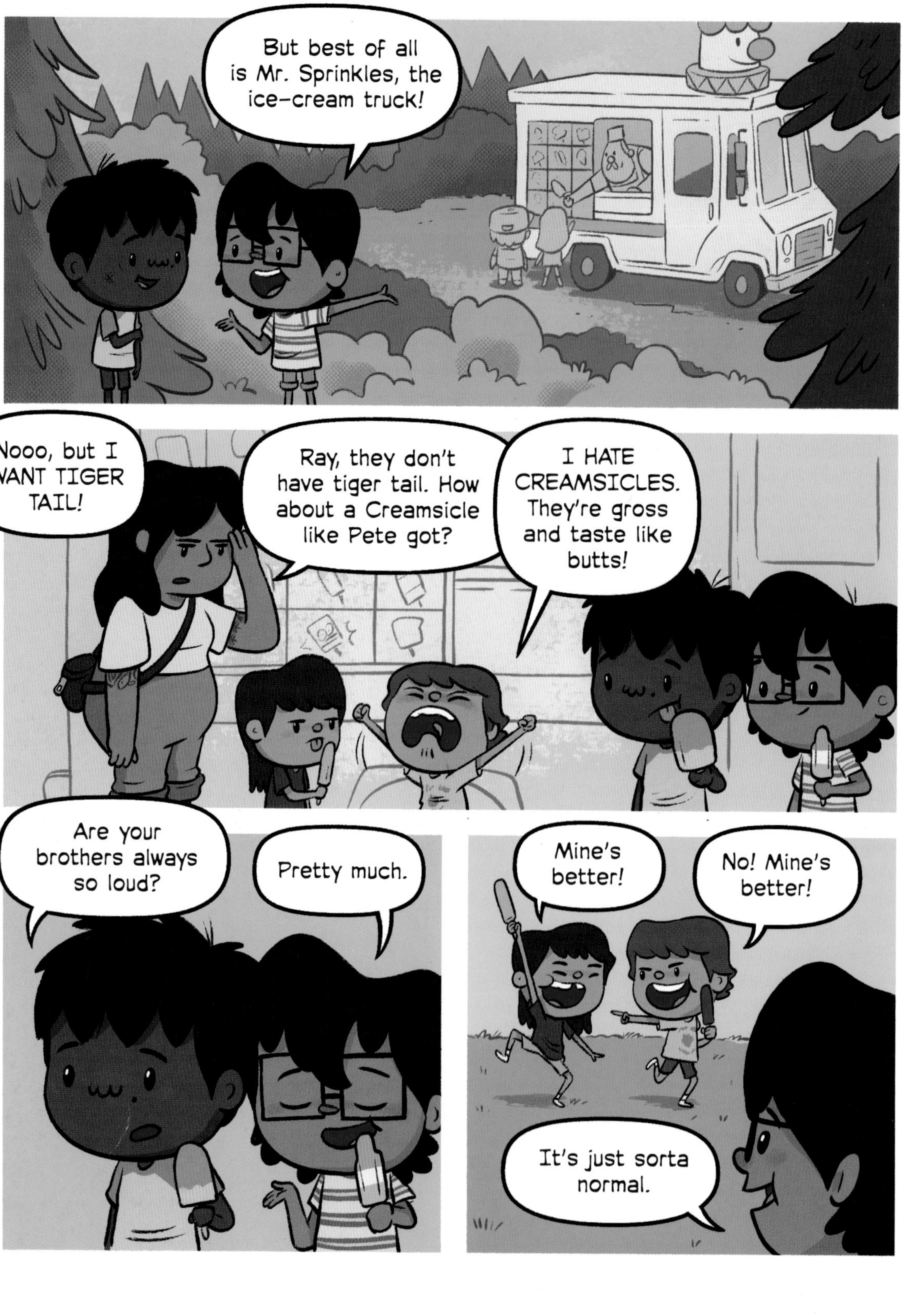
But best of all is Mr. Sprinkles, the ice-cream truck!
Nooo, but I WANT TIGER TAIL!
Ray, they don't have tiger tail. How about a Creamsicle like Pete got?
I HATE CREAMSICLES. They're gross and taste like butts!
Are your brothers always so loud?
Pretty much.
Mine's better!
No! Mine's better!
It's just sorta normal.

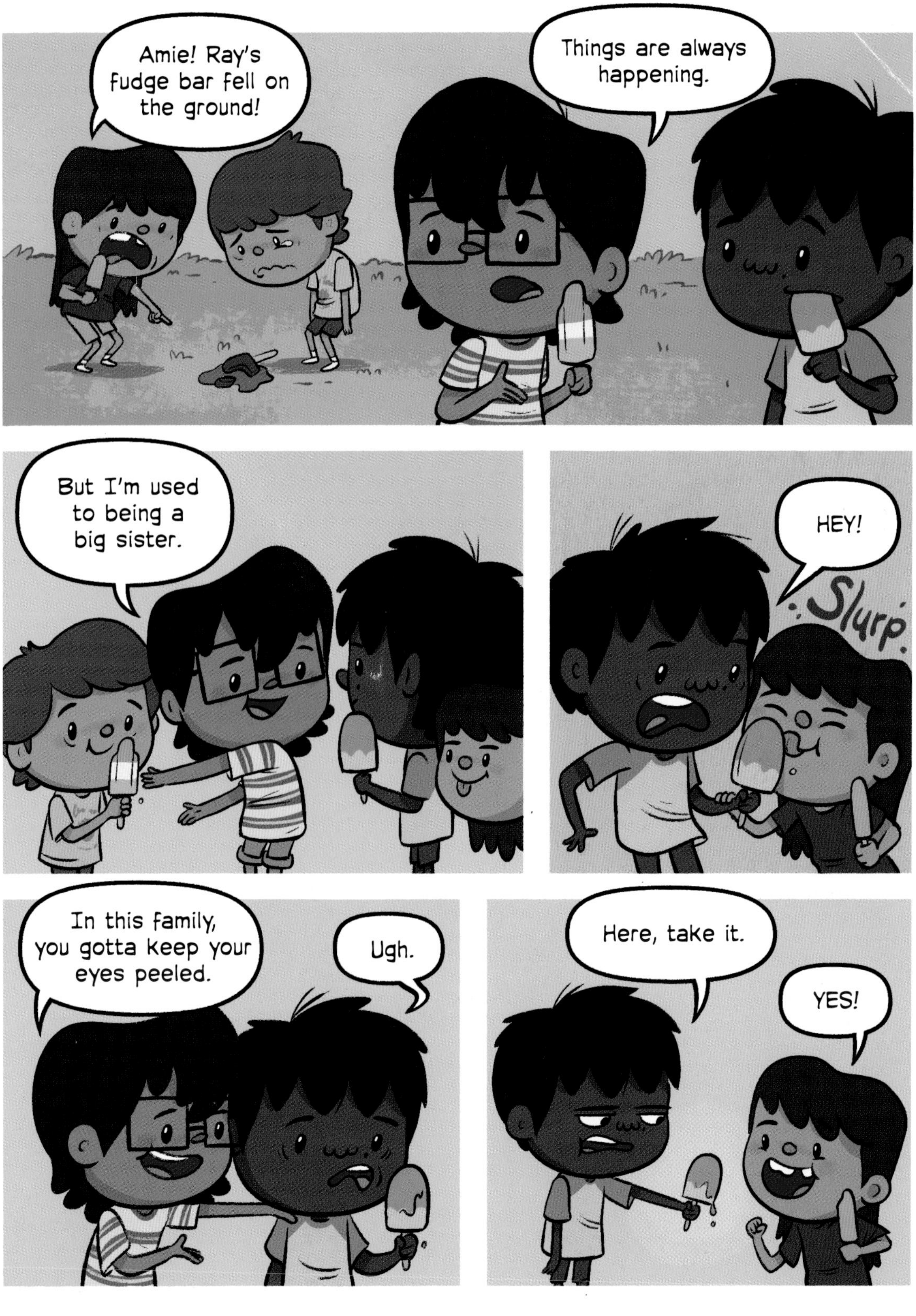
Amie! Ray's fudge bar fell on the ground!
Things are always happening.
But I'm used to being a big sister.
HEY!
Slurp.
In this family, you gotta keep your eyes peeled.
Ugh.
Here, take it.
YES!

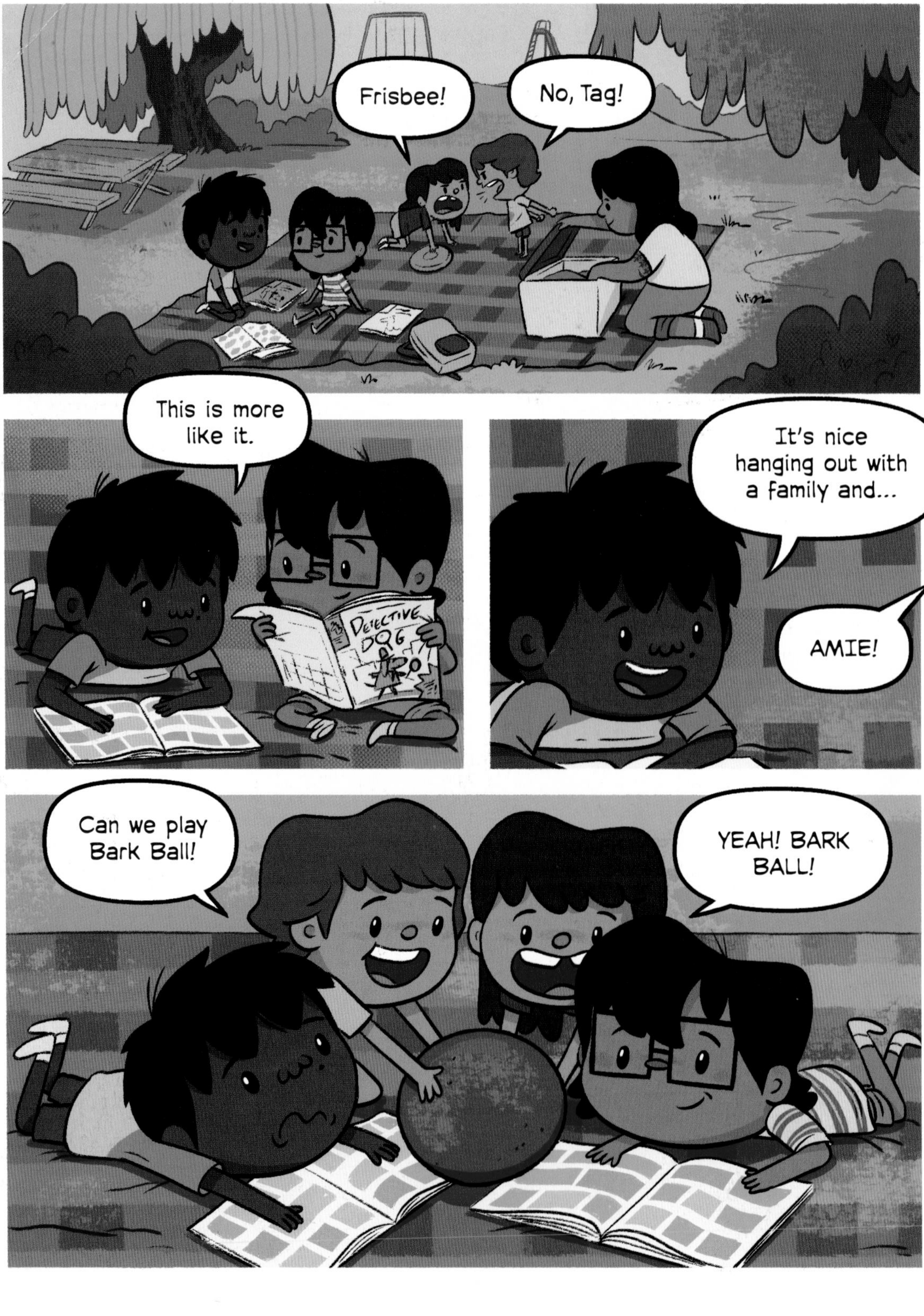
Frisbee!
No, Tag!
This is more like it.
It's nice hanging out with a family and...
AMIE!
Can we play Bark Ball!
YEAH! BARK BALL!

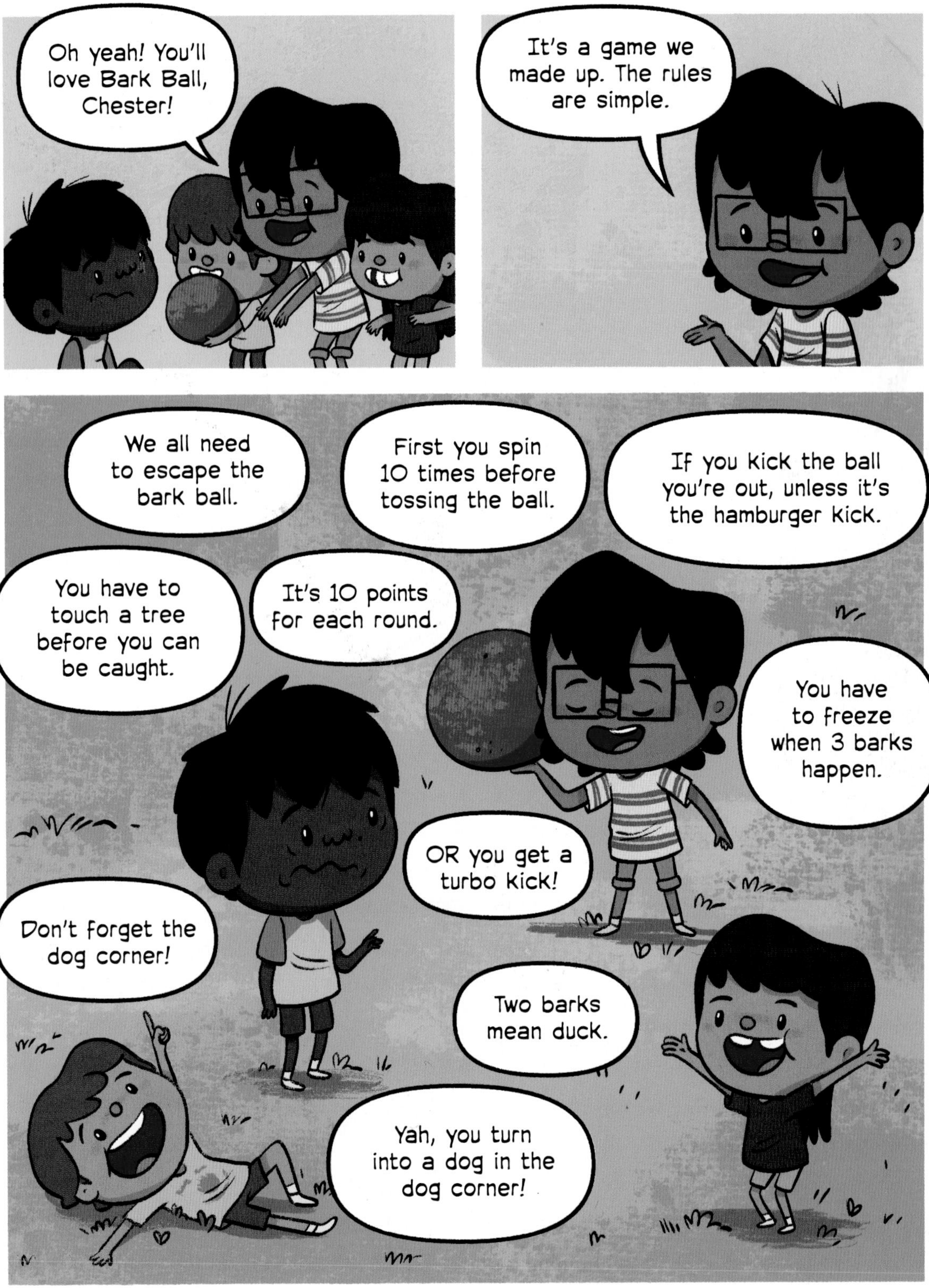
Oh yeah! You'll love Bark Ball, Chester!
It's a game we made up. The rules are simple.
We all need to escape the bark ball.
First you spin 10 times before tossing the ball.
If you kick the ball you're out, unless it's the hamburger kick.
You have to touch a tree before you can be caught.
It's 10 points for each round.
You have to freeze when 3 barks happen.
OR you get a turbo kick!
Don't forget the dog corner!
Two barks mean duck.
Yah, you turn into a dog in the dog corner!

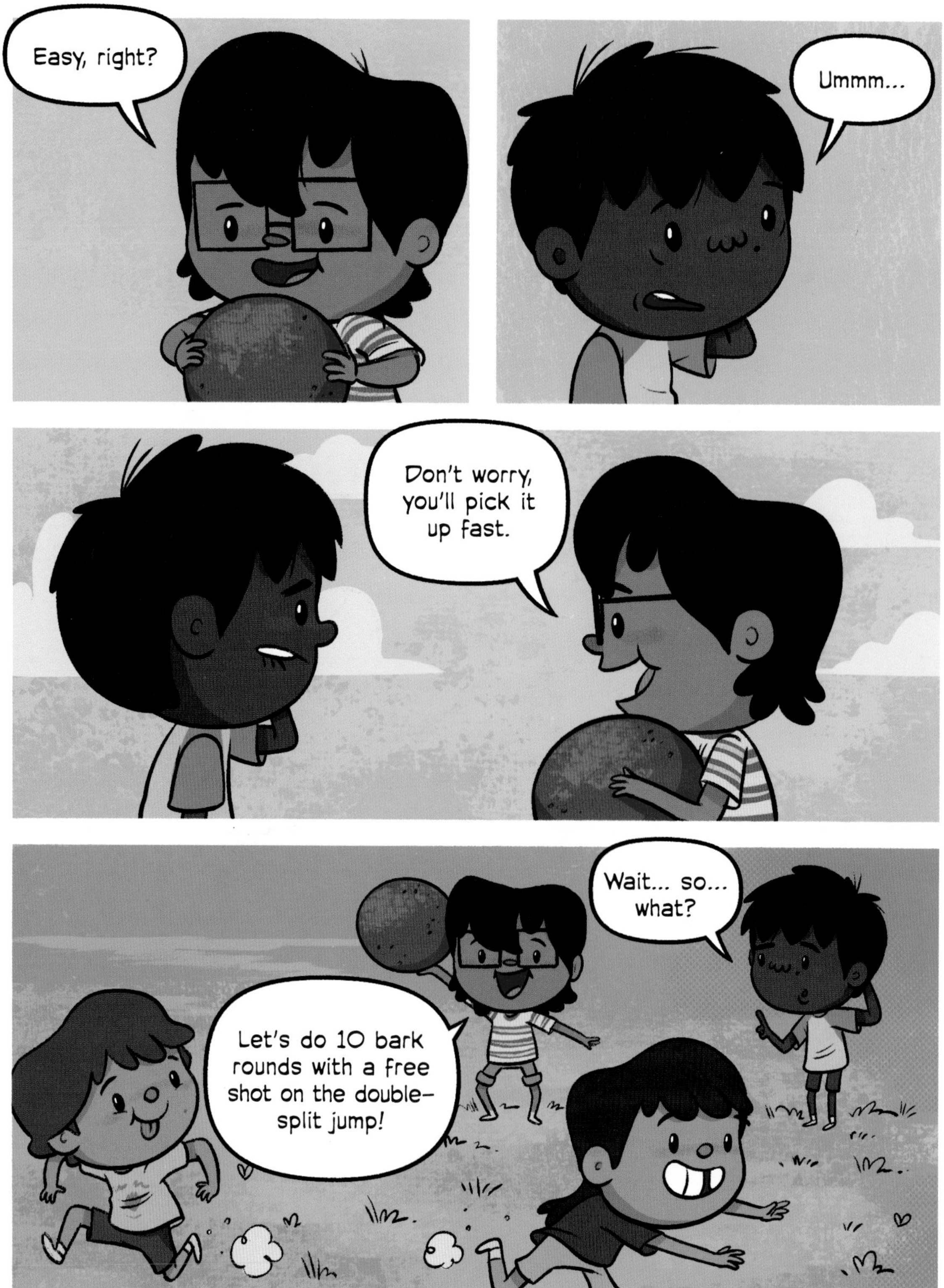
Easy, right?
Ummm...
Don't worry, you'll pick it up fast.
Wait... so... what?
Let's do 10 bark rounds with a free shot on the double-split jump!

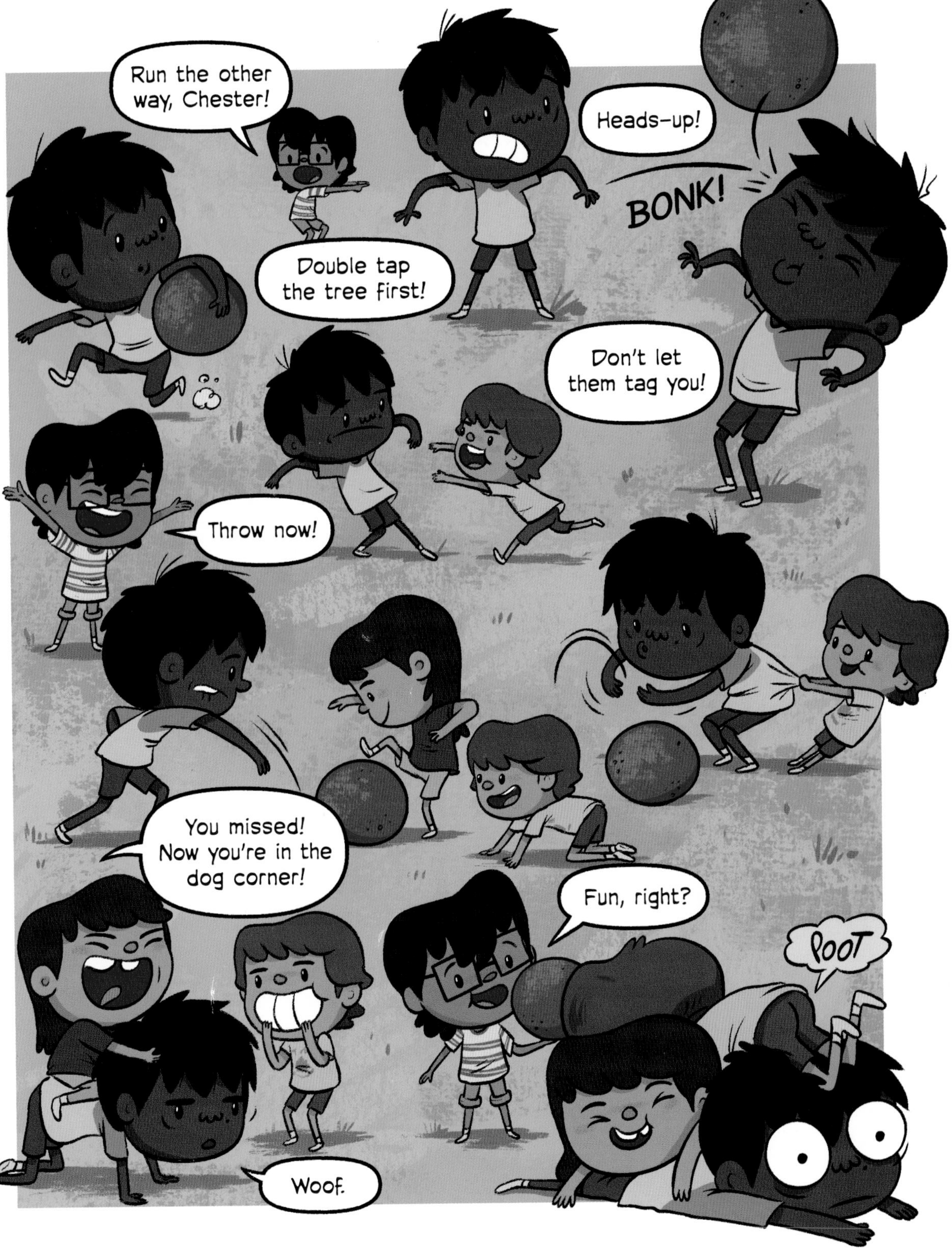
Run the other way, Chester!
Heads-up!
BONK!
Double tap the tree first!
Don't let them tag you!
Throw now!
You missed! Now you're in the dog corner!
Fun, right?
POOT
Woof.

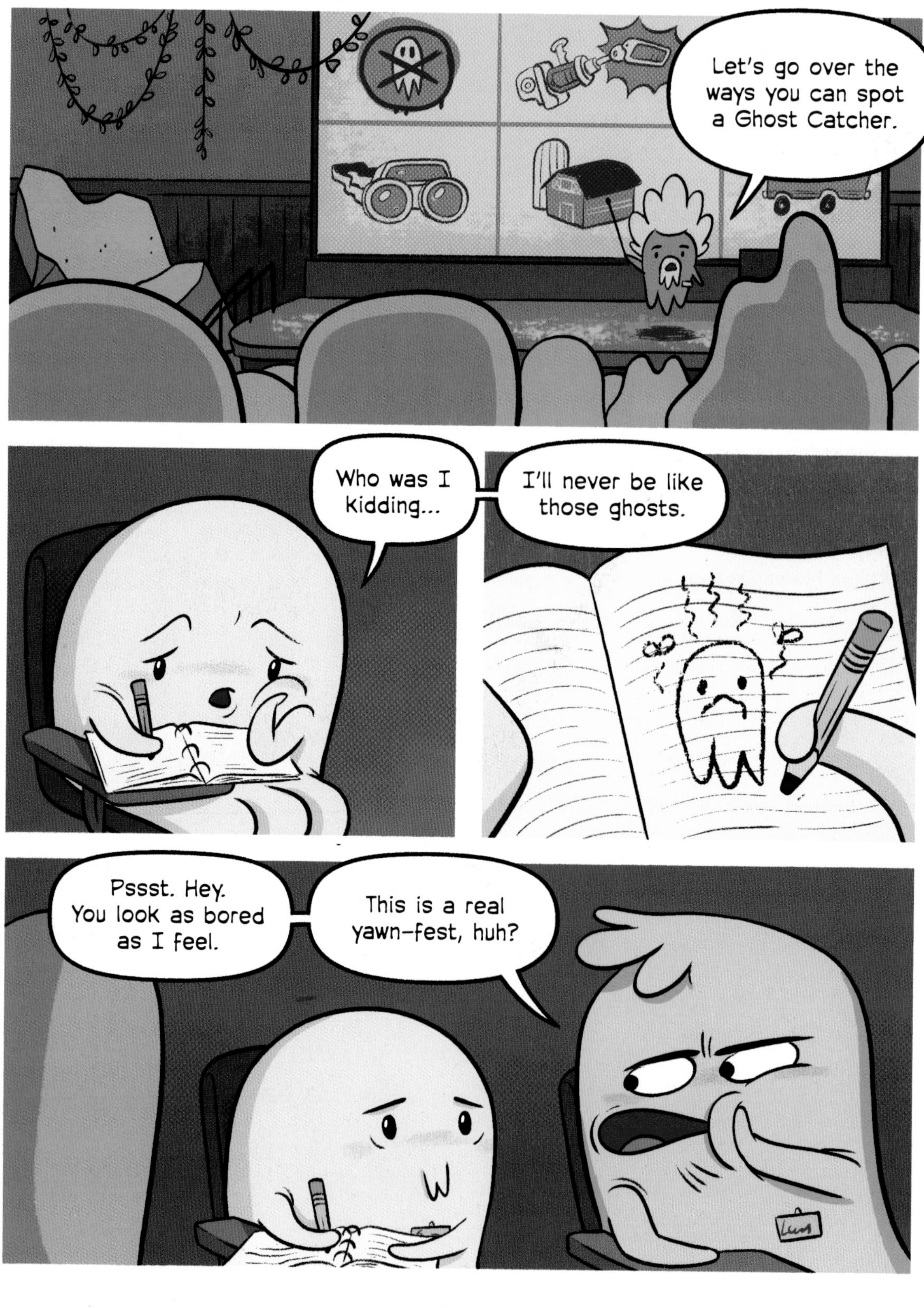
Let's go over the ways you can spot a Ghost Catcher.
Who was I kidding...
I'll never be like those ghosts.
Pssst. Hey. You look as bored as I feel.
This is a real yawn-fest, huh?

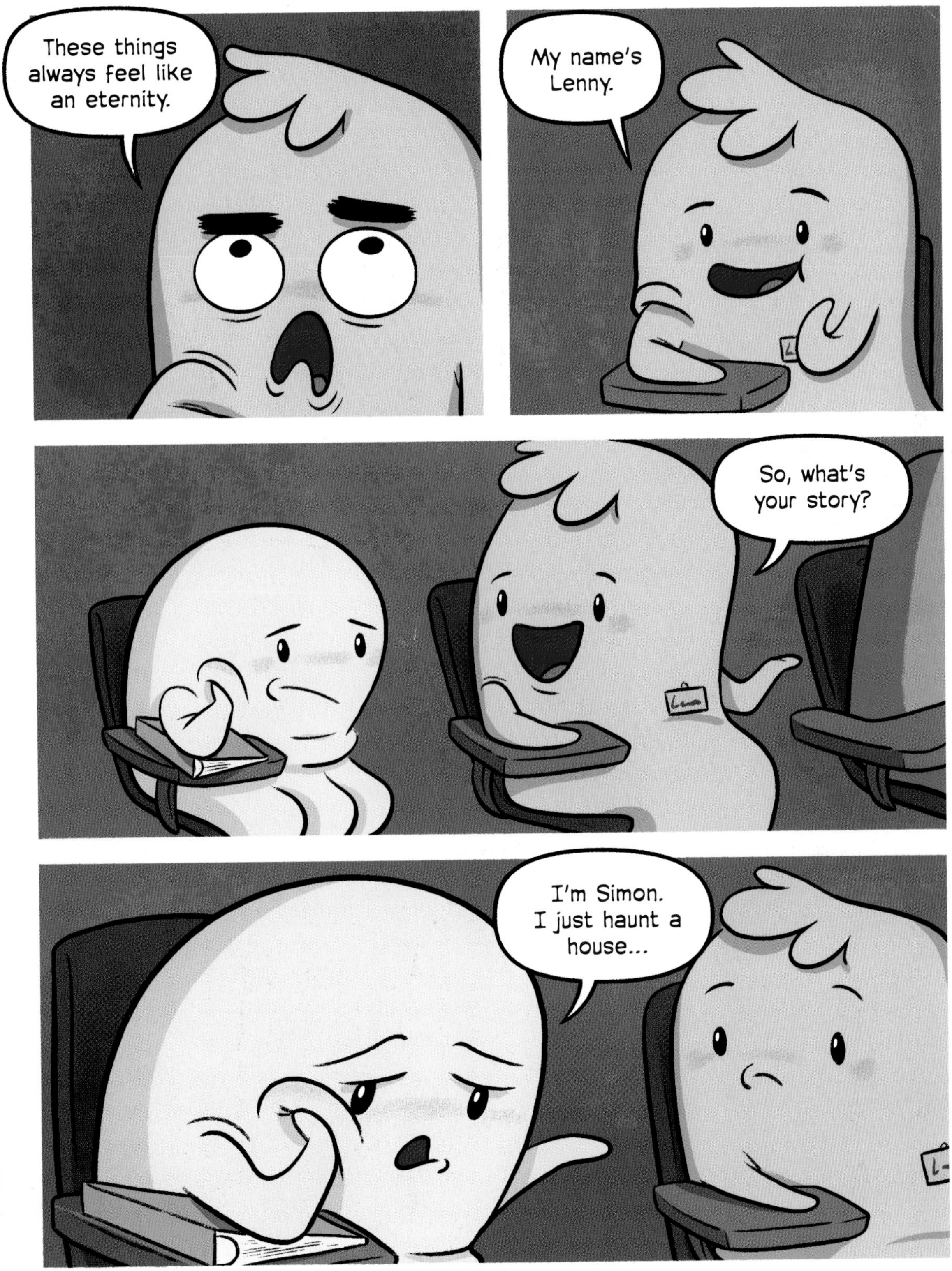
These things always feel like an eternity.
My name's Lenny.
So, what's your story?
I'm Simon. I just haunt a house...

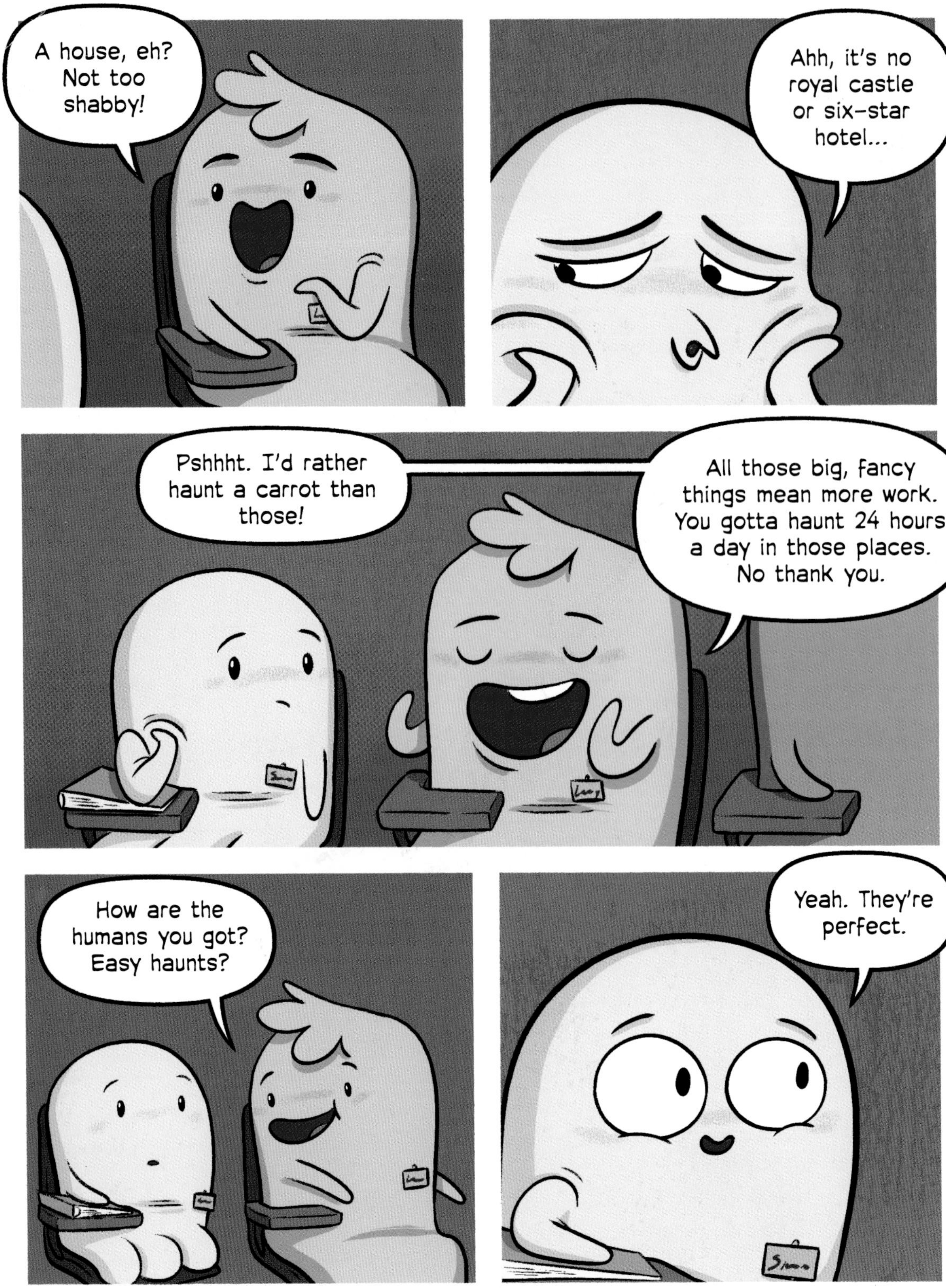
A house, eh? Not too shabby!
Ahh, it's no royal castle or six-star hotel...
Pshhht. I'd rather haunt a carrot than those!
All those big, fancy things mean more work. You gotta haunt 24 hours a day in those places. No thank you.
How are the humans you got? Easy haunts?
Yeah. They're perfect.

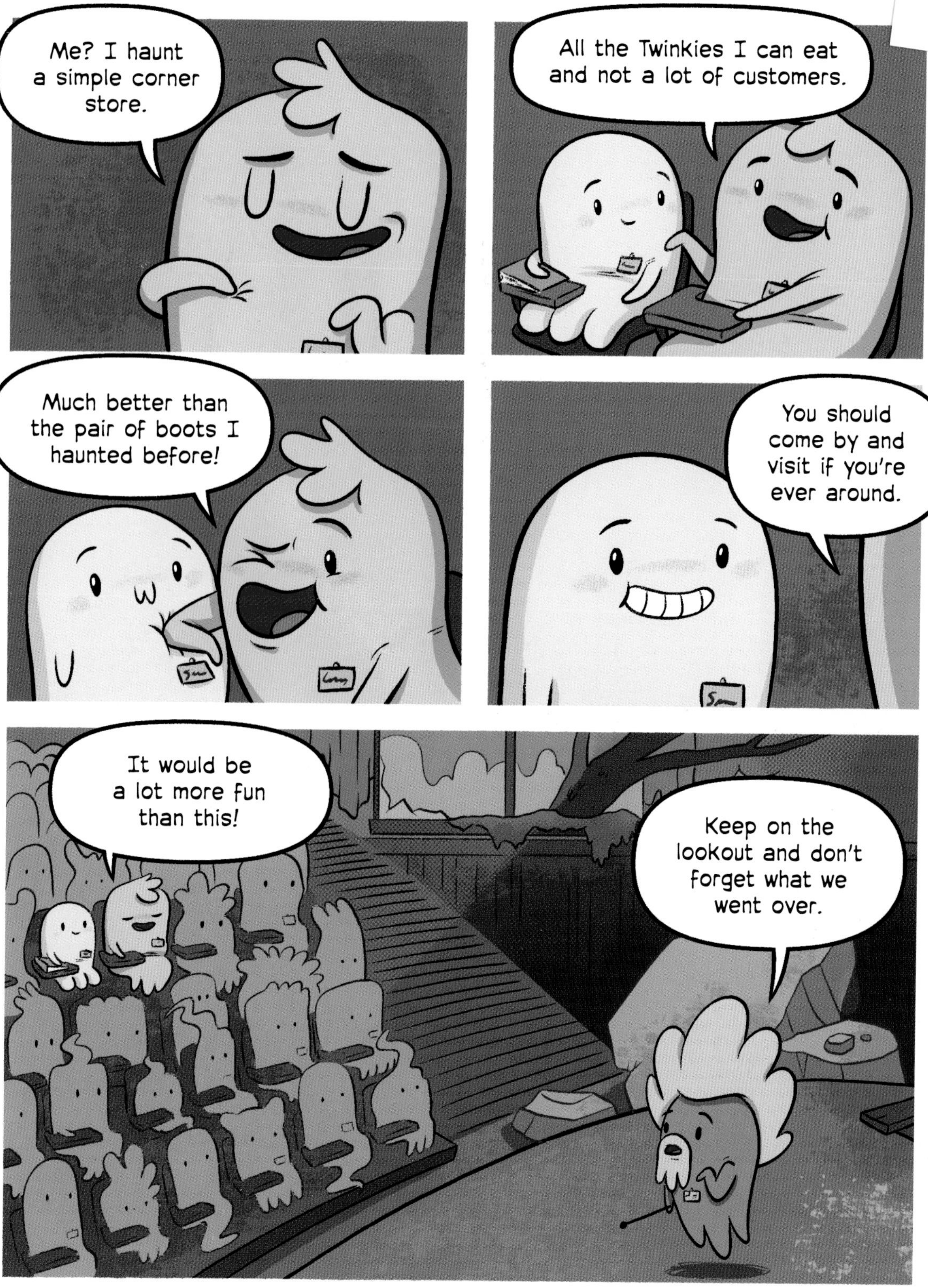
Me? I haunt a simple corner store.
All the Twinkies I can eat and not a lot of customers.
Much better than the pair of boots I haunted before!
You should come by and visit if you're ever around.
It would be a lot more fun than this!
Keep on the lookout and don't forget what we went over.

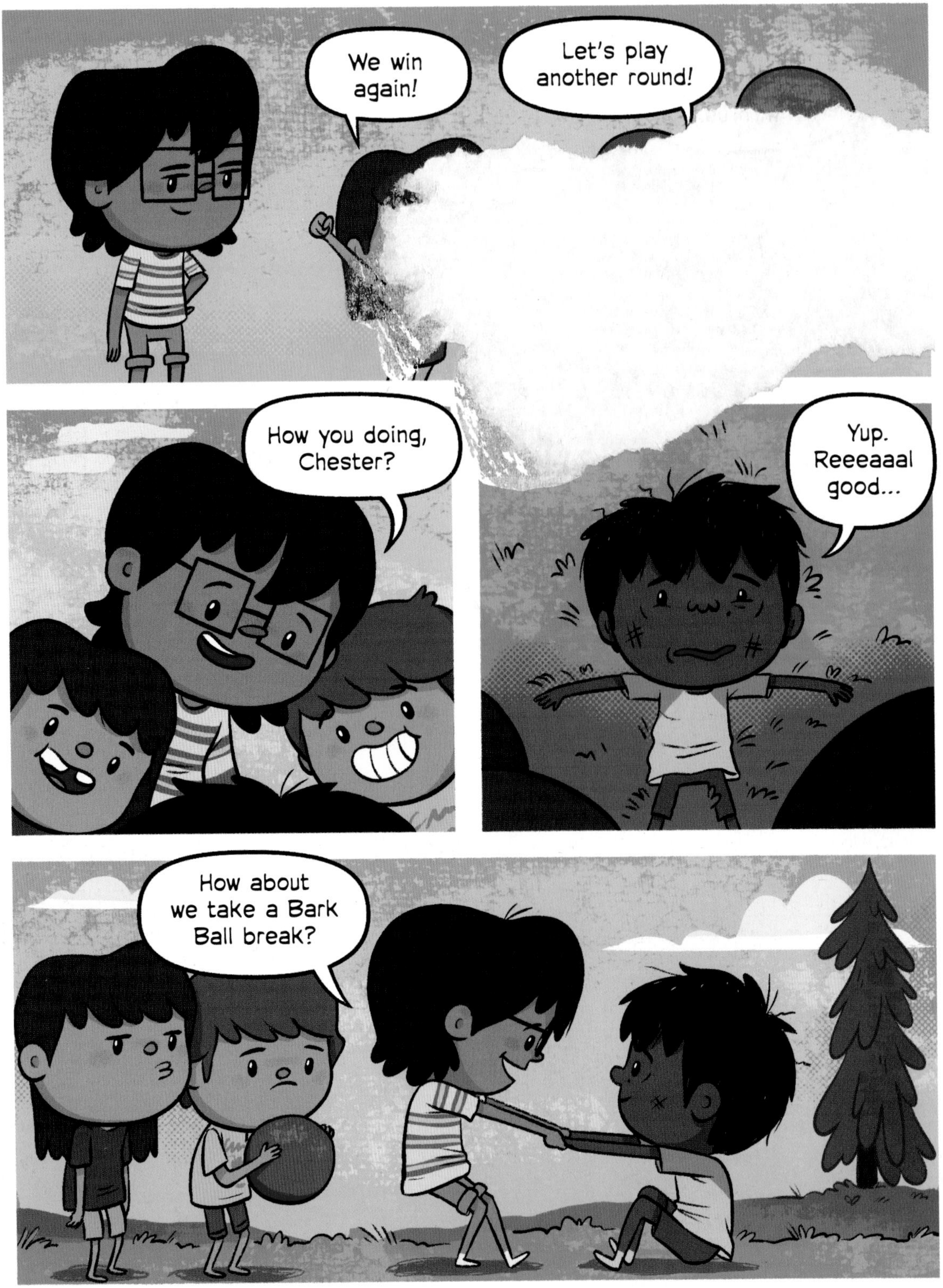
We win again!
Let's play another round!
How you doing, Chester?
Yup. Reeeaaal good...
How about we take a Bark Ball break?

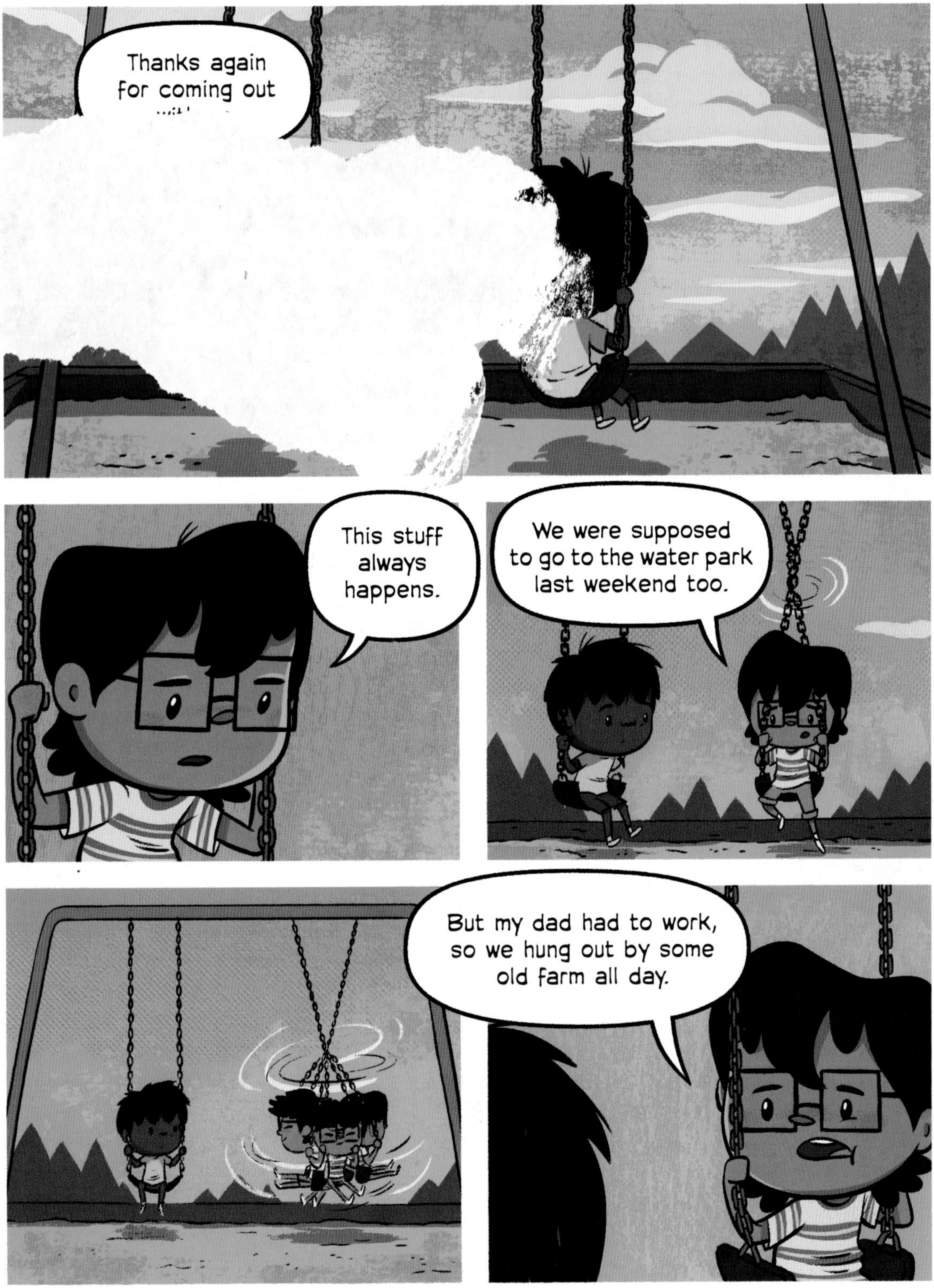
Thanks again for coming out
This stuff always happens.
We were supposed to go to the water park last weekend too.
But my dad had to work, so we hung out by some old farm all day.

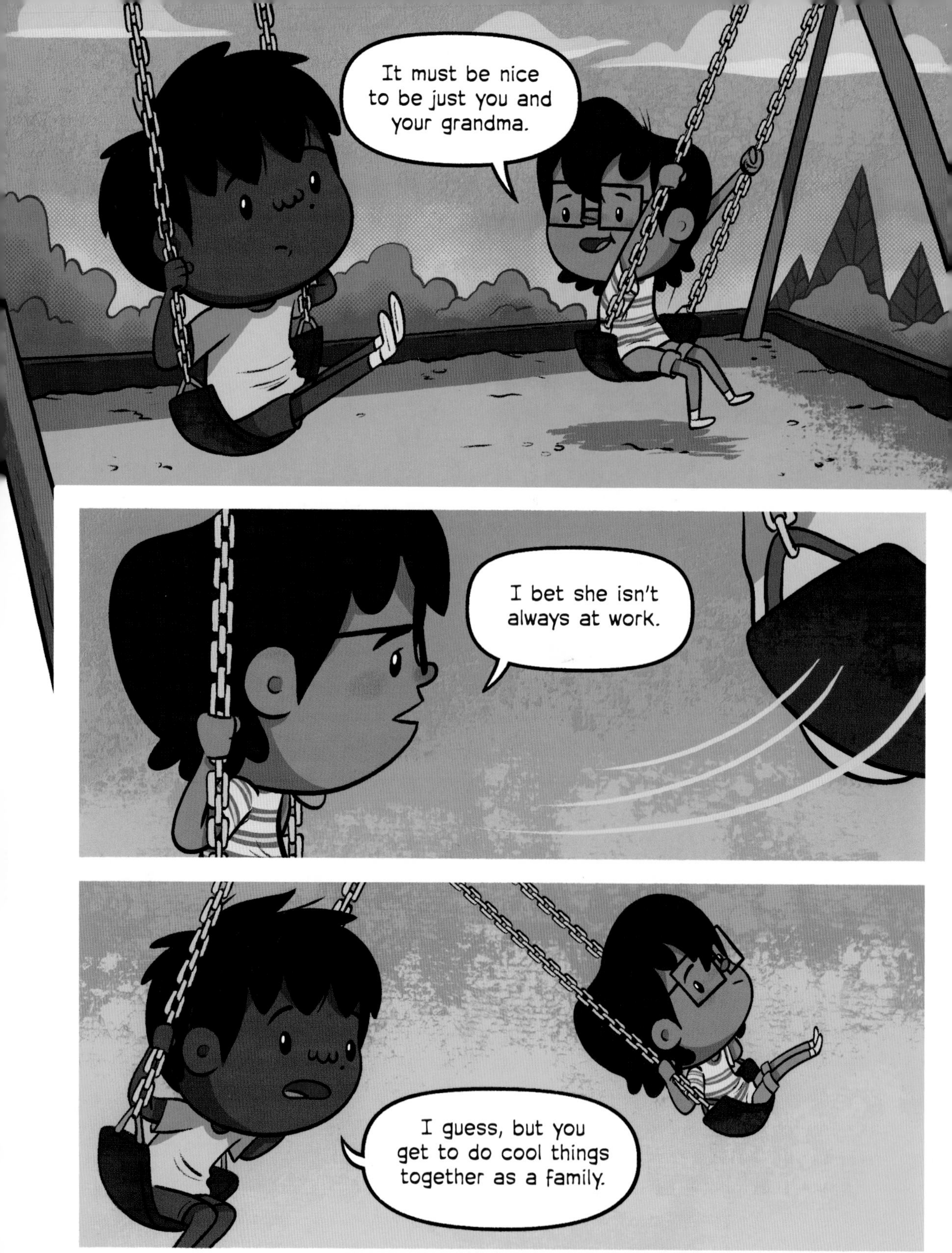
It must be nice to be just you and your grandma.
I bet she isn't always at work.
I guess, but you get to do cool things together as a family.

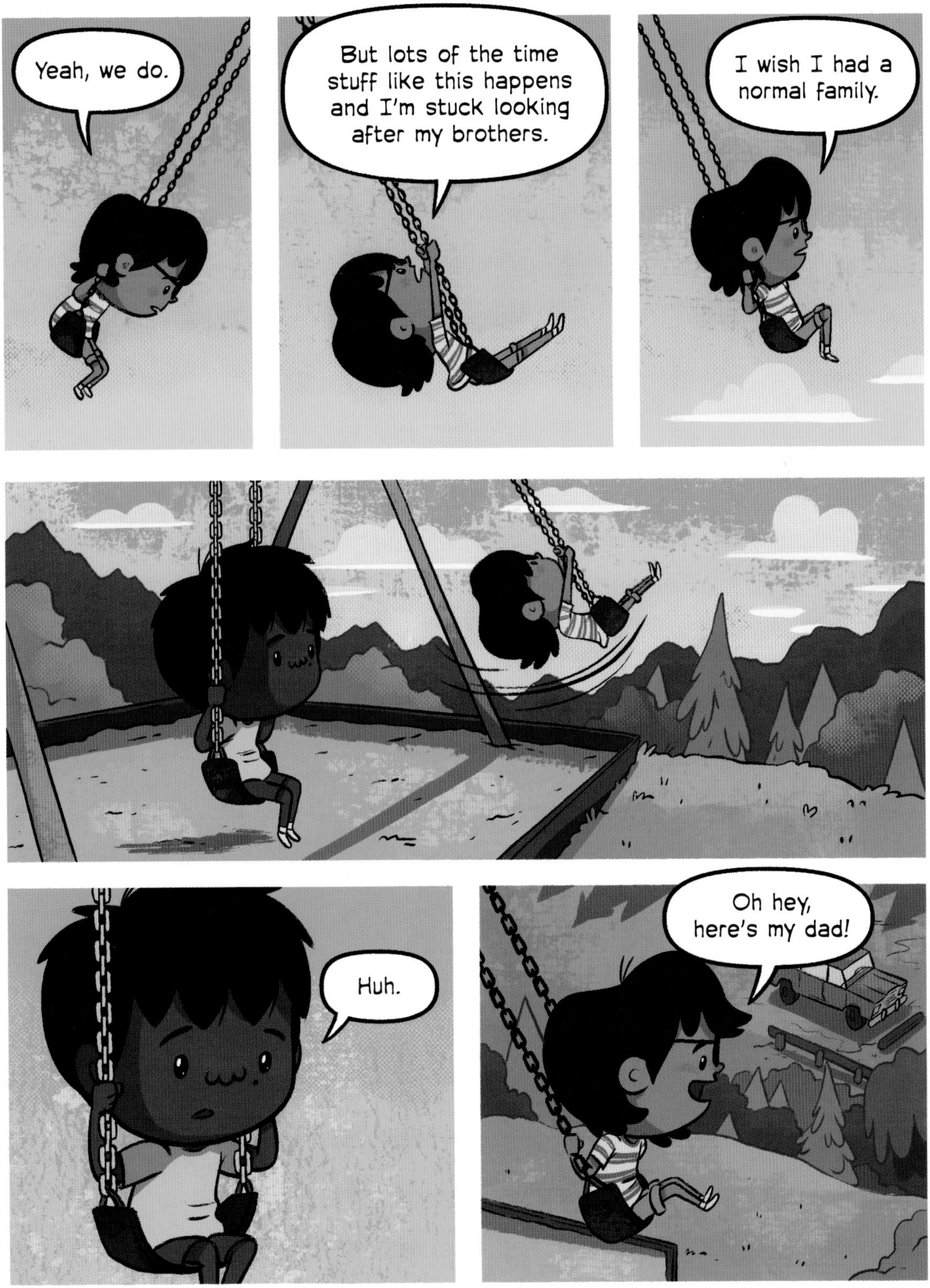
Yeah, we do.
But lots of the time stuff like this happens and I'm stuck looking after my brothers.
I wish I had a normal family.
Huh.
Oh hey, here's my dad!

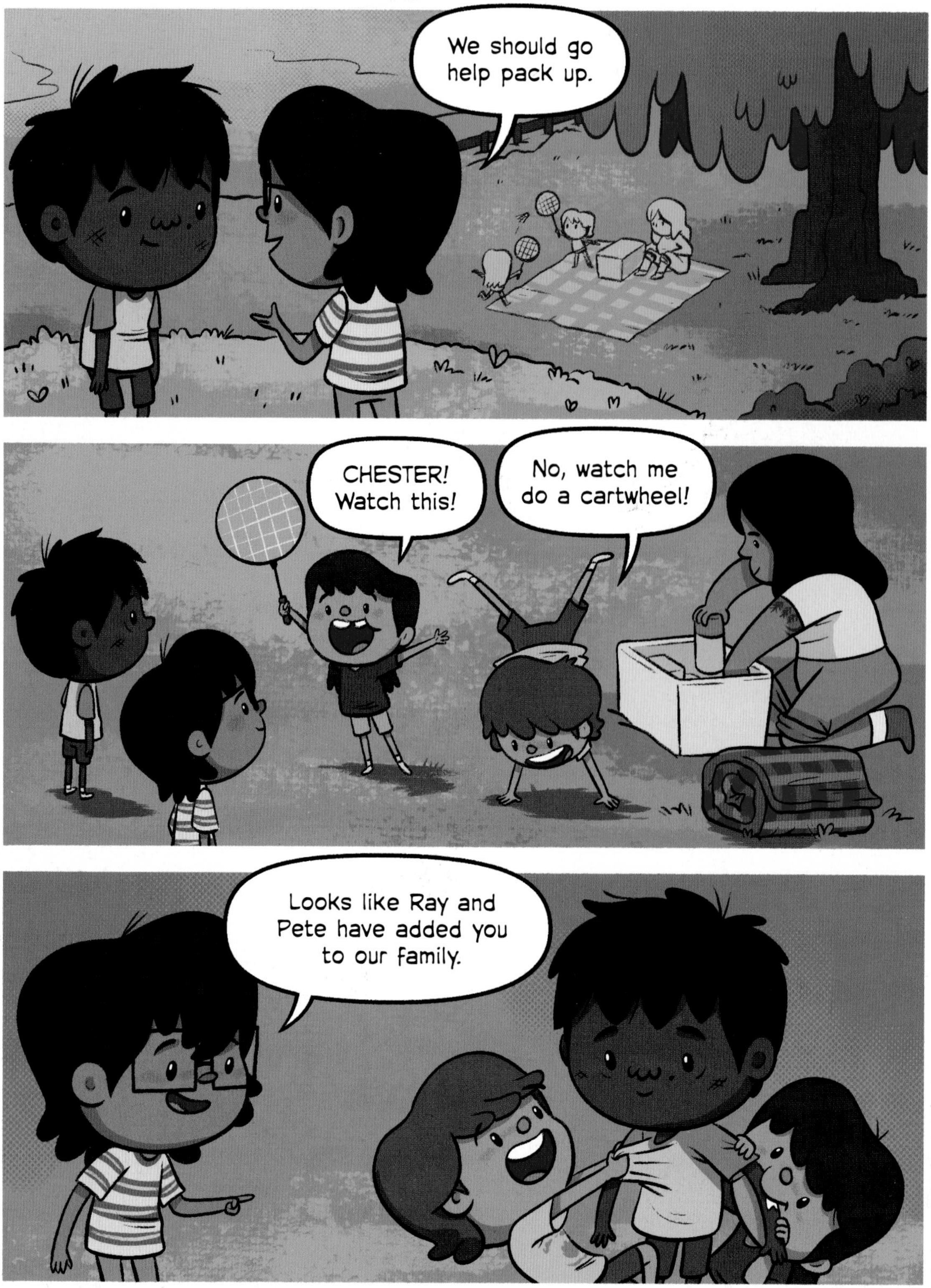
We should go help pack up.
CHESTER! Watch this!
No, watch me do a cartwheel!
Looks like Ray and Pete have added you to our family.

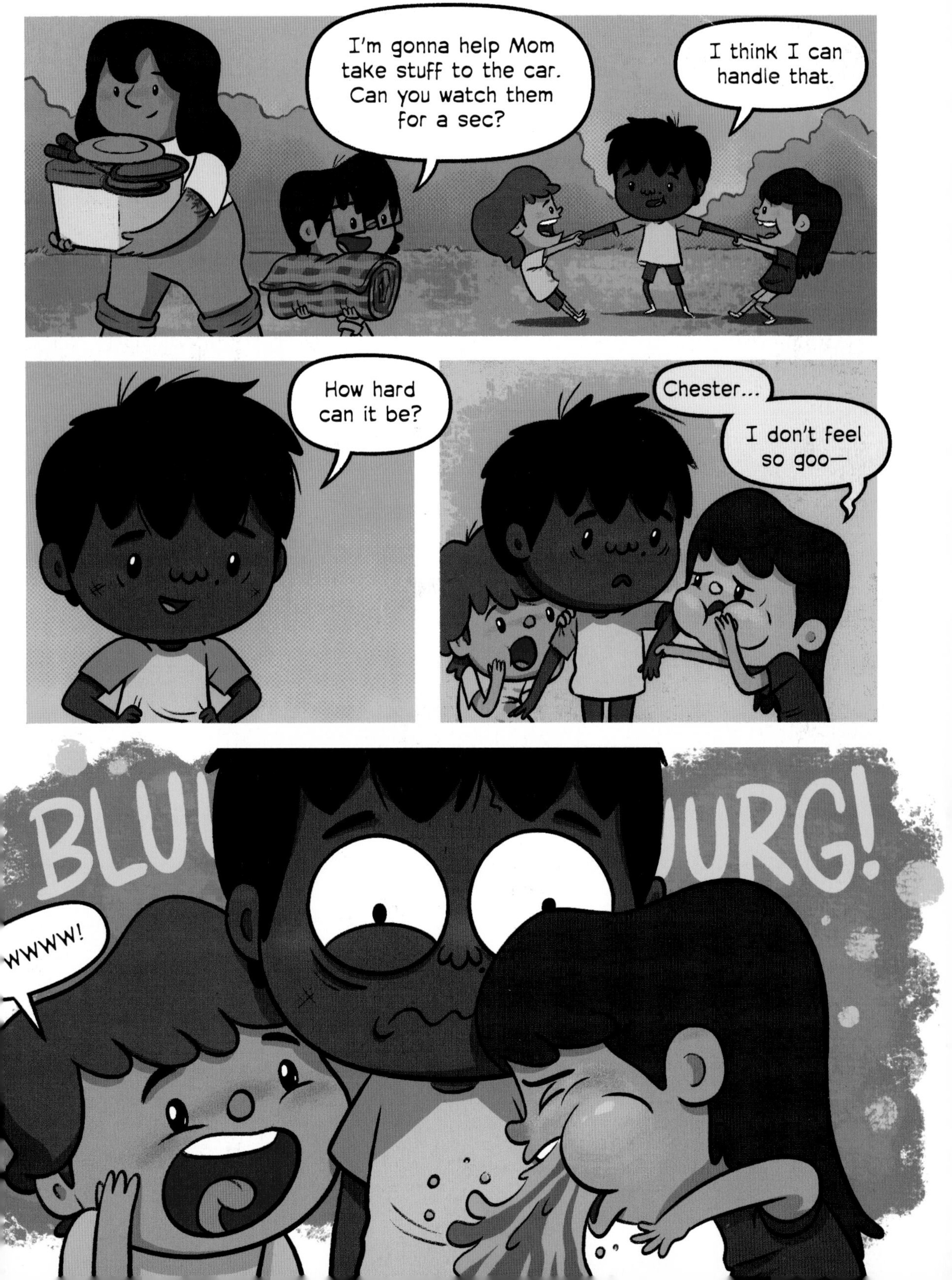
I'm gonna help Mom take stuff to the car. Can you watch them for a sec?
I think I can handle that.
How hard can it be?
Chester...
I don't feel so goo—
BLU
URG!
WWWW!

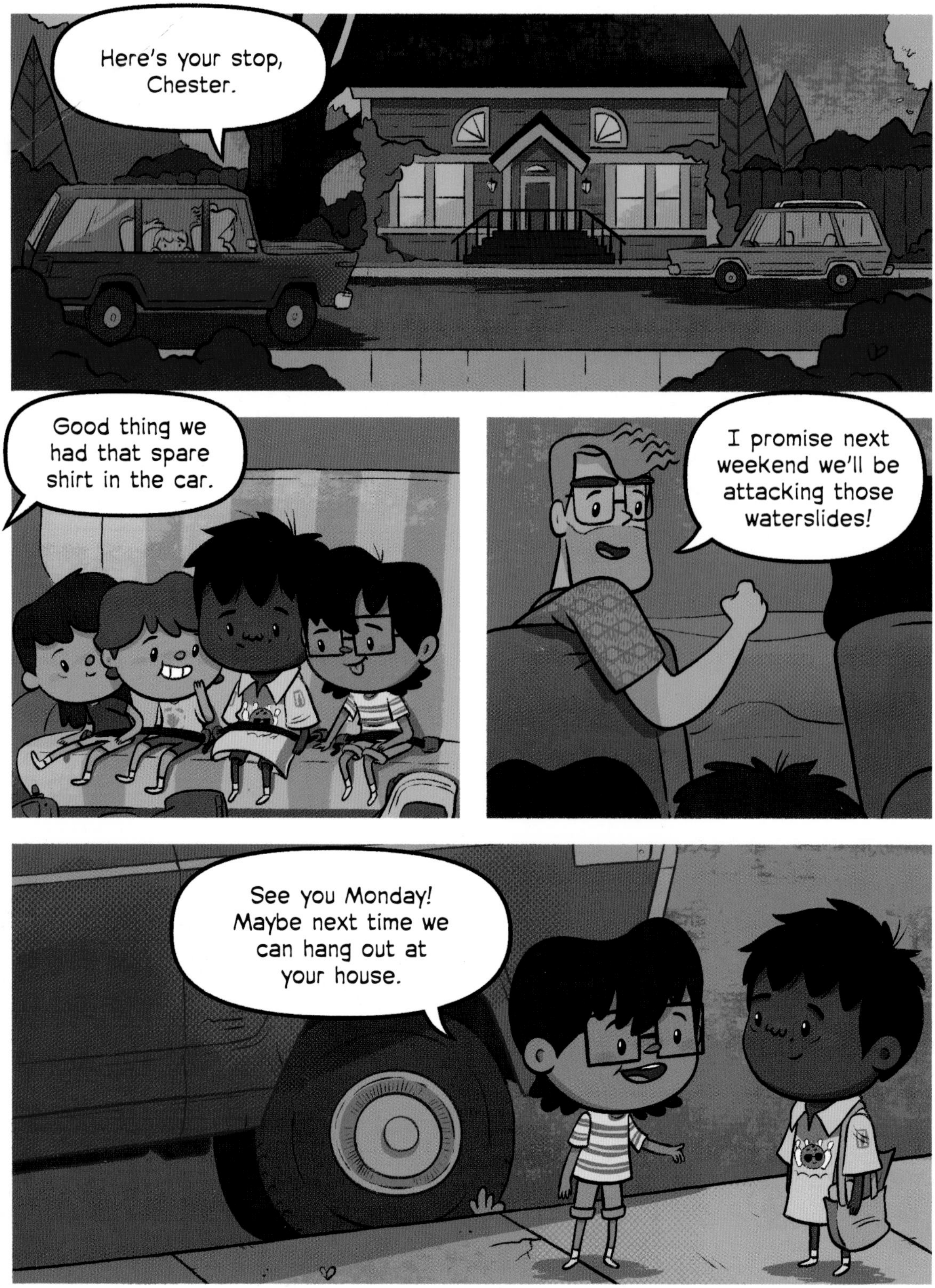
Here's your stop, Chester.
Good thing we had that spare shirt in the car.
I promise next weekend we'll be attacking those waterslides!
See you Monday! Maybe next time we can hang out at your house.

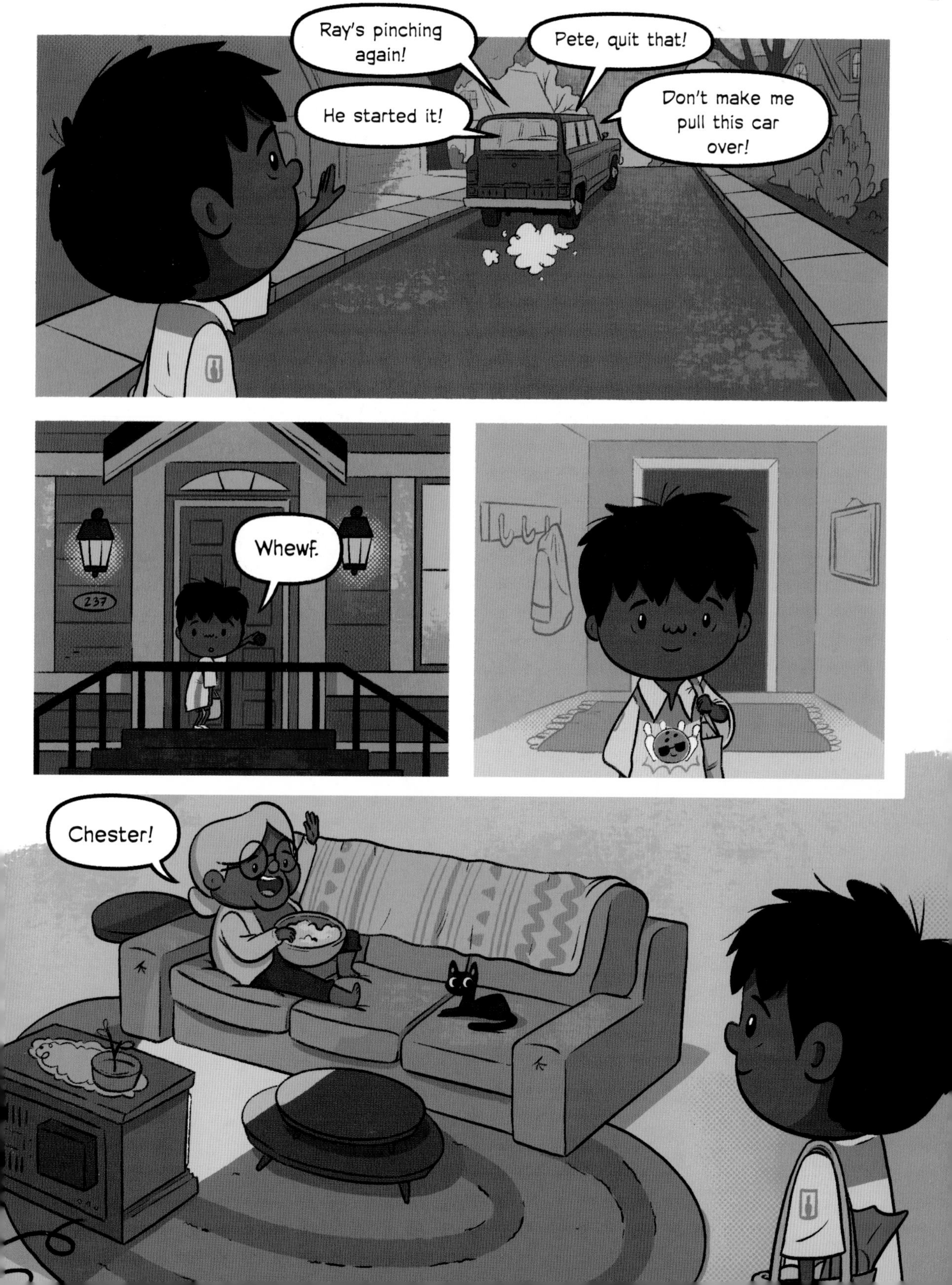
Ray's pinching again!
He started it!
Pete, quit that!
Don't make me pull this car over!
237
Whewf.
Chester!

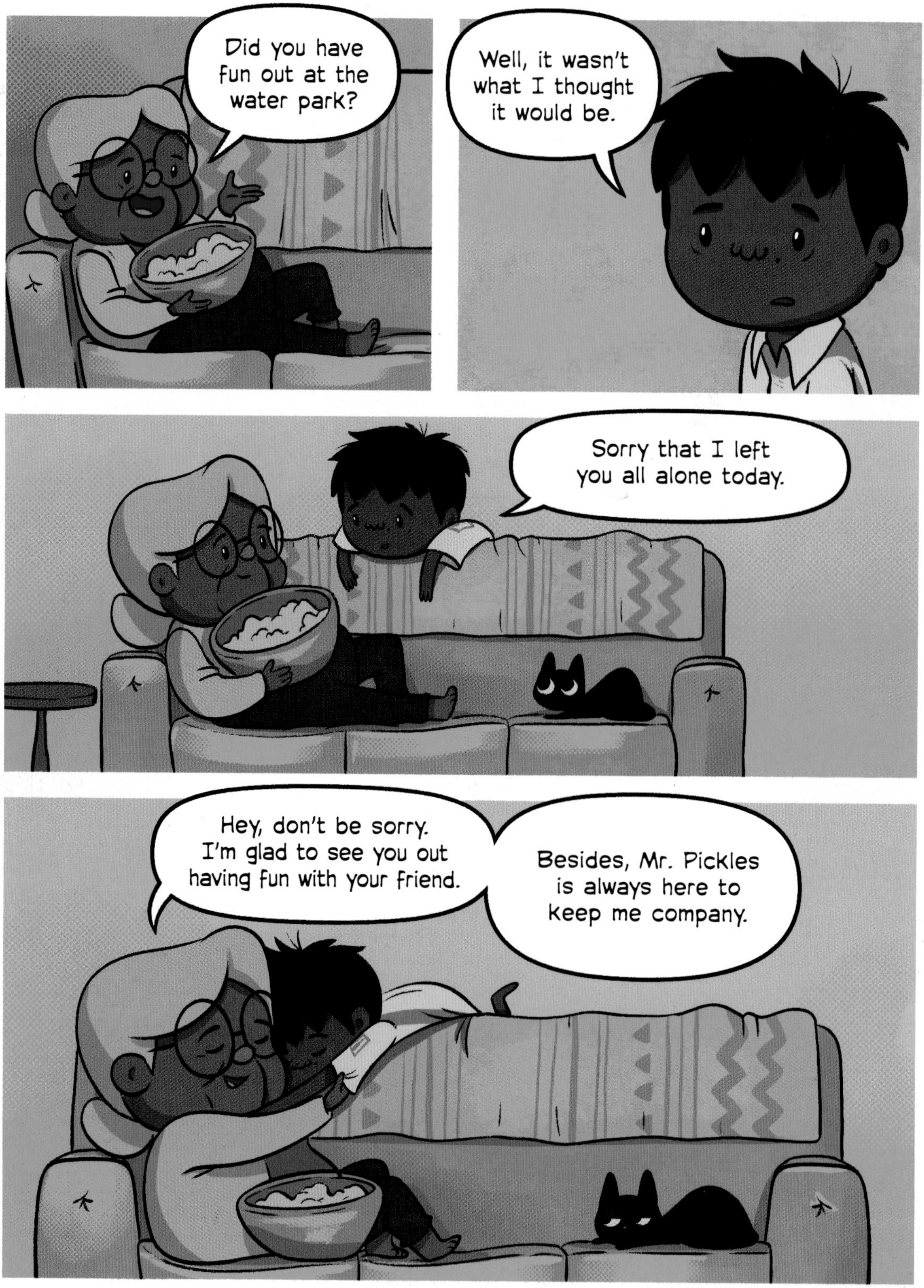
Did you have fun out at the water park?
Well, it wasn't what I thought it would be.
Sorry that I left you all alone today.
Hey, don't be sorry. I'm glad to see you out having fun with your friend.
Besides, Mr. Pickles is always here to keep me company.

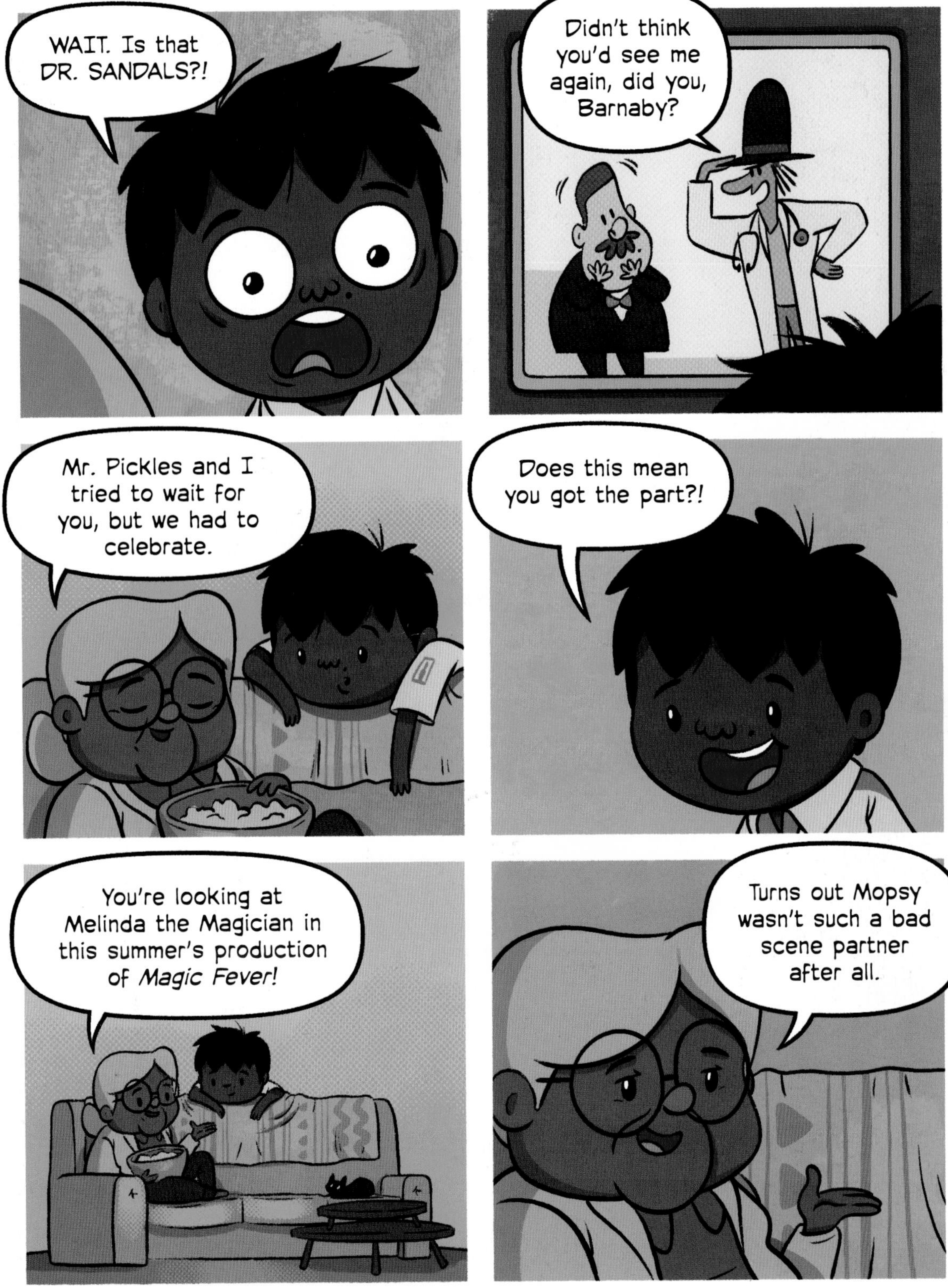
WAIT. Is that DR. SANDALS?!
Didn't think you'd see me again, did you, Barnaby?
Mr. Pickles and I tried to wait for you, but we had to celebrate.
Does this mean you got the part?!
You're looking at Melinda the Magician in this summer's production of *Magic Fever*!
Turns out Mopsy wasn't such a bad scene partner after all.

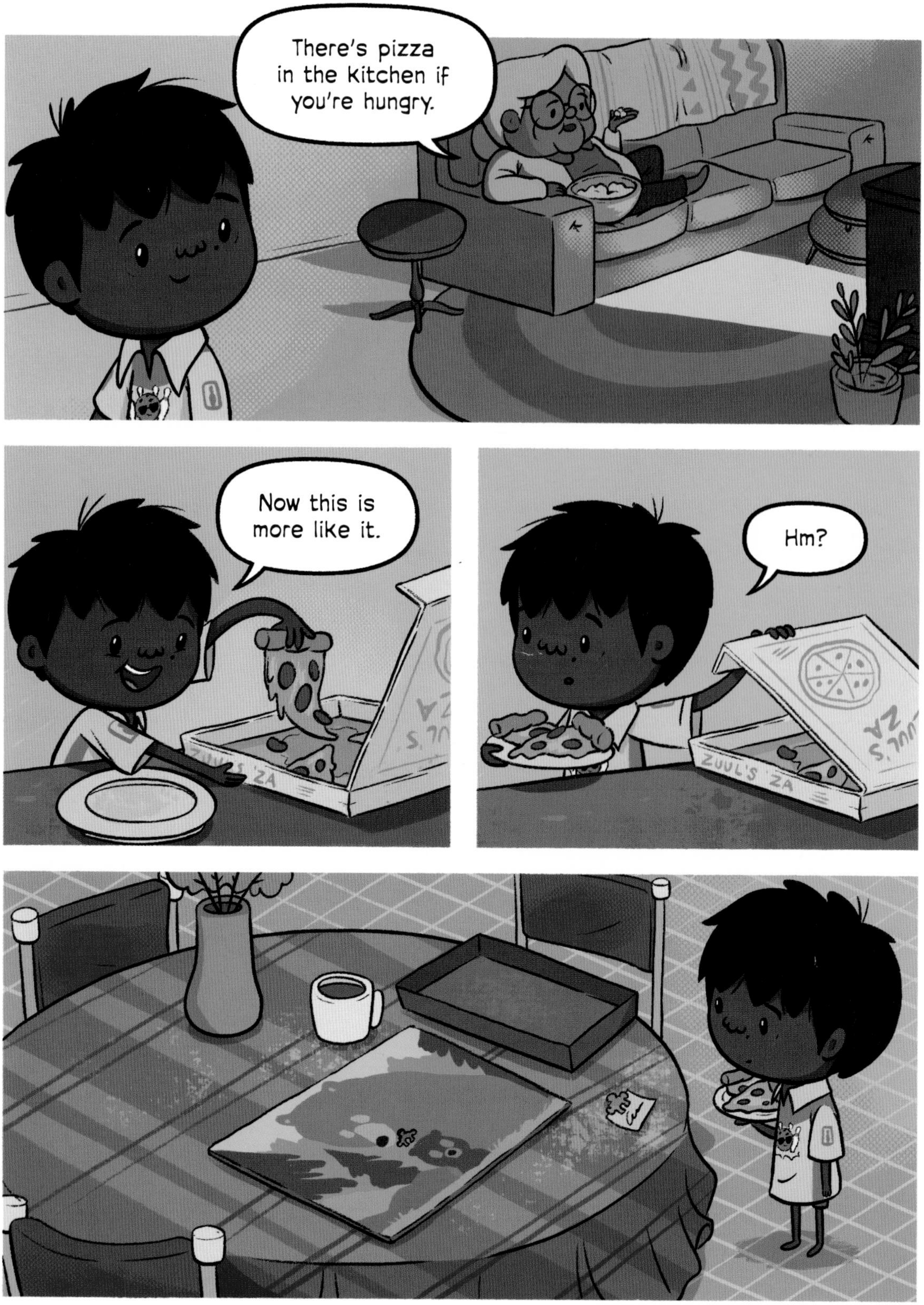
There's pizza in the kitchen if you're hungry.
Now this is more like it.
ZUUL'S 'ZA
Hm?
ZUUL'S 'ZA

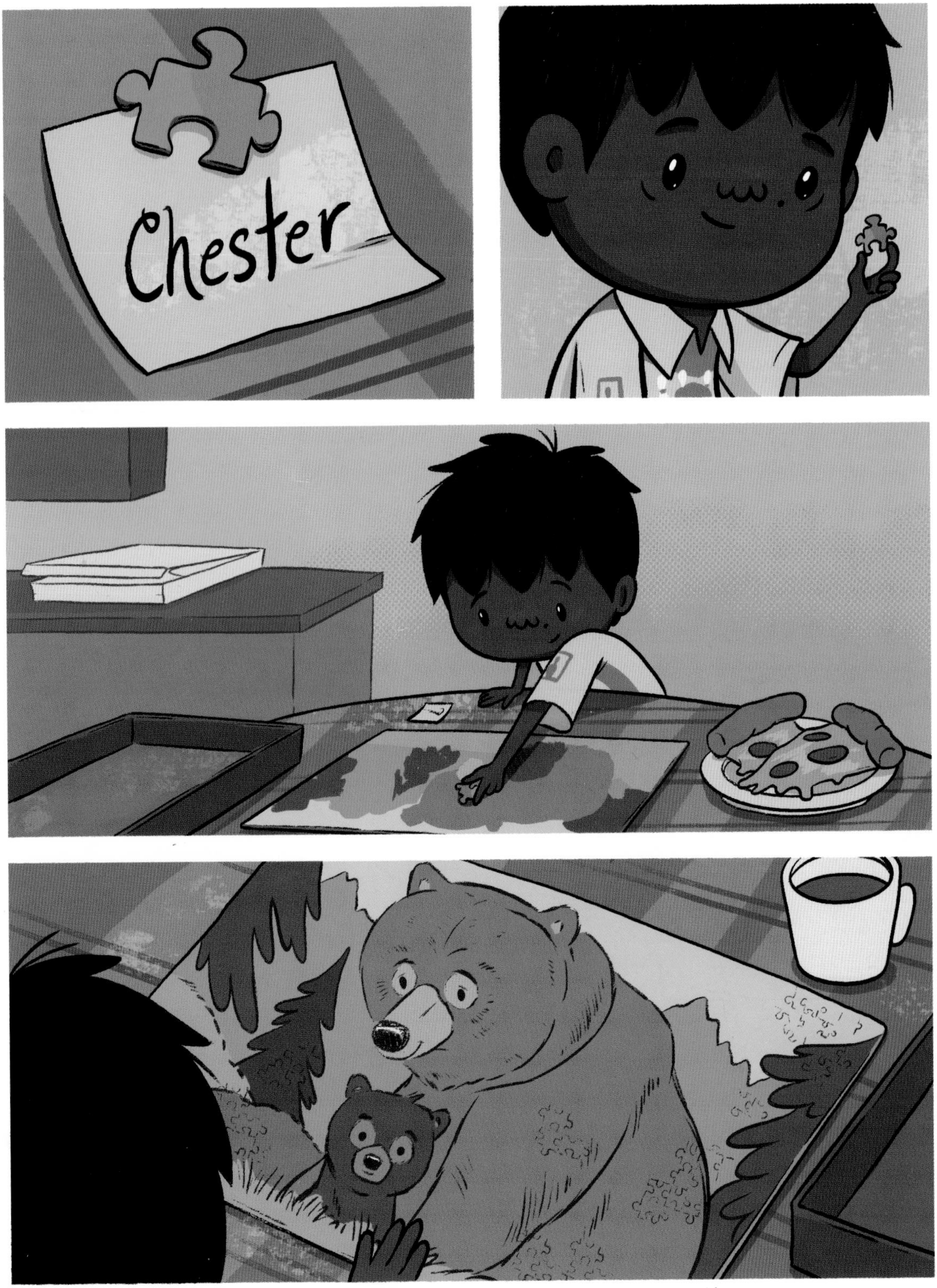
Chester

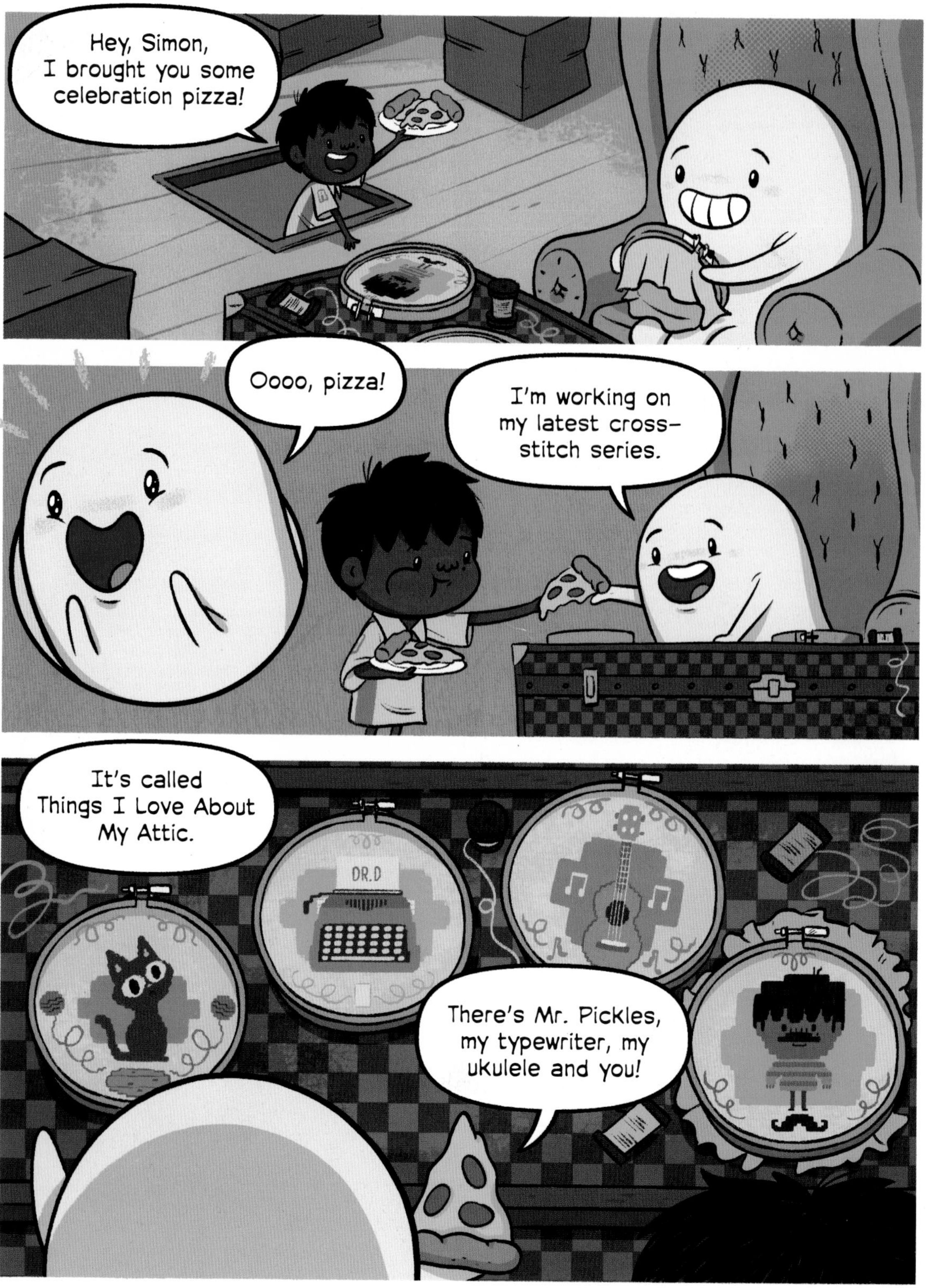
Hey, Simon,
I brought you some celebration pizza!
Oooo, pizza!
I'm working on my latest cross-stitch series.
It's called Things I Love About My Attic.
DR.D
There's Mr. Pickles, my typewriter, my ukulele and you!

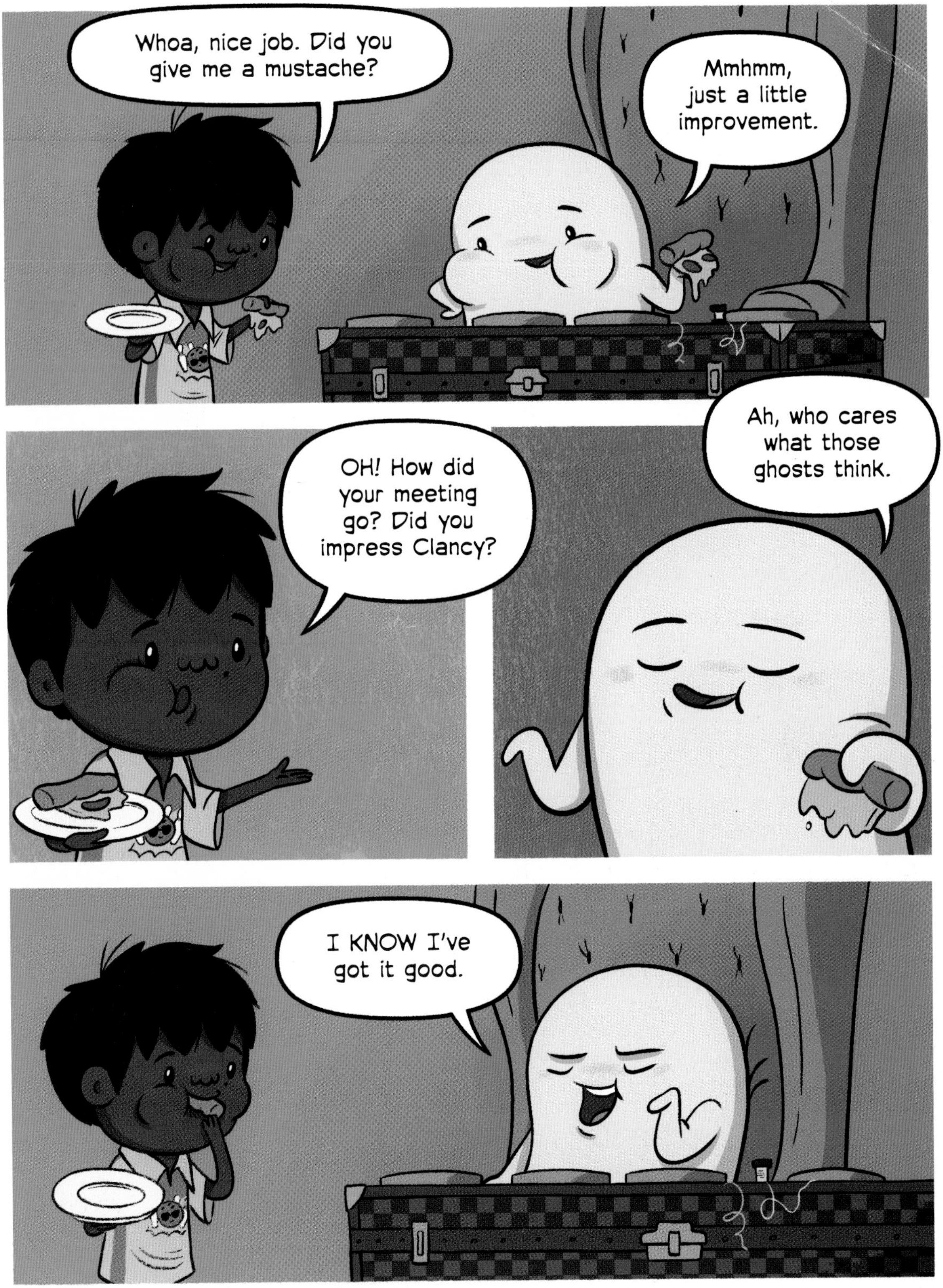

Whoa, nice job. Did you give me a mustache?
Mmhmm, just a little improvement.
OH! How did your meeting go? Did you impress Clancy?
Ah, who cares what those ghosts think.
I KNOW I've got it good.

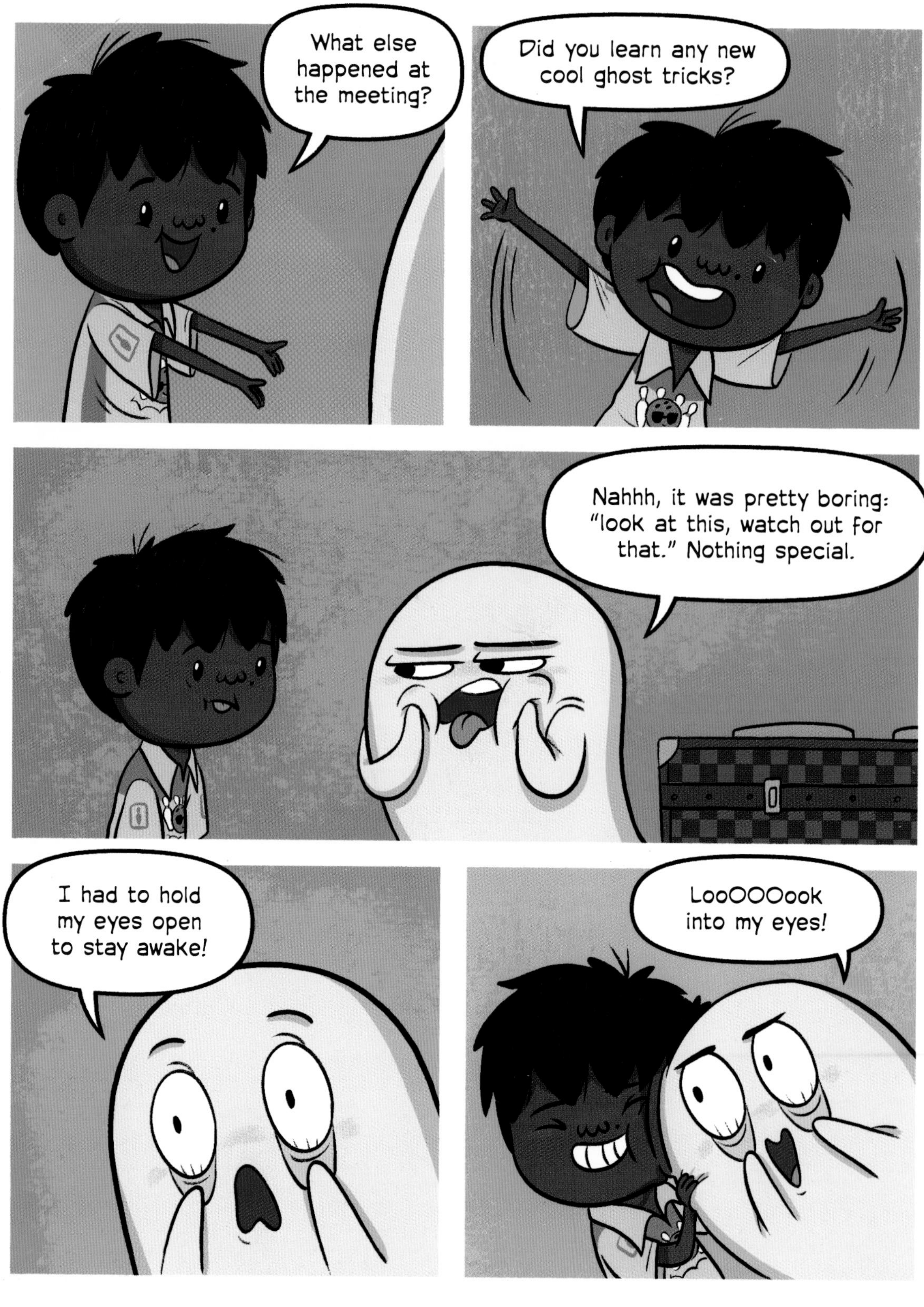
What else happened at the meeting?
Did you learn any new cool ghost tricks?
Nahhh, it was pretty boring: "look at this, watch out for that." Nothing special.
I had to hold my eyes open to stay awake!
LooOOOook into my eyes!

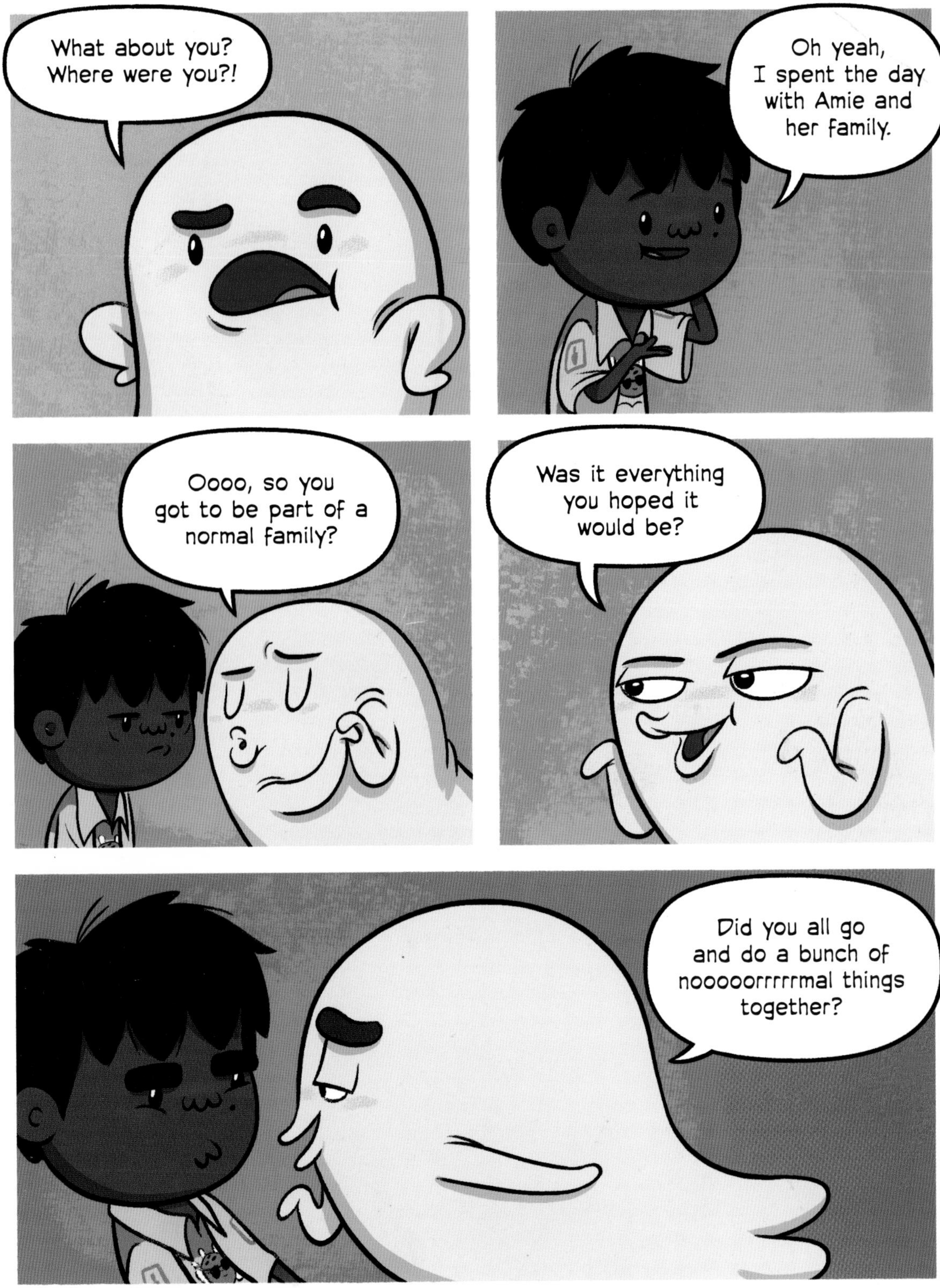
What about you? Where were you?!
Oh yeah, I spent the day with Amie and her family.
Oooo, so you got to be part of a normal family?
Was it everything you hoped it would be?
Did you all go and do a bunch of nooooorrrrrmal things together?

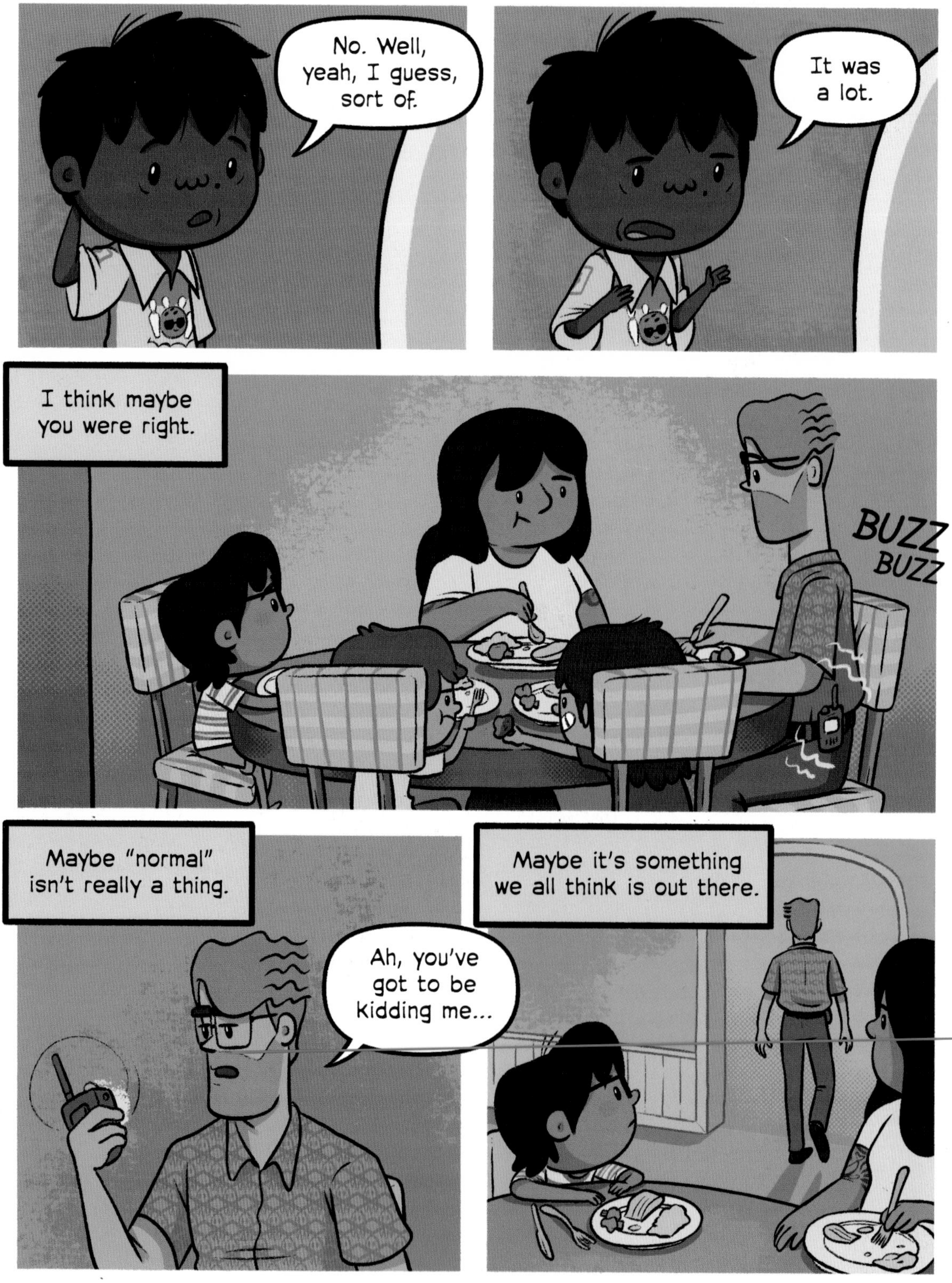
No. Well, yeah, I guess, sort of.
It was a lot.
I think maybe you were right.
BUZZ BUZZ
Maybe "normal" isn't really a thing.
Ah, you've got to be kidding me...
Maybe it's something we all think is out there.

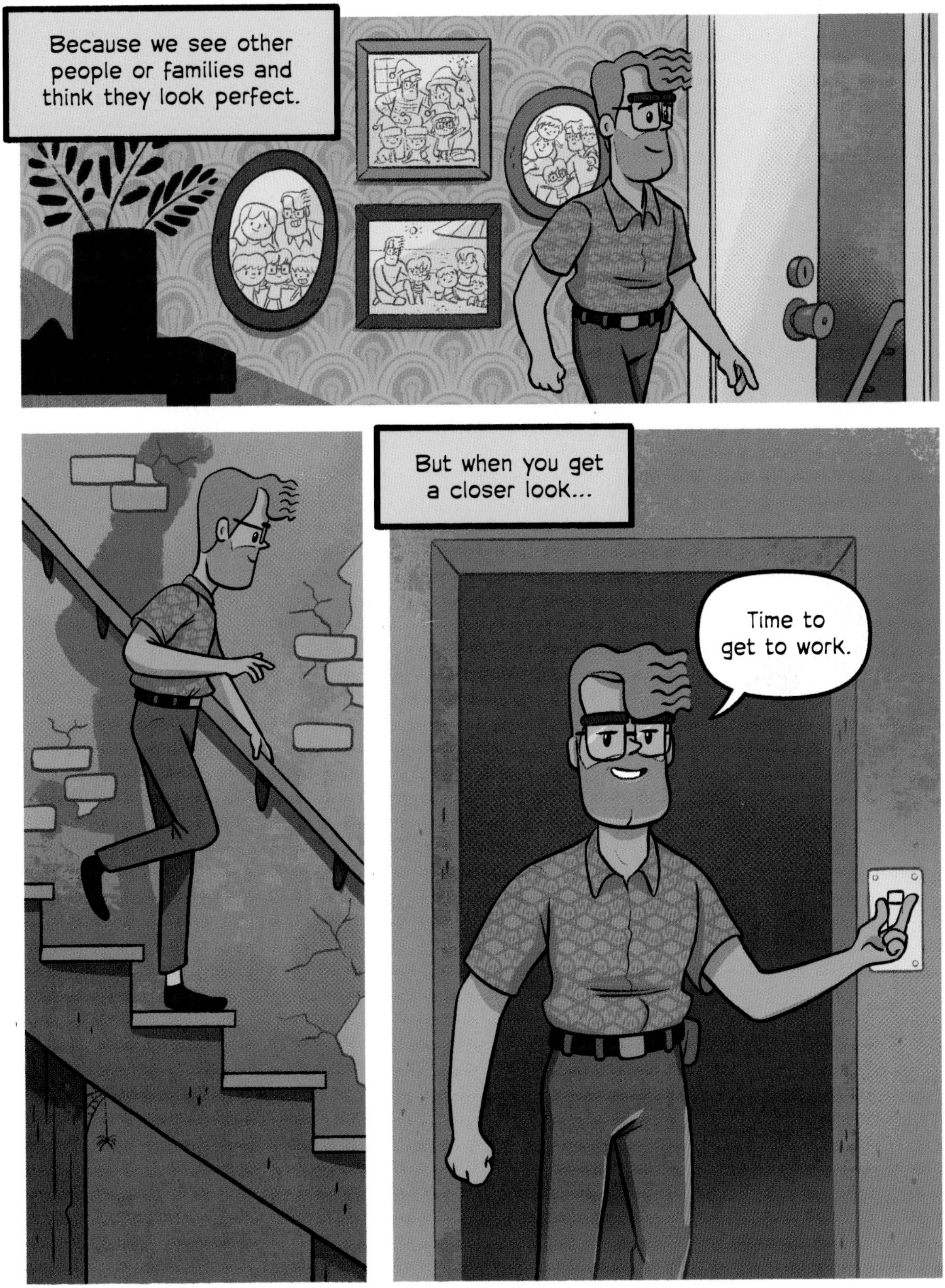
Because we see other people or families and think they look perfect.
But when you get a closer look...
Time to get to work.

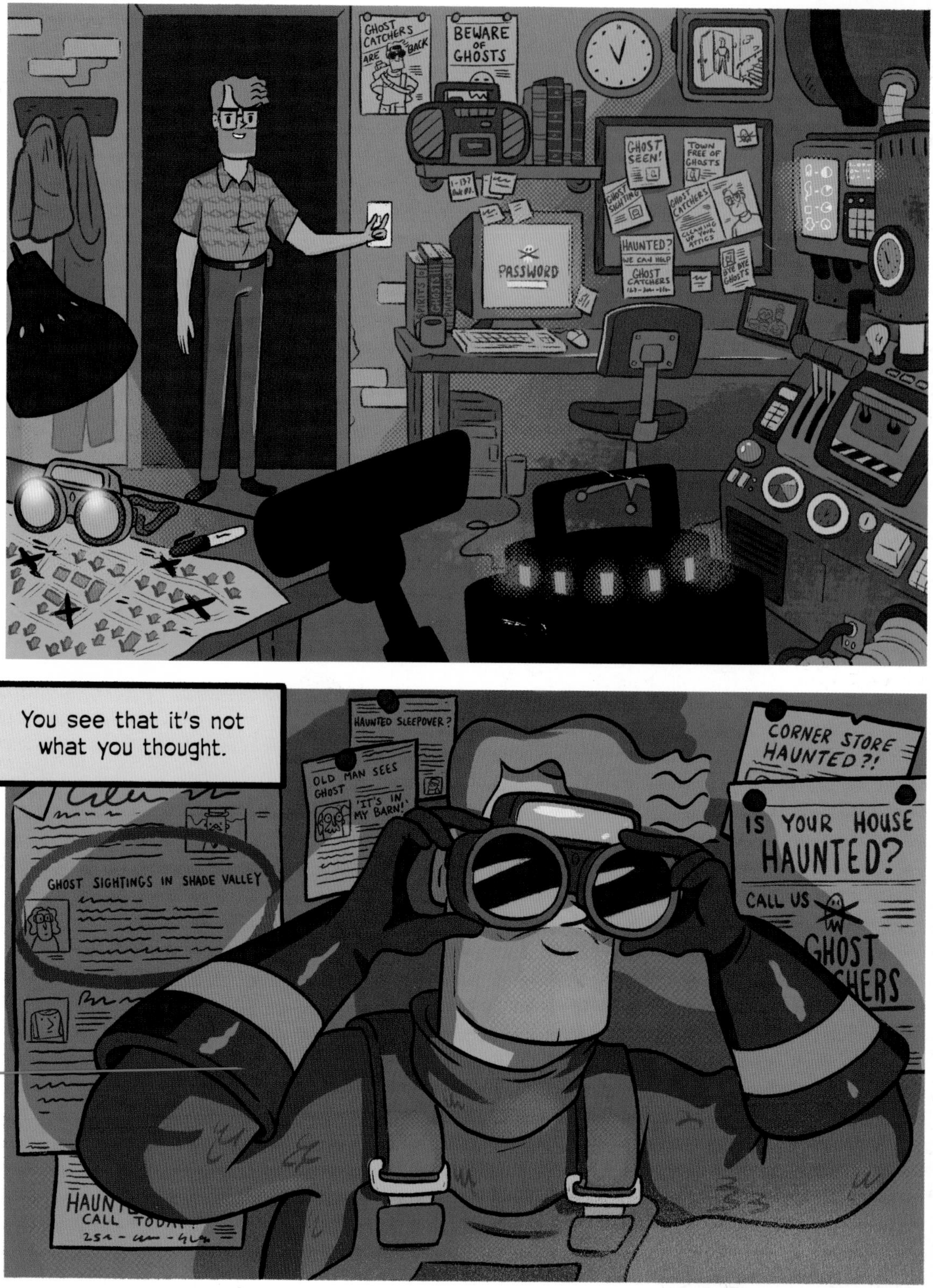

GHOST CATCHERS ARE BACK
BEWARE OF GHOSTS
GHOST SEEN!
TOWN FREE OF GHOSTS
GHOST SIGHTING
GHOST CATCHERS CLEANING UP YOUR ATTICS
HAUNTED? WE CAN HELP GHOST CATCHERS
BYE BYE GHOSTS
PASSWORD
SPIRITS
GHOSTS
PHANTOMS
You see that it's not what you thought.
HAUNTED SLEEPOVER?
OLD MAN SEES GHOST
'IT'S IN MY BARN!'
GHOST SIGHTINGS IN SHADE VALLEY
CORNER STORE HAUNTED?!
IS YOUR HOUSE HAUNTED?
CALL US

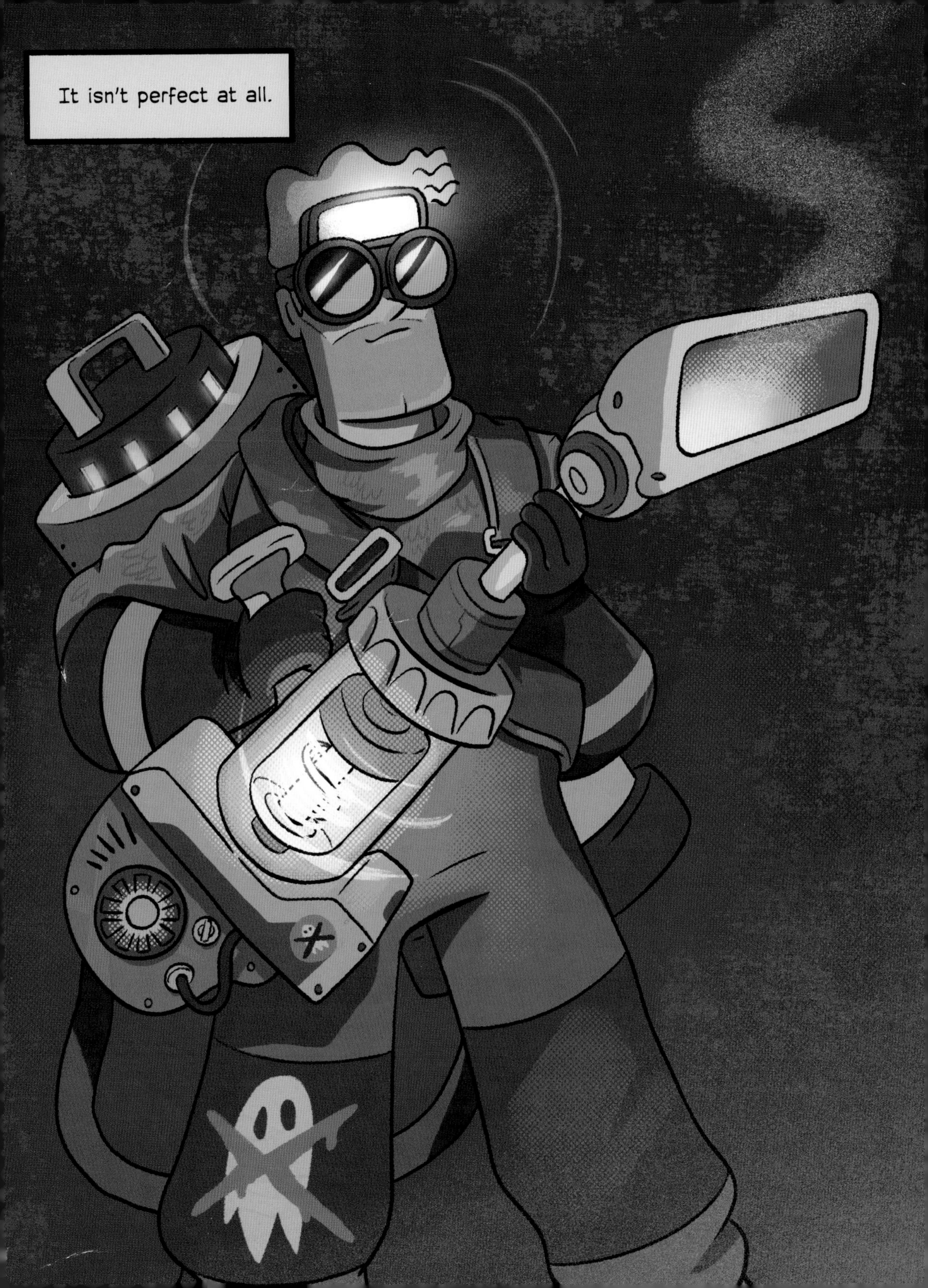
It isn't perfect at all.

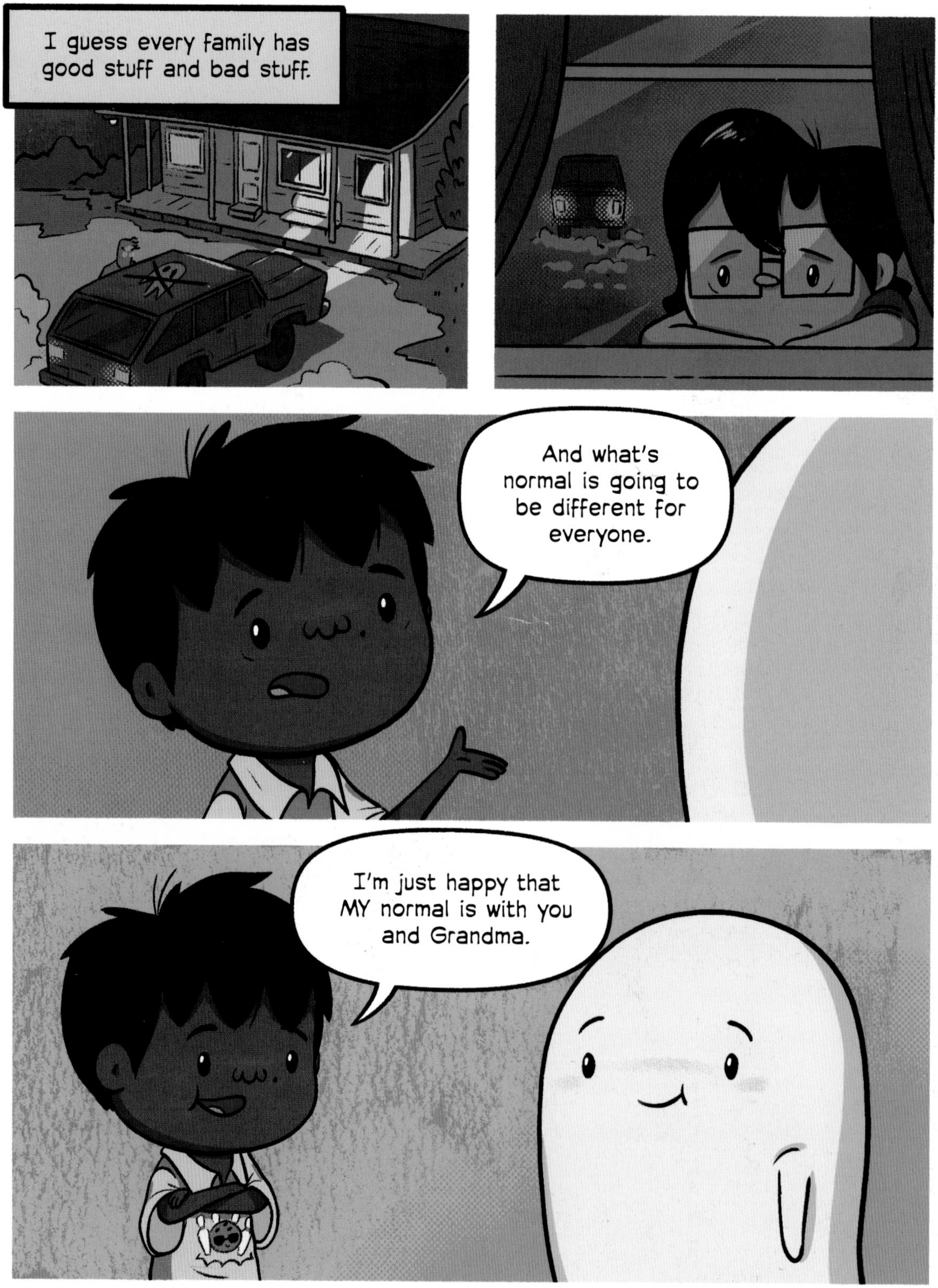
I guess every family has good stuff and bad stuff.
And what's normal is going to be different for everyone.
I'm just happy that MY normal is with you and Grandma.

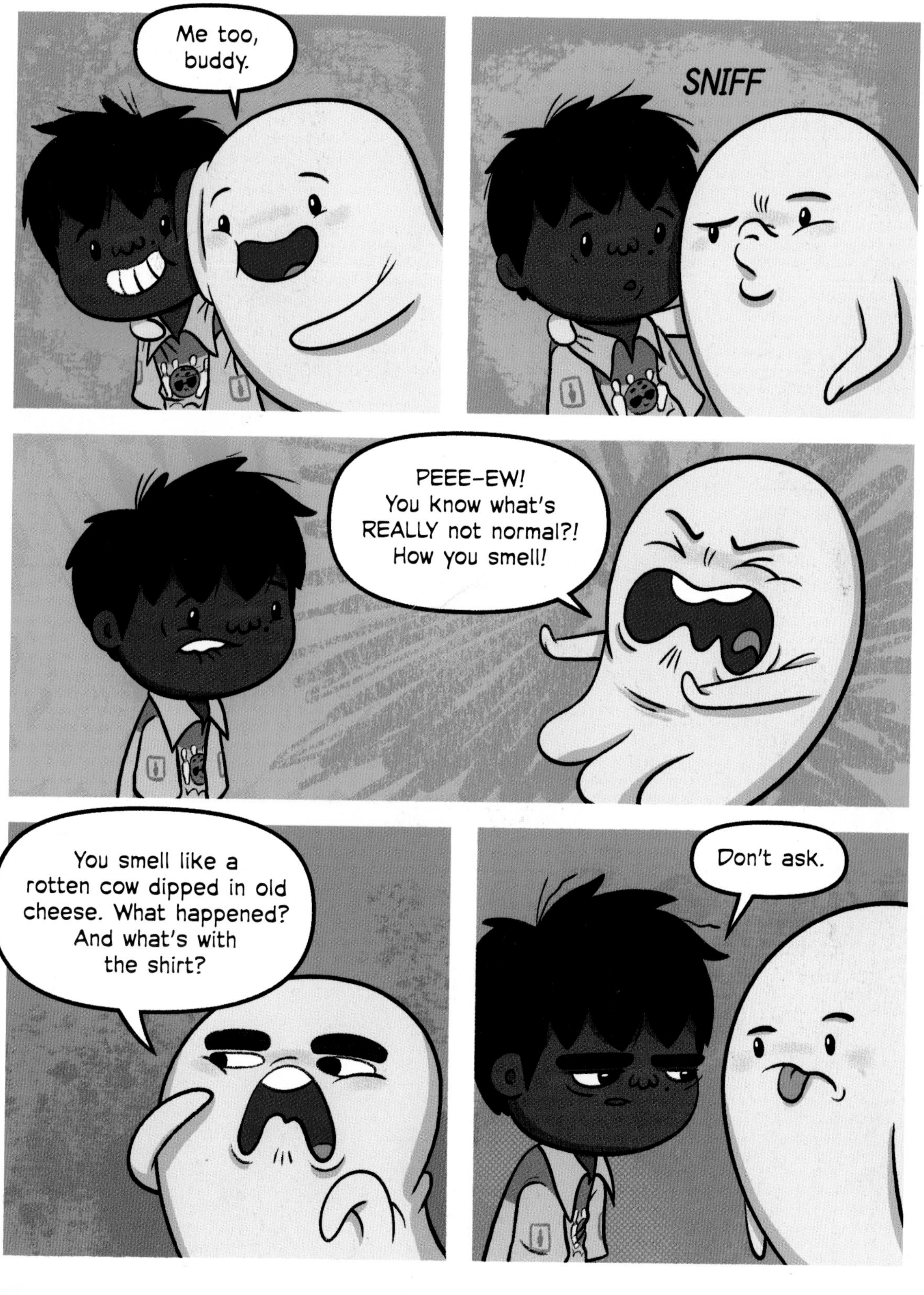
Me too, buddy.
SNIFF
PEEE-EW! You know what's REALLY not normal?! How you smell!
You smell like a rotten cow dipped in old cheese. What happened? And what's with the shirt?
Don't ask.

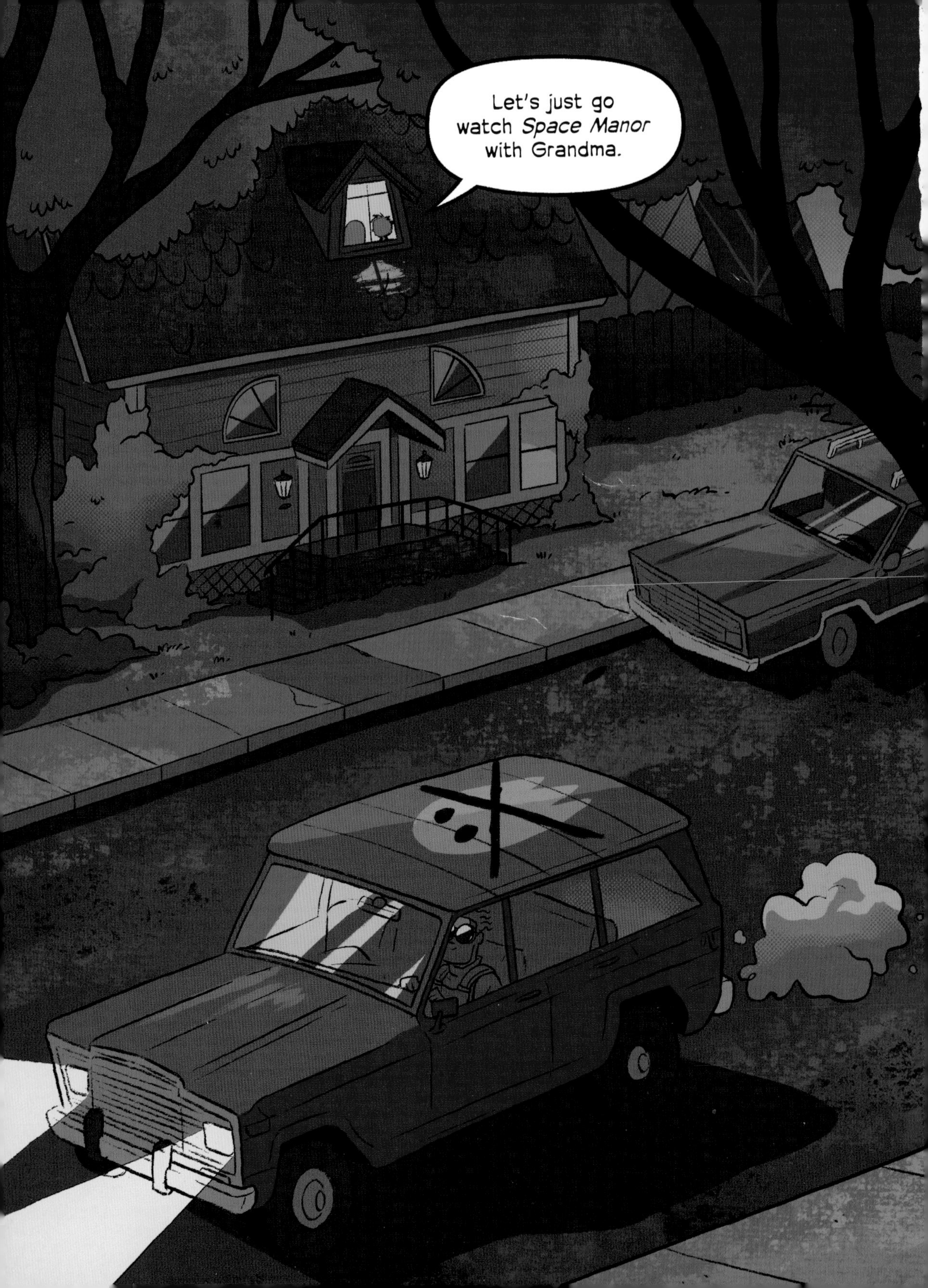
Let's just go watch *Space Manor* with Grandma.

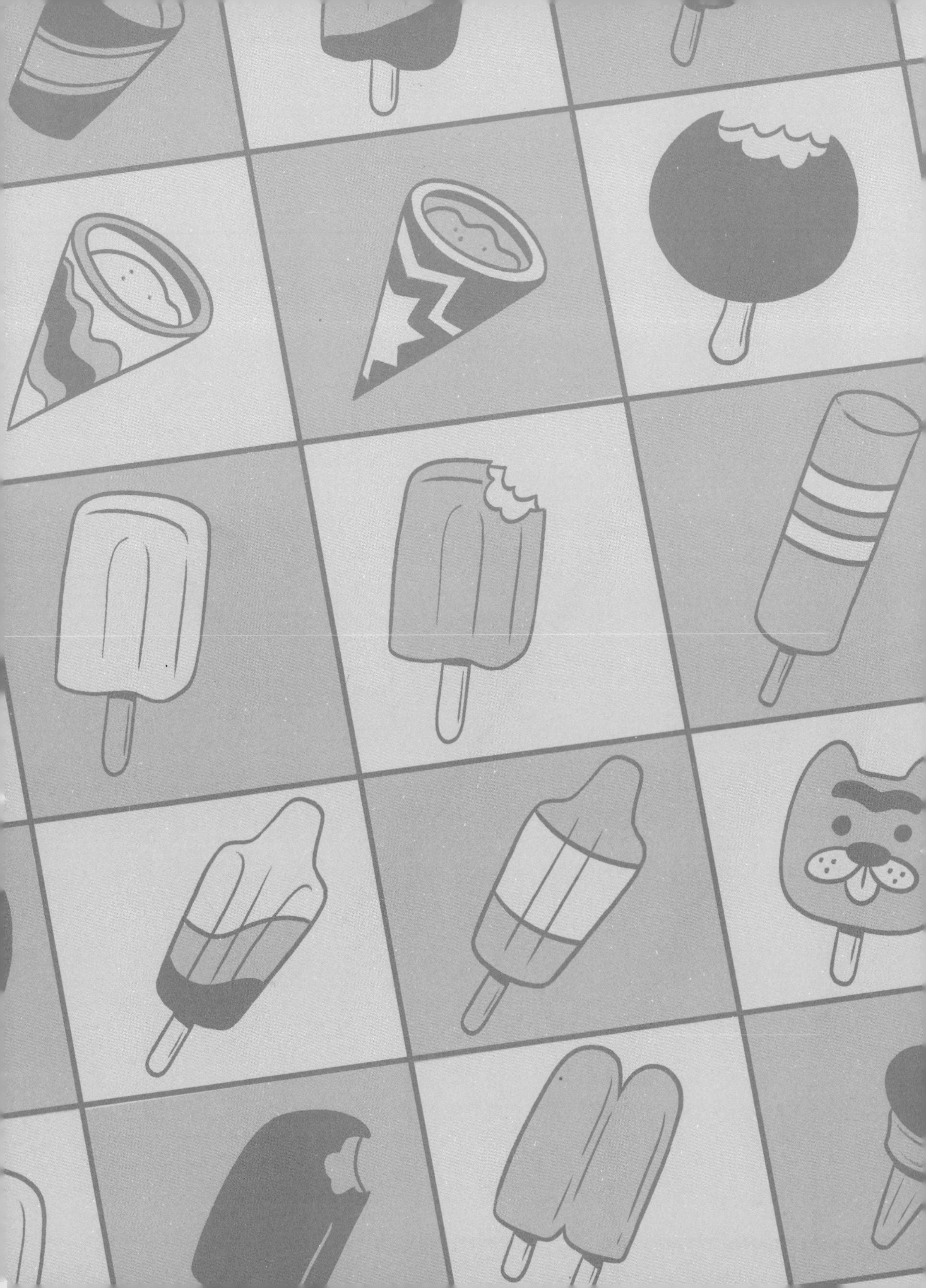